ROYAL EXPECTATIONS

Praise for Jenny Frame

Longing for You

"Jenny Frame knocks it out of the park once again with this fantastic sequel to *Hunger For You*. She can keep the pages turning with a delicious mix of intrigue and romance."—*Rainbow Literary Society*

Hunger for You

"[Byron and Amelia] are guaranteed to get the reader all hot and bothered. Jenny Frame writes brilliant love scenes in all of her books and makes me believe the characters crave each other."—*Kitty Kat's Book Review Blog*

"I loved this book. Paranormal stuff like vampires and werewolves are my go-to sins. This book had literally everything I needed: chemistry between the leads, hot love scenes (phew), drama, angst, romance (oh my, the romance) and strong supporting characters."—*The Reading Doc*

The Duchess and the Dreamer

"We thoroughly enjoyed the whole romance-the-disbelieving-duchess with gallantry, unwavering care, and grand gestures. Since this is very firmly in the butch-femme zone, it appealed to that part of our traditionally-conditioned-typecasting mindset that all the wooing and work is done by Evan without throwing even a small fit at any point. We liked the fact that Clementine has layers and depth. She has her own personal and personality hurdles that make her behaviour understandable and create the right opportunities for Evan to play the romantic knight convincingly…We definitely recommend this one to anyone looking for a feel-good mushy romance."—*Best Lesfic Reviews*

"There are a whole range of things I like about Jenny Frame's aristocratic heroines: they have plausible histories to account for them holding titles in their own right; they're in touch with reality and not necessarily super-rich, certainly not through inheritance; and they find themselves paired with perfectly contrasting co-heroines…Clementine and Evan are excellently depicted, and I love the butch:femme dynamic they have going on, as well as their individual abilities to stick to their principles but also to compromise with each other when necessary."
—*The Good, The Bad and The Unread*

Still Not Over You

"*Still Not Over You* is a wonderful second-chance romance anthology that makes you believe in love again. And you would certainly be missing out if you have not read *My Forever Girl*, because it truly is everything."—*SymRoute*

Someone to Love

"One of the author's best works to date—both Trent and Wendy were so well developed they came alive. I could really picture them and they jumped off the pages. They had fantastic chemistry, and their sexual dynamic was deliciously well written. The supporting characters and the storyline about Alice's trauma was also sensitively written and well handled."—*Melina Bickard, Librarian, Waterloo Library (UK)*

Wooing the Farmer

"The chemistry between the two MCs had us hooked right away. We also absolutely loved the seemingly ditzy femme with an ambition of steel but really a vulnerable girl. The sex scenes are great. Definitely recommended."—*Reviewer@large*

"This is the book we Axedale fanatics have been waiting for…Jenny Frame writes the most amazing characters and this whole series is a masterpiece. But where she excels is in writing butch lesbians. Every time I read a Jenny Frame book I think it's the best ever, but time and again she surprises me. She has surpassed herself with *Wooing the Farmer*."—*Kitty Kat's Book Review Blog*

Royal Court

"The author creates two very relatable characters…Quincy's quietude and mental torture are offset by Holly's openness and lust for life. Holly's determination and tenacity in trying to reach Quincy are total wish-fulfilment of a person like that. The chemistry and attraction is excellently built."—*Best Lesbian Erotica*

"[A] butch/femme romance that packs a punch."—*Les Rêveur*

"There were unbelievably hot sex scenes as I have come to expect and look forward to in Jenny Frame's books. Passions slowly rise until you feel the characters may burst!…Royal Court is wonderful and I highly recommend it."—*Kitty Kat's Book Review Blog*

Royal Court "was a fun, light-hearted book with a very endearing romance."—*Leanne Chew, Librarian, Parnell Library (Auckland, NZ)*

Charming the Vicar

"Chances are, you've never read or become captivated by a romance like *Charming the Vicar*. While books featuring people of the cloth aren't unusual, Bridget is no ordinary vicar—a lesbian with a history of kink...Surrounded by mostly supportive villagers, Bridget and Finn balance love and faith in a story that affirms both can exist for anyone, regardless of sexual identity."—*RT Book Reviews*

"The sex scenes were some of the sexiest, most intimate and quite frankly, sensual I have read in a while. Jenny Frame had me hooked and I reread a few scenes because I felt like I needed to experience the intense intimacy between Finn and Bridget again. The devotion they showed to one another during these sex scenes but also in the intimate moments was gripping and for lack of a better word, carnal."—*Les Rêveur*

"The sexual chemistry between [Finn and Bridge] is unbelievably hot. It is sexy, lustful and with more than a hint of kink. The scenes between them are highly erotic—and not just the sex scenes. The tension is ramped up so well that I felt the characters would explode if they did not get relief!...An excellent book set in the most wonderful village—a place I hope to return to very soon!"—*Kitty Kat's Book Reviews*

"This is Frame's best character work to date. They are layered and flawed and yet relatable...Frame really pushed herself with *Charming the Vicar* and it totally paid off...I also appreciate that even though she regularly writes butch/femme characters, no two pairings are the same."—*The Lesbian Review*

Unexpected

"If you enjoy contemporary romances, *Unexpected* is a great choice. The character work is excellent, the plotting and pacing are well done, and it's just a sweet, warm read...Definitely pick this book up when you're looking for your next comfort read, because it's sure to put a smile on your face by the time you get to that happy ending."—*Curve*

"*Unexpected* by Jenny Frame is a charming butch/femme romance that is perfect for anyone who wants to feel the magic of overcoming adversity and finding true love. I love the way Jenny Frame writes.

I have yet to discover an author who writes like her. Her voice is strong and unique and gives a freshness to the lesbian fiction sector."
—*The Lesbian Review*

Royal Rebel

"Frame's stories are easy to follow and really engaging. She stands head and shoulders above a number of the romance authors and it's easy to see why she is quickly making a name for herself in lesfic romance."—*The Lesbian Review*

Courting the Countess

"I love Frame's romances. They are well paced, filled with beautiful character moments and a wonderful set of side characters who ultimately end up winning your heart...I love Jenny Frame's butch/femme dynamic; she gets it so right for a romance."—*The Lesbian Review*

"I loved, loved, loved this book. I didn't expect to get so involved in the story but I couldn't help but fall in love with Annie and Harry...The love scenes were beautifully written and very sexy. I found the whole book romantic and ultimately joyful and I had a lump in my throat on more than one occasion. A wonderful book that certainly stirred my emotions."—*Kitty Kat's Book Reviews*

"*Courting The Countess* has an historical feel in a present day world, a thought provoking tale filled with raw emotions throughout. [Frame] has a magical way of pulling you in, making you feel every emotion her characters experience."—*Lunar Rainbow Reviewz*

"I didn't want to put the book down and I didn't. Harry and Annie are two amazingly written characters that bring life to the pages as they find love and adventures in Harry's home. This is a great read, and you will enjoy it immensely if you give it a try!"—*Fantastic Book Reviews*

A Royal Romance

"*A Royal Romance* was a guilty pleasure read for me. It was just fun to see the relationship develop between George and Bea, to see George's life as queen and Bea's as a commoner. It was also refreshing to see that both of their families were encouraging, even when Bea doubted that things could work between them because of their class differences...*A Royal Romance* left me wanting a sequel, and romances don't usually do that to me."—*Leeanna.ME Mostly a Book Blog*

By the Author

A Royal Romance

Courting the Countess

Dapper

Royal Rebel

Unexpected

Charming the Vicar

Royal Court

Wooing the Farmer

Someone to Love

The Duchess and the Dreamer

Royal Family

Home Is Where the Heart Is

Sweet Surprise

Royal Exposé

A Haven for the Wanderer

Just One Dance

Royal Expectations

Wild for You

Hunger for You

Longing for You

Dying for You

Living for You

Wolfgang County Series

Heart of the Pack

Soul of the Pack

Blood of the Pack

Visit us at www.boldstrokesbooks.com

ROYAL
EXPECTATIONS

by
Jenny Frame

2024

ROYAL EXPECTATIONS

ISBN 13: 978-1-63679-591-1

This Trade Paperback Original Is Published By
Bold Strokes Books, Inc.
P.O. Box 249
Valley Falls, NY 12185

First Edition: September 2024

Credits
Editor: Ruth Sternglantz
Production Design: Stacia Seaman
Cover Design by Tammy Seidick

Acknowledgments

Thanks to Rad, Sandy, and all the BSB team for all their hard work. I couldn't hope for a more supportive publishing team.

Huge thanks to Ruth, who helps and encourages me so much.

And finally, thanks to my family for being so supportive in all that I do.

For my Barney Boy.
Always and forever in our hearts.

PROLOGUE

The sun beat down on the Windsor Estate. It was a perfect English summer day. Teddy and Summer had finished a simple picnic under the shade of their favourite tree, an eight-hundred-year-old oak tree that they both felt had a magic to it.

It stood in front of a large home on the Windsor grounds that was long uninhabited. It had a romantic feel because it was from an older, simpler time, with a spirit of place that spoke to Teddy especially, and she had dreams of refurbishing it one day.

Teddy lay in Summer's lap, as Summer stroked the hair from her brow, which the gentle breeze buffeted as it rushed under the tree.

"There's so much we can do to help the organizations that mean so much to us," Teddy said. "We'll have so much land when I inherit the Duchy of Cornwall. I know it's meant to fund the office of the Prince or Princess of Wales, but that's more than covered by a fraction of the money the land generates."

"Yes," Summer said, "I'd love you to set up a respite care charity and give parents the break they need. I know how much my illness took out of my mum and dad. Cornwall is a perfect place for people to recuperate. It could be a sister charity to your mama's Timmy's hospice trust."

"We'll do it, anything you want," Teddy said excitedly. "There are so many properties we can use on the Duchy land, and the title of Princess of Wales will bring so much publicity to all the causes that mean so much to us."

Summer laughed. "*We'll* do it?"

"Of course us. You know I want you. I want to be married and have lots of kids. At least five anyway."

Summer raised an eyebrow then joked. "At least five? You haven't even asked me to marry you yet."

"I will, you know I will," Teddy said.

"You're nineteen, Ted. Who knows, you might hate the sight of me in five years."

"You're three years older than me. You'd think you were an old woman. I've loved you forever. My parents love you, probably as much as me, and so do the rest of the family. Your family love me."

"But our parents still think we should spend some more time apart," Summer said. "And we have. Six long months apart, of the year our parents made us promise to spend working apart."

"Yes," Teddy said, "that was just Mum making sure we had our own experiences and didn't rush into our forever. We live for our holidays, and here we are, six months down. You've worked as an intern for Queen Rozala, and I've been helping build schools in Africa, which was amazing, and now I'm going to study agriculture at Cambridge for the rest of the year."

"You're forgetting—I've got to go to university, and you have Royal Marines officer training," Summer said.

Teddy reached up to Summer and caressed her cheek. "And we will get through all of that. What we have is perfect, a perfect love story, Cinderella," Teddy said.

Summer stroked her cheek. "The story of the princess and her Cinderella?"

"Why do I hear doubt in your voice?" Teddy asked.

"Because anyone you marry will be a princess and eventually a queen. You know my health—"

Teddy grasped Summer's forearm and kissed the spot where the nano medical device sat under her skin. It kept Summer alive. Without it, Summer wouldn't have survived past her childhood years.

Teddy hated to think about Summer being sick. She had visited Summer in hospital so many times before this tech had been fitted, and Summer's illness made Teddy feel impotent, fearful, and uber-protective.

"Your health is fine," Teddy said.

"It is just now. You know I had a relapse that stopped me starting uni for a while. I have my bad days when I'm tired, and pressure makes it worse. The whole world will be watching my every move when they find out about us."

Teddy kissed her nose and each cheek. "The doctor fixed your implant. You've been fine since. They won't find out about us anytime soon. We always go out in a big group, and everyone knows that you're close with Annie—they'll assume you're there with her."

Summer sighed. "I just worry that the press will find out when I go to university. It would be a nightmare if we were outed."

"It's like we've always planned. You went to do an internship with Aunty Roza for a year, you'll be ready to go back to uni soon, now that you're well. By the time you're finished with uni, I'll be well established as a Royal Marine, as prepared as I can be before becoming Princess of Wales, and you Lady of Wales."

Teddy let Summer roll her over. "Planned down to the last minute. Then what?"

Teddy smiled. "Then I go down on one knee like a true fairy-tale princess and ask Cinderella to marry me, we get a dog like we both want to, move in together and renovate this beautiful forgotten house, then get married. Fairy tale complete. The perfect five year plan."

Summer laughed. "Fairy tale complete? You really are sure about this, aren't you. About where we'll be in five years' time?"

"I am. There is no one else in this world who I would marry. So you're it, Cinders."

CHAPTER ONE

Five years later

Summer Fisher opened her eyes and saw the beautiful sight of Windsor Castle ahead of her. It was a sight that she never really got used to, no matter how often she saw it.

As a non-royal member of the royal household, Summer had seen it more than most. She had been coming here for playdates since she was a young girl, first to play with Princess Teddy and then, as they got older, as a companion to Princess Adrianna—or Anna, as she was known.

Although ten years the princess's senior, Summer was extremely close with Princess Anna, and when Anna had need of a private secretary, hiring Summer seemed the logical next step. Summer had studied business, administration, and management, a perfect background to help her friend.

Summer stiffened slightly as the nano pump that sat under her skin dispensed medicine into her bloodstream. Summer had a rare genetic disorder that attacked the heart and kidneys. She'd spent a lot of time in hospital as a child and had met the royal family when she had taken part in a charity day that Queen Georgina's cousin, Queen Rozala of Denbourg, organized with Queen Beatrice for children with chronic illness or special needs, or in need of hospice care.

The driver asked, "Do you want to be dropped at the entrance, Ms. Summer?"

"The stables, please."

Princess Anna was a huge horse lover, and most of her free time was spent training and riding them.

Summer felt a buzz of energy wave over her body as the medication surged its way through her system. A chip monitored her and automatically medicated her when she needed it. This technology kept her living a routine life, nothing like the restricted life she'd had to live as a child.

She heard a beep from her watch and opened her news app, which sprang up before her eyes. Summer scrolled down the newsfeed until a picture caught her eye, a picture of Princess Teddy leaving a nightclub with her newest girlfriend. The headline read "Is Pandora Priestly going to be our new Lady of Wales?"

Summer tensed, then congratulated herself on dodging a bullet. She had been best friends with the princess as they grew up together, and they became childhood sweethearts—until it ended abruptly when Teddy was twenty and she was twenty-four. Since then, the Teddy she knew had disappeared as the princess moved from woman to woman, showing her true colours.

She shut down the screen quickly. *Don't think about it.*

The car drove into the stables just as Princess Anna and her horse trotted back from a ride in Windsor Park. Not far behind her was her protection officer, Laura Lane-Hastings, chosen for her experience with horses in the Household Cavalry Mounted Regiment and her subsequent move to the elite police force Protection Command. The Queen wanted someone who would share her daughter's love of horses, but who could also protect her from harm. Quincy, head of Royal security, recommended Captain Lane-Hastings, and she fit the bill exactly.

Anna spotted her, slid off her horse, and shouted with glee, "I beat Laney back, Summer."

Summer chuckled when she saw Laney jump off her horse and wink at her. Anna rolled her eyes. "I can see you laughing, Summer."

Anna turned quickly and put her hands on her hips with indignation. "You could at least let me enjoy ten minutes thinking I beat you back."

"Ma'am," Laney said, "would I let you win? I'm a sportswoman. Fair play and all that."

"Yes, you would. Not with anyone else, but you let me win at least once a week."

Summer loved the sweet big-sister relationship Captain Lane-Hastings had with Anna. She'd do anything for the princess. Laney was built like a rugby player and would protect Anna with her life, but she could be extremely sweet and let her win a horse race. From what she had been told, Laney was virtually born in a saddle. Her parents owned racehorses, and her mother had represented the UK at the Olympics for showjumping.

Anna, like the Queen, was brought up with horse riding as part of daily life, and Anna loved it, although she'd never persuaded Summer to ride with her. When Summer was a child, she'd taken a fall off a little pony, and that had been enough to put her off riding for life.

"Give Laney a break, Annie. She's being nice."

"Nice," Laney said with a huff. "I've never been accused of such a thing."

Anna kissed Summer on both cheeks in welcome. "I suppose, but no going easy on me next time."

Anna pointed a finger at Laney. "That's an order, Captain Lane-Hastings."

Laney laughed. "Yes, ma'am. I shall leave you in my dust next time."

"We'll see."

The gravel crunched as a boy and three dogs came running at them. It was Anna's ten-year-old brother, Prince Rupert Reginald Buckingham, Roo for short, and the family dogs.

The boss of the group, a five-year-old female Airedale terrier called Freya, was followed by a black Labrador named Bear, and Ollie the brown and tan smooth-haired miniature Dachshund who was trying to catch up with the bigger dogs.

Ollie had been a present from the Queen to her wife, adopted from Battersea Dogs' Home. He was dumped at only six weeks old at the back alley of a fish-and-chip shop, with injuries and cuts. But now he had a castle for a home and loved his life with his packmates.

"Annie," Roo said, "you promised I could go riding. Why didn't you wait for me?"

"Because you were playing VR games and most probably on a different planet."

"Hi Summer."

Summer put her arm around him and kissed his dark, floppy hair. "Hi Roo."

Annie and Laney made a fuss over the dogs while the horses watched on. They were very used to the family dogs and other dogs on the estate.

"Where's Artie?" Annie asked.

Artie had been the family nanny since Katya, who just happened to be the Princess of Vospya working undercover as a nanny, left to take up the throne of Vospya.

"I told him Simon was coming with me," Rupert said.

Simon was his protection officer.

Annie crooked her finger and beckoned him to her. Summer lifted Ollie up into her arms and kissed his little snout.

"Roo, you know you're not supposed to sneak out. Anything could happen."

"*You* did. You told me so," Roo said.

"It's do as I say, Roo, not do as I do."

Laney took the reins of Anna's horse as well as her own. "I'll take the horses and Roo back to the stables for you if you're going straight back to the castle." She turned to Rupert. "Do you want to help with the horses?"

"Yes, Captain." Roo saluted.

"Thanks, Laney."

Anna kissed her horse's nose and said, "See you tomorrow, Honey."

Summer put Ollie down and ruffled Roo's messy locks of hair. "See you later, Roo."

"Bye."

The horses, Laney, Roo, and the gaggle of dogs set off for the stables.

"That boy is lucky he's adorable. He gets off with murder," Anna said.

Summer laughed. "All he has to do is bat those big blue eyes of his."

Anna looped her arm through Summer's and said, "I've been summoned to lunch with my mums."

"Surely you haven't been up to no good?" Summer joked.

"Me? No, I'm the good kid. Teddy is the wild one, although Roo gets away with it because he's the baby of the family."

Prince Rupert Reginald Buckingham was a late baby to the Queens. Queen Bea had always wanted a big family, but after Anna was born, life became extremely busy, and there never seemed to be a right time.

But as Bea was getting older, that need for another child became ever sharper. And with the help of their fertility doctors, Roo was born. Now ten years old, he kept his two mums and his sister on their toes.

Summer stopped and said, "I can go and settle in while you have lunch."

"No way, I'm not facing lunch with my mothers alone."

"Why? You have lunch and dinner with them all the time."

Anna sighed. "That's just lunch, but if I'm asked to *lunch*, that's completely different. It means something's wrong, or Teddy's done something wrong, or I'm being asked to do something they know I won't like. Besides, they invited you, and you know they love you."

Summer did know that, and she loved the two Queens right back. She had respect for their position, but since she knew them from when she was a child, Summer didn't have the nervousness around them that others might have.

But both her friendship with Summer and her love and respect for Queen Georgina and Queen Bea could lead to awkwardness.

They were the parents of her ex—her first love, Teddy—and so she had to be in Teddy's company from time to time. It was tense, and Summer tried to keep her distance, but if they did end up next to each other, they usually exchanged a few sarcastic or sometimes cutting comments.

Teddy had always been confident, but since they'd gone their separate ways, confidence had grown into arrogance. The girl she fell in love with had been kind, generous, caring, full of love, but now she spent all her time going from vacuous heiresses to celebrities, who spent their time being seen at the right places and contributed nothing to society.

It was a change in Teddy that Summer couldn't understand.

"Are you okay?" Anna interrupted her thoughts.

"Yes, sorry. Lunch sounds great."

❖

"Georgie, don't get uptight."

Bea took a glass of sparkling lime water from the footman and took a sip. George and Beatrice were in one of the smaller private rooms where there was a dining table set out with four places.

George was leaning against the fireplace nursing a pre-lunch drink, looking more frustrated by the minute.

"This is important, Bea. Teddy's taking on the title of Princess of Wales is a duty, making a vow to the nation, and she wants me simply to make a statement to the media?"

"I know."

George started to pace. "This is a solemn undertaking, Bea. She also becomes Duchess of Cornwall. An estate of five hundred and thirty four kilometres, across twenty-three counties. Do you think she's ready for that?"

Bea sighed. "No, but she has the potential. Teddy has all the tools, but she's pushing away from the responsibility."

George sat down in a leather armchair despondently. "She's pushing away from me too. We were always so close. Teddy was my shadow growing up. We did everything together."

Bea remembered George putting Teddy on her shoulders and going for a walk in the forest to teach her about types of trees and the animals that lived there. It was a beautiful relationship. George was and continued to be Teddy's hero, Bea was sure of that, but something was making Teddy push back.

"She doesn't mean to push you away, Georgie. She's just struggling to find her place, her worth in this family and to the country. She reminds me so much of you when we met."

George narrowed her eyes. "I wasn't dating rich girls and neglecting my duties."

Bea chuckled. "No, you weren't dating rich girls."

George was so inexperienced when she first met her, and it had made her adorably sweet.

"But you felt you had a lot to live up to. You struggled to feel worthy of your father's crown, worried you weren't as good with the public as Theo."

George's brother Theo was confident, had an easy way of talking to people he didn't know, much like Anna. But like Anna, Theo didn't have the burden of responsibility that their firstborn sibling did.

"I had one thing to help me that Teddy doesn't have." George smiled. "You, my darling."

Bea's heart fluttered. Bea understood how much George had relied on her. Bea was the one person in the world that saw past the calm, strong, dutiful Queen to the vulnerable George underneath.

"If only she could have someone like you, my darling."

"She did have. Summer was that person." Bea sighed. "She would be the perfect daughter-in-law and Lady of Wales."

"I know," George said, "but it wasn't to be."

"We can't pick or choose our daughter's girlfriends," Bea said, "as much as I'd love to."

"Instead we have a succession of entitled rich girls who distract her from her duty," George said.

"I've tried really hard to get on with her girlfriends, but not one of them has had a social conscience unless it would enhance her social media following," Bea said.

The door opened, and in strode their youngest daughter Anna, followed by Summer.

"Hi Mums."

George opened her arms and said, "Little bug."

Anna hugged George while Summer curtsied and then kissed Bea on each cheek.

"Summer, so nice to see you," Bea said. "You haven't spent the weekend with us at Windsor for a while."

"It's nice to be back, Your Majesty."

"How often have we had the *your majesty* conversation, Summer?"

"Sorry, ma'am. I like to do things the right way."

Bea squeezed her hand. If only Teddy could see how perfect Summer was.

Teddy never liked to talk about how she and Summer had broken up. Teddy had been heartbroken. But from what little Anna had told them, it had been partly due to the public scrutiny. Bea knew how that felt. In fact, she and George had broken up for a time in their courtship too.

She turned to George, who had her arm around Anna. "If you're quite finished, could I get a hug from my daughter?"

Anna smiled and went straight into her mama's arms, while Summer gave George a kiss on each cheek.

"Have you seen Roo, Annie?" George said. "He came and took the dogs and said he was going to find you."

Anna glanced at Summer. "Yes, Laney took him to the stables."

"He went out without Artie or Simon again, didn't he?" Bea asked.

"Well…" Anna sputtered.

George shook her head. "That boy is like Houdini. I need to have a word with him."

"So why have I been summoned?" Anna asked.

"Does there need to be something wrong to have lunch with your parents?" Bea said. "We have lunch all the time."

Bea led them over to the dining table, and while George pulled out Bea's chair, Summer said, "I can tell, believe me. What have I done?"

The footmen started to serve the lunch—poached salmon for

George, Bea, and Anna, and a light Thai salad with marinated tofu for Summer.

It touched Summer's heart that George and Bea provided vegan food, without her even asking. They treated her like one of the family, even making sure there was a non-alcoholic wine to go with lunch. They knew her meds meant she couldn't drink.

They ate a few bites, and Anna said again, "So? Is it me or my darling sister?"

Bea looked at George, inviting her to speak. George put her knife and fork down and took a sip of wine.

"It's not you, bug. We need some help with your sister."

Summer's stomach twisted. This was the awkwardness of still being part of her girlfriend's family.

"I guessed as much. What's going on?" Anna asked.

George continued, "We talked last summer about creating Teddy Princess of Wales this year, and she's done nothing but resist and block it."

Bea covered George's hand. "Teddy doesn't want the big ceremony in Wales, like your mum had with Grandfather. It was important to your mum, but Teddy thinks it doesn't hit the right tone with the public, with the economy the way it is."

Anna pushed her food around the plate. "Can I be honest?"

"You can always be honest with us," Bea said.

Anna glanced at Summer. "I agree with her. I think that kind of ceremony is in the past. We need to be relevant to today's world."

"Monarchy is rooted in the past," George said. "It's magical, a connection with all the other generations before us. To take ceremony out of the monarchy leaves it tarnished. Irrelevant."

Summer could hear the frustration in the Queen's voice.

"We can make new traditions, Mum. You can't connect with young people and people who are struggling with money by having an expensive coronation event."

"That's true, George," Bea said. "When I was part of the anti-monarchy group, that's the first thing I'd put on my placard. *Wasting public funds.*"

Summer could feel the tension around the table, but she suspected it was due to George's hurt feelings rather than anything else.

George dabbed her mouth with her napkin and was silent for a few seconds. "Well, it's too late to organize a ceremony in Wales anyway, but she has to come up with alternatives. I will not create her Princess of Wales through a press release. She is becoming a full-time working royal. She has a billion pound estate to run. I sent her to Cambridge to learn about farming and agriculture, she's been to Sandhurst and passed out as an officer, but nothing seems to make Teddy take her role seriously."

"That's where you two come in," Bea said. "Anna, we want to launch you to the public as well. That way you can help your sister."

"In what way?" Anna asked.

Summer could feel the way this was going, and she didn't like it. She squeezed her knife so tightly that her knuckles turned white.

George looked at Anna seriously. "You, Teddy, and Roo are the future of this family, and I want my people to know that. Roo is too young to take part, but you can be a big help. I cannot create you Princess Royal for as long as your Aunt Grace lives, so as well as Teddy becoming Princess of Wales, I intend to give you a royal dukedom and create you Duchess of Edinburgh."

Bea immediately said, "We want you to be a team, for the public to see a clear line of succession and a modern monarchy—and that's you two."

Summer's stomach twisted. She couldn't do this. There were too many memories, too many hurts, and too much anger to work alongside Teddy.

Bea turned to Summer. "I know it's awkward for you, but I ask this as a personal favour, Summer. Anna needs your organizational skills to support her in her duty."

How could she say no to that? "What about Teddy's private secretary? Doesn't he have a firm grasp of Teddy's schedule?"

"He only has a firm grip of the new nightclub openings or holidays in Saint-Tropez, whatever that girlfriend of hers wants to do," George quipped.

"I'll call her," Bea said. "It's time for Teddy to face her future."

CHAPTER TWO

Teddy dug her spade in the vegetable bed and turned over a heap of soil. She stopped briefly to push her dark fringe out of her eyes.

"It's going to be a bumper crop this year. I can feel it in my bones." Across the vegetable bed, her grandfather rested on his shovel.

"It will be, Grandpa."

Reg Elliot was her only grandpa. Teddy's other grandfather, the late King, died before she was born, and it made her treasure this relationship even more. Ever since Teddy could remember, she had been planting and digging out flower and vegetable beds with Grandpa.

He'd been a gardener all of his adult life and took the time to build up the bond between them, working in the garden, teaching her all about plants and the care of them.

Grandpa and her Grandma Sarah lived in a beautiful cottage on the Windsor Estate. They moved there after their daughter's marriage to the Queen to be close to Bea, and to be protected from royal watchers.

Teddy not only loved coming to see her grandparents, but also loved the physical labour of gardening, and seeing results from a hard day's toil. It was a break from the closeted world of the royal life, where there was a footman around every corner, to cater to your every need.

It was also a welcome break from the world where she was looked upon by everyone she met, and every camera that was trained on her. It was, quite simply, her escape.

"So, the lettuce will go here, and the carrots in the other bed?" Teddy said.

Her grandpa balanced his spade against his leg, then pulled out his notebook. He couldn't get to grips with modern technology, so he relied on pencil and paper.

"Yeah, carrots and onions, kale, beetroot, and squash in the beds over there." He pointed to the vegetable beds farthest away from them.

Jack, her police protection officer, was digging out one of those beds. He always got stuck in and helped.

"Then there's Roo's bed over there. He wanted to plant potatoes and sweet potatoes."

"Good choice," Teddy said.

Roo loved to spend time with his grandparents and came to have sleepovers with them all the time.

There were many cottages on the Windsor Estate. Some were normal-sized houses that fit the term *cottage* and some were huge homes that were also named cottages.

Her grandparents chose this one, Bramble Cottage, because of the huge garden, with enough room for Grandpa to cultivate his vegetables and flowers, and a large greenhouse.

"Tea's up," Grandma Sarah shouted. She walked towards them with a tray of mugs of tea just as Teddy was getting a secure message from the Queen's private secretary, Sebastian.

She opened the message. Teddy liked Bastian, as they all called him, but when she got a secure message from him, Teddy knew she was most likely in trouble.

And she was right. Teddy felt so frustrated. Why couldn't her mum speak to her face-to-face?

After a few minutes Sarah handed her a cup of tea.

"What's wrong, Teddy?" Sarah asked.

Teddy sighed. "Mum has ordered me to come to a planning meeting, for being invested as Princess of Wales. Apparently, Annie is going to be helping me."

"That's okay. Annie will be a great help to you," Grandpa said.

"It's not that. Mum keeps pressuring me. I know I'm right. The country doesn't want an expensive medieval ceremony. The title causes enough sensitivity in Wales as it is."

Jack had retreated tactfully.

Grandma Sarah handed Teddy her tea. "Come up with alternatives then. If you go in with no ideas of your own, you'll both be at a stalemate."

Grandpa nodded. "Think of all the things that are important to you and what your new title could bring to causes or movements that are important. Little Annie will help you."

"Just remember," her grandmother said, "your mum probably feels a little hurt that you don't want to share the same traditional thing as she went through with her father. I remember watching that ceremony live on TV from Caernarfon. I never imagined my granddaughter would become Princess of Wales too."

Teddy smiled and put her arm around the shoulders of her much smaller grandmother and kissed her head. She didn't want to say it out loud, but she was never going to live up to her mother as Princess of Wales, in the public's eyes.

Instead she said, "Usually it's my love life that Mum and Mama want updates on."

"They just want you to be happy," her grandfather said, "and whoever you're going out with draws the public interest."

"When are we going to meet your young lady?" Grandma Sarah asked.

Never.

❖

Teddy was travelling to Buckingham Palace for the dreaded meeting about her new role. She wasn't looking forward to it. Her mum's private secretary, Sebastian, would be there, as well as Annie and her own secretary.

She liked Bastian, as he was less formally called. She had grown up with him, but he stood for Queen Georgina's generation, and Teddy was looking to do things differently.

She was thankful that her two mums had engagements today. Not that she didn't adore her parents, but if the Queen was there, everyone would be looking to her for the direction she wanted to go, and Teddy hadn't figured out what way she wanted to go yet, but she knew it had to be different.

Jack turned around from his front seat. "We'll be five minutes."

"Thanks, Jack."

Teddy's phone rang, and she answered from her watch, a small holo screen popping up in front of her. It was Pandora.

"Teddy? Dinner tonight at the Fire Club? It's all booked."

Not even a *hello* or a *how are you doing today*. But Teddy was used to that from Pandora.

She'd met Pandora three months ago. They were introduced at a party one of her old school friends had organized. After that, Pandora always seemed to be at any social event Teddy was at.

Eventually they got together. It wasn't serious, none of her girlfriends were, but it was fun, mostly, and it kept her family off her back. They wanted her to settle down. She was never going to settle down, but they didn't know her plans.

For most people her age, marriage was a destination only if they wanted it. But it was expected—by her family and the country—that she would marry and produce an heir and a spare. That wasn't going to happen. She wasn't going to have her heart broken again for love.

Teddy had long since realized that there wouldn't be another woman who would share her throne—she would do it alone. There had only ever been one woman who she pictured sharing her life, and that had been a youthful fantasy.

Teddy's parents weren't going to rush her down the aisle with women like Pandora, rich girls with very little social conscience.

Teddy said, "I've got a meeting at the palace this afternoon. I don't know what time I'll finish." Teddy wasn't in the mood tonight. She'd had her fill of cameras in her face, people gawking at her, and stories about her in the papers for the last few weeks.

"You're not going to be in a meeting till eight o'clock tonight, Teddy."

"No," Teddy sighed. "Okay, as long as it's private, Pandora. I don't want a big scene."

Pandora smiled. "It's a private dining room, Teddy. Don't worry. Publicity is good. I don't know why you are so against it. It keeps you relevant."

"I'm not a celebrity, and I'm not relevant."

"Okay, grumpy. Just pick me up at seven thirty, and we can have the most delicious meal at the Fire Club. Bye."

Pandora hung up, and just as she did a call came through from her PR guy, Kurt. Teddy met him at university, before she went to officer training at Sandhurst. He helped her do all the things she never got to do in her teenage years while living under the royal microscope.

"Hi, Teddy, I'm running twenty minutes late. I'll be there as soon as possible."

"Okay, see you soon."

"Oh, do you want me with you tonight?"

"Where?" Teddy was confused.

"At the restaurant. The Fire Club," Kurt said.

Teddy squinted. "How did you know?"

"Pandora called me to put it in your diary."

Before I even knew about it or agreed? Teddy was feeling like a pawn on a chessboard.

"Fine. I'll see you soon."

Teddy's car drove through the gates of Buckingham Palace, past the tourists that crowded around the decorative iron fence surrounding it. She looked up to the roof. The Sovereign's Standard wasn't flying above, meaning Queen Georgina was still out on her royal engagement for the day.

She wished she didn't have a sense of relief. Her mum had always been her hero, her best friend, but Teddy always thought she fell short of her mother's expectations, and the country's.

So why try?

That intrusive thought had been torturing her since she was a teenager, when she fully understood the enormity of her destiny, and the act she had to follow.

The car stopped at the entrance, and Teddy tried to banish the thought from her mind.

One of the footmen opened the car door for her. "Thank you, Tom."

The deputy sergeant of the royal household bowed his head and escorted her in.

"Where are we, Sierra?" Teddy asked.

"The small dining room on the first floor, Your Royal Highness."

"Lead the way."

Teddy followed her upstairs and along to the room. Sierra stopped at the door and said, "The Queen's private secretary will be with you shortly."

"Thanks."

Teddy walked in and was taken aback to see Summer sitting at the table alone. She had not expected her to be part of this. But if Anna was involved, maybe she should have. Summer looked up and immediately stood, curtsied, and said, "Your Royal Highness."

Teddy balled her fists tightly. She hated Summer curtsying to her. They had known each other intimately, but by doing that Summer was building a wall between them.

"Where's Annie?" Teddy asked.

"She's just getting changed. We were at an engagement with the Abigail Trust, we just got back."

Teddy nodded and walked to the head of the table. The Abigail Trust was named in her mama's sister's name. She had died when her mama was young, and she loved horses. Queen Bea started the charity to give city kids the chance to be taken out to the countryside to ride and work with horses.

When Anna came of age, it seemed only natural for her to take on that charity as a patron, in view of her love of horses. Teddy could ride well, but she didn't have the passion for horses that Anna had.

Teddy put one hand in her pocket and stared down at the report waiting on the table: *The Investiture of the Princess of Wales.*

Teddy's stomach clenched with tension. Her whole life had been hurtling towards this moment, the first step towards her destiny to become Queen, which she prayed was many, many years ahead.

She wanted to run and never be caught. Summer being here only made things worse.

Teddy sat down at the head of the table. Normally, Teddy was in a large group whenever she saw Summer. They maybe exchanged a few pithy remarks, but this, being alone, eyeball to eyeball, was another thing altogether.

The silence hung heavily between them. The only sound was the ticking of the antique clock that seemed to be louder than it should be.

She had to break the silence, but just as she opened her mouth, the clock struck on the hour and covered her words.

"Sorry?" Summer said.

"How have you been?"

"Well, thank you. How about you?"

Teddy hated this small talk. How could you have small talk with someone you've been captivated by passionately, touched passionately, loved passionately? It was wrong.

"I'm okay. You and Annie have been beavering away being the good children, I hear, topping the charts for the number of royal visits this year, behind the Queens and Aunt Grace, of course," Teddy said sarcastically.

"And you, Teddy?"

"I've been busy."

Summer raised her eyebrows. "So I've read."

That was a dig. "What do you mean?" Teddy said defensively.

"Just that you couldn't fail to hear about the club openings and parties you've been to with—sorry, is it Penelope?"

"Pandora. My girlfriend's called Pandora."

"Oh yes. How could I forget?" Summer said.

Summer looked down to her computer pad, making Teddy all the more annoyed. "It's not my fault if the media choose to focus on the places I go in my private life, and not my royal visits."

Summer never looked up, but said, "You can control where you go. You know where you're likely to be photographed."

Teddy felt such anger inside. Who was Summer to criticize her? They'd had a great relationship, loving, caring, with great ambitions for the future.

They used to spend lazy Sunday afternoons walking the grounds of Windsor, planning what causes they would promote when they got older, when Teddy became Princess of Wales, when Teddy would become Queen—before it all unravelled between them.

"Listen, I'm not the one asking the photographers to turn up. In fact I go out of my way to have a private life," Teddy said.

Still Summer didn't look up, and it infuriated Teddy.

"And yet they still manage to find you."

Teddy opened her mouth, ready to let her frustration rip, when Sebastian and her sister walked into the room, laughing together.

Summer stood out of respect for Annie, and Bastian bowed quickly to Teddy. "Your Royal Highness."

"Hey big sister," Anna said as she kissed Teddy's head and gave her a hug.

"Hi pipsqueak. Little sister coming to keep me in check?" Teddy smiled, her anger now dissipating.

"I'm the good child, remember?" Annie joked.

"Oh, I know. So, we're being launched onto the public like a rocket, Duchess of Edinburgh?"

Anna flounced onto the chair. "I know, makes me sound ancient."

"If it would be all right for me to chair the meeting, I can kick off, Your Royal Highnesses. Or would you like me to wait for your PA, ma'am?" Bastian said to Teddy.

"No, carry on."

Kurt didn't usually do well in meetings like this. After university, he worked in magazines and TV. He wasn't exactly au fait with royal protocol, but at least he was on her side.

"The Queen is quite anxious that Your Royal Highnesses are created Princess of Wales and Duchess of Edinburgh before the end of this year. I understand the traditional ceremony isn't thought to suit you, ma'am?"

Teddy leaned back in her chair and crossed her legs. "No, it wouldn't suit people in my own age group. Especially when you have a cost of living crisis, and government benefits are being cut left, right, and centre by our government."

She looked over at Summer and saw her jaw tense up. "And before you say it, Bastian—or anyone else around this table—I do know I can't say that in public."

It was a natural thing for Teddy to do when she felt she'd made a big statement. When they'd been together, Teddy relied on Summer to make sure she was saying or doing the right thing. They had an almost telepathic link, and Teddy instinctively turned to her, even though she didn't want to.

Anna piped up. "I don't always agree with my sister, but she is right. I've told our mums that. Monarchy needs to be able to adapt, and a traditional ceremony like the Queen had just won't hit the right tone."

"Summer? Any thoughts?"

Here we go.

"I'm in complete agreement. It has to be something different, an event where the princess can give her vow of service to the nation, but framed by a different kind, a more modern kind, of event."

Summer agreed? Would wonders never cease?

There was a time when they agreed on everything, had the same goals, but not any more. Teddy knew Summer was disapproving of her lifestyle, her not taking her role seriously, her not working as hard as Annie.

But at least Summer was honest about this.

"Do you have any ideas, ma'am?" Summer said.

That made fiery anger race through her body. Every time Summer used a curtsy or a title, she was mentally distancing herself from Teddy. Shoving and pushing her away.

"No, I don't, *Ms. Fisher*, but I'm sure that you know best, and between you, my sister, and Bastian you'll come up with the right idea." Teddy stood. "So if you all decide what *I* should be doing, let me know, and I'll play along like a good little puppet."

"Teddy," Annie said, "calm down. We're just talking here."

"I have an appointment this evening, so if you'll excuse me, I need to get ready."

"A charitable event?"

Summer was mocking her even more. She knew how to wound her more than anyone else.

Teddy didn't answer. Summer looked back down at the desk and shook her head.

She could feel the disgust and disappointment with every shake of Summer's head.

Teddy walked out of the room and didn't look back.

❖

Teddy picked up Pandora that evening and they headed to the restaurant Pandora had chosen. Teddy zoned out of Pandora's incessant chatter. This afternoon's meeting had left Teddy with a lot on her mind.

Anger, frustration, and a suffocating sense of responsibility that she didn't want to bear.

Teddy had pushed her responsibilities away to the future for so long, and now the future was here. It was a shock.

Not only did she have this new title, but she also had the Duchy of Cornwall and the enormity of the land there. Having Summer there to witness her unsuitability for the role only made matters worse. It hadn't always been that way, and seeing Summer today reminded her of a happier, simpler time, when they'd so looked forward to this time in their life that they'd made their five-year plan underneath their favourite tree.

They had been together since Teddy's eighteenth birthday party, and when they were just about to make things much more serious, when Teddy turned twenty, their dreams were left in tatters, and now, five years later, they were leading separate lives. It still hurt like hell.

The flash of a camera knocked Teddy from her thoughts. Pandora leaned into her. "Smile. I want a picture for my socials."

"You know I don't like you posting pictures with me," Teddy said sharply.

"Why not? You're my girlfriend," Pandora said equally as sharply.

Teddy wasn't comfortable with that term, but she let it slide. "I get enough pictures taken of me without more being put out there. Respect my privacy, okay?"

"You're so touchy, Teddy. Fine."

Jack lowered the privacy screen from the front seat and turned around. "The restaurant entrance is full of press, ma'am."

"What? How could they know?" Teddy looked at Pandora. "You said it would be private. How did they find out?"

"I don't know." Pandora shrugged.

Teddy did not feel like this today. This afternoon had left her feeling melancholy for a whole number of reasons, and fighting her way through the press was not going to make her feel any better.

"Drive on past, Jack. We'll cancel the reservation," Teddy said.

"No way," Pandora said angrily. "You promised me. First you won't take a picture with me, and now you want to cancel dinner…"

Teddy closed her eyes as Pandora continued to rant. She would never get any peace if they didn't go to dinner.

"Fine. Jack, stop at the restaurant. When we go in, find out if we can leave from a back entrance."

A smile lit up Pandora's face, and she clapped her hands excitedly. "Thank you."

"We need to find out how this leaked out."

"Okay, okay, Teddy. Chill out and enjoy tonight first."

The car stopped in front of the restaurant. The driver got out and opened the car door, while Jack was a barrier between them and the press pack.

The noise and flashes from the small drone cameras hit them while the press shouted questions at them.

"Are you getting engaged, ma'am? Is Pandora your Lady of Wales?"

"Princess Edwina? Teddy?"

Jack and the driver managed to get them through the front door, but all the while Teddy's anger and stress were building.

The noise and the confusion dropped away as they were finally in the club. Teddy looked around, and the whole room was silent and watching them intently. She felt like an exhibit at the zoo.

Pandora didn't appear to feel the stress. The attention brought out the biggest smile on her face.

The maître d' hurried towards them. "Your Royal Highness. Thank you for coming. I have your table ready in the corner over there."

He pointed to a table at the back wall of the dining area, where they could be seen by everyone.

"I thought our table was in a private room?" Teddy asked.

The maître d' looked confused. "We don't have private rooms, ma'am."

There was an awkward silence, and Teddy could feel everyone looking at them.

Pandora whispered, "Don't make a fuss."

Teddy had no choice. She complied and walked over to the table. It turned out to be the most unpleasant meal. Teddy hardly ate anything, not because of the food but because of the attention and Pandora's reaction to it.

Pandora was *loving* the attention, talking loudly, laughing, exaggerating every story she told. It was like a performance to her. Teddy was always aware she was some kind of trophy to Pandora, a trophy to display for attention and likes on her social media accounts, but since Teddy was in a sense using her to keep her family off her back, it had been a fair trade-off in Teddy's eyes.

This was going too far. Seeing and working with Summer today reminded Teddy why she kept her love life casual, and using her girlfriends to keep the family from insisting she take relationships seriously was reaching its limit.

Teddy's mum had lived a conventional life. She waited until she fell in love with her perfect partner and settled down to the dynastic business of creating heirs. Teddy once thought that she would follow her mum's example. She'd met her childhood sweetheart when she was a toddler and her mums took her to a children's charity event, organized by her aunt Roza.

Queen Roza of Denbourg was actually Queen Georgina's cousin, but they were all so close and had children of similar ages, so Queen Roza and Crown Consort Lennox were aunts to Teddy, Annie, and Rupert.

Apparently she and Summer met at that event, and they'd been friends ever since.

"Teddy, are you listening to me?" Pandora said.

"What? No."

"People are listening, Teddy."

Teddy looked around, and when she did, people's heads snapped back quickly to their plates or their partners. There were some secretly trying to video them too. They thought it was not noticeable, but Teddy spotted it easily. It was something she'd lived with for years.

Teddy had enough. She signalled to Jack, who was standing by the entrance.

"What is it?" Pandora asked.

"We're leaving."

Pandora tried to convey her frustration by whispering, so it wasn't so easily heard. "What are you talking about? We've only had the first course."

"Jack, can you pay the bill and find out if we can leave by the back door?"

"Yes, ma'am. That won't be a problem," Jack said.

If looks could kill, Teddy would have been dead many times over by the time they got into the car. Pandora was furious.

As soon as they were on their own, Pandora exploded. "What were you thinking?"

"I was tired of being looked at like a zoo exhibit."

"You humiliated me in front of the whole restaurant," Pandora said.

"By leaving because we had no privacy? I have none in my public life—I'm not going to be on display in my private life."

She silently thanked Jack when he put up the screen to give them more of that privacy.

"Why do you care? What's the big deal about letting me have some attention?" Pandora said angrily. "You have it all. You don't have to fight for publicity and attention. You get it by just walking into a room. People like me have to work hard at it. To stay relevant."

"You can have it. I've lived under a microscope since before I was born. I won't have any more attention than I need to. You promised me a private room."

"It's not my fault, is it? I didn't know the press would be there, or that the restaurant would get the wrong booking from Kurt."

That's exactly what Teddy feared. She had a bad feeling that Pandora had orchestrated this whole evening. If she couldn't trust her, time was up on their brief relationship.

They both sat in silence till they arrived at Pandora's. Teddy got out and said to Jack, "I'll just take Pandora up to her door. I won't be long."

Pandora lived with her mother in the family home in Mayfair. Her mother liked to travel around the nicest parts of the world, so Pandora mostly had the house to herself.

They walked up the steps, and Teddy knew she needed to end it.

Pandora unlocked the door and said, "Are you coming in?"

Teddy put her hands in her pockets. "No, I'll head home."

Pandora grasped her arm. "I'm sorry about tonight, okay? It won't happen again."

That made Teddy more suspicious. "How can you be sure of that? Do you know who called the press?"

"Of course not. I mean, we should have left the way you wanted to when we arrived," Pandora said.

Was she wrong for suspecting Pandora? Maybe she was too jaded. It was so hard to trust people who hadn't proved themselves over many years. Perhaps she should sleep on it. Just because Teddy wanted to end this didn't mean it had to be done after such a catastrophic date.

"Let's forget about it. I'll call you soon."

Pandora leaned in for a kiss, but Teddy kissed her cheek instead. "Goodnight."

"Have you asked if I can come to the Windsor Horse Trials yet?"

Pandora had been going on about being invited to a family event since she'd met her, but Teddy kept putting her off. Pandora and her family would be like oil and water, and Teddy didn't want to share that close family intimacy with someone she didn't trust one hundred per cent or care enough about to let her guard down.

The Windsor Horse Trials were a public event, but the family had a drinks party in the evening. They all shared a love of horses, and many of them took part in events throughout the trials, so it was a special time.

"Not yet. I will. I'll let you know. Goodnight," Teddy said.

As she walked back to the car, she thought of what a coward she was. She was worried about how Pandora would take rejection, honestly, not because she cared about Teddy, but because of the attention she would lose.

Yet more attention Teddy didn't want to think about.

❖

Summer lay back on her couch working on her computer while she watched TV. Anna's diary was so busy that she had to keep on top of it constantly. Summer loved her job. She liked being busy, and helping her best friend made it perfect for her.

Once she updated her diary, she stared at the computer screen. It was time to start her new project.

"Computer, make new file." Summer hesitated. "Princess of Wales Project."

Summer had been dreading this since she got home. During the day she had managed to block out the noise of her mind, her memories, and what this would mean, but now here in the quiet of her own living room, there was nowhere to hide.

It had been many years since they had broken up, but it was a bad break-up, and not something she cared to remember. Although they had seen each other since then, they'd never been alone together.

Today they had been in a big empty room with nothing but awkwardness and discomfort. Summer wasn't a fool. She knew that Teddy felt the same, and yet they had to do this. Summer wondered if there was any small part of Teddy that still hurt, or was she really just full of bullshit and sarcastic jokes? That was what she showed to Summer every time they met.

Today Teddy had flounced out angrily rather than deal with the reality of her new role. It was so typical of who Teddy was now, but things had once been so different, so simple when they were young and in love. She opened up her photo and video file and hesitated over a folder called *Charming and Cinderella*.

They had called themselves that since childhood. After watching the classic film together as young children, they had quite naturally taken on those roles. When they grew up and became involved seriously, the names became sweet terms of endearment.

Why she didn't have the strength to delete these pictures and videos, she didn't know. Summer opened it once in a blue moon when memories drifted across her consciousness. Memories that would never leave her.

She called up a picture of Teddy and her, sitting under their favourite tree. They used to dream there, dream of a time when Teddy would become a working royal, Princess of Wales, and she and Summer would try to make the world a better place.

Summer moved on to a picture of them as young kids, a picture her mum took of them both playing together at a charity play day. She was dressed up like a fairy-tale princess and Teddy like a knight in shining armour.

It was a day like the first day they met. She'd been around six years old, and Teddy a few years younger.

Summer held on to Princess Rozala's hand as they walked around the play day. There was noise and laughter as the children chased around the room. All the kids were wild and excited, apart from one.

Summer saw a little girl on the other side of the room hanging on to an adult, and trying her best to hide.

"Roza? Who is that girl?"

Roza knelt down. "That's my cousin's daughter, Princess Teddy. Would you like to meet her?"

"Yeah, she's sad."

"I think she's shy. Maybe we can help her."

"Yeah," Summer said. She skipped over to the girl, who was dressed in cute blue dungarees and had dark brown hair.

"Teddy, I'd like you to meet my friend Summer."

"Hi Teddy, you want to come and see the clown with me?" Summer reached out her hand.

Teddy still looked nervous but took her hand, and the pair of them ran off together.

That had been the start of their intense friendship. Teddy had the deepest blue eyes. She'd noticed that at their first meeting. The image of Teddy relaxing and taking her hand stayed with Summer.

Something few people knew about Teddy was she lacked confidence, and Summer's friendship and love had supported her and allowed Teddy to flourish.

That had been the case, but in the years since they'd parted, who knew? It wasn't the image that Teddy created now. Teddy gave the impression that she hadn't a care in the world, everything was a laugh and a joke, and that she took few things seriously.

For the future of the royal family, Summer hoped that wasn't the case. But even if it was, it was Summer's job to create a plan that would show the public otherwise, no matter the truth of it, and no doubt she'd have to fight Teddy's PA all the way.

Summer closed the file and sat up. "Computer, delete file Prince—" Something was holding her back. Why couldn't she get rid of the baggage she was carrying around? "Forget it," Summer said in frustration.

She was angry at herself that she still couldn't let the memories go, when clearly, going by the number of women she had been with, Teddy could.

The phone rang—her mum and dad. Just what she needed to distract her. They were currently on a cruise, living life to the full.

Summer encouraged them to. They had such a difficult and painful time during her childhood, with hospital visits, worry that she wasn't going to make it, and the highs and lows of new treatments. Now that Summer's condition was controlled, it was time for them to fully enjoy life.

But they still called her every day. They were the best parents Summer could hope for.

"Hi Mum, Dad. How's Jamaica?"

"Look, darling!" Summer's mum spun the phone around.

Her mum and dad were holding each other at the railings of the ship, and there was blue sky and blue ocean as far as the eye could see.

Summer smiled. "Don't go all *Titanic* on me. I want you both back in one piece."

"Don't worry," her dad said. "I'll keep your mum safe." He wrapped his arms around her. "So tell me, how's work?"

Tell the truth, or withhold the information that would make them worry?

Both her parents had treated Teddy like a second daughter, and when they broke up and Teddy quickly moved on, it hurt them as it did her.

She chose for them not to worry. "Everything's great. Annie's got the Windsor Horse Trials coming up, so it's all horsey stuff. You know how focused she gets on competition."

"Just don't let her talk you into going up on one again," her mum said.

"Don't worry, Mum." Once bitten, twice shy.

CHAPTER THREE

It had been two days since Teddy's very public date with Pandora, and just as expected their pictures and videos were all over social media, both from outside and inside the restaurant. Teddy just wanted to hide, so she deleted all her social media apps and stuck her head in the sand.

Pandora had called a few times, but she didn't answer. She couldn't deal with her now, and yet couldn't end it either.

Luckily today she could have some privacy and be treated like a normal human being—well, as normal as she could be. Twice a week, public engagements permitting, Teddy volunteered at a charity for the unhoused called Street Kitchen.

This was one part of her life that was private. Here in this busy kitchen in her jeans, T-shirt, and beanie hat, she was just one of the volunteers. Nobody was overawed by her presence because she'd been coming here since she was a young child, with Annie.

Their mum had brought them here, not as an official visit but privately, to let her children both understand how lucky they were, and to instil in them the need to serve and contribute without there being cameras everywhere.

Teddy had been volunteering regularly since she was a teenager. Annie did two days a week as well, at a sister Street Kitchen over in the East End of London. Here she was just one of the volunteers and known just as Teddy.

Marco, the head cook, directed all the staff. "Teddy? How are those beans looking?"

"Good to go." Teddy poured the food into a metal serving dish and took it over to the bain-marie serving display that looked out to the dining area.

"Thanks, Teddy," Kim, one of the serving staff, said.

Years of working here with mostly the same people gave it a relaxed atmosphere for Teddy. Only new volunteers found it strange to see Princess Edwina serve here, and it required an adjustment for them.

Apart from when she was with her family, Teddy felt the most normal here. It was somewhere she could give back to a great cause. Her mums always made it crystal clear to her, Annie, and Roo how privileged they were, and that a life of service was important because of that.

"I'll take the tea and coffee out now, Marco," Teddy said.

The large tea urn had been brewing for long enough and was ready to go out. She took the trolley. As she started to push it to the kitchen door, Jack came out of the storeroom, carrying three boxes.

In front of him was the indomitable catering manager, Kath, with her notepad. "Put those boxes down by the sink and collect the other three, thank you."

Jack rolled his eyes and Teddy sniggered. They always put Jack to good use while Teddy was here. Jack pretended to be annoyed, but she knew it meant a lot to him, helping out here.

Teddy rolled the trolley out into the dining room. It was full for breakfast and as usual there was a line of people waiting for a place at the table to open up.

It suited Teddy to come here in the morning. She woke at four and arrived here by five to help with set-up and food prep. The two days here always gave a sense of stability to her week.

Teddy pushed the trolley to the first table. "Tea? Coffee?"

"Tea, please?" A middle-aged woman held her cup up.

"No problem. Milk?" Teddy offered.

"Yes, please."

Teddy filled up the cup and handed it over. With her casual clothes, nobody tended to give her a second glance. It's not the place you would expect to meet Princess Edwina, heir to throne, serving tea, so she mostly went unnoticed.

But sometimes the regulars worked it out. Amazingly, though, they built up such a regard for her that they didn't talk and respected her anonymity. It was a protection she didn't take lightly.

Once she went around most of the tables, she saw her fellow volunteer Andy talking with a young girl she hadn't seen before. Andy had himself once been unhoused. She had known him since she was a teenager.

Street Kitchen had helped him find housing and get through a landscaping college course. Now he was a self-employed gardener and volunteered here to give back and help people the way he had been helped.

Teddy arrived at the table just as the young woman walked away. "Is she new?"

Andy nodded. "A runaway. She was physically abused by her stepfather."

Teddy's phone was on silent but she felt it vibrate in her pocket. She ignored it. "Will she let us help?"

"She's promised to come back tomorrow and get some help for housing," Andy said.

Street Kitchen had expanded over the years and was now a one-stop shop for food, shower facilities, and housing, as well as legal and employment advice.

"I hope so. She looked lost."

"I know how that feels," Andy said, "but we can help her, just like I was."

Teddy's phone vibrated again. It was Pandora. She'd called many times, and Kurt too.

She stuffed her phone back in her pocket. Both of them knew that her mornings here were sacrosanct. When she thought about that young woman and the differences in her life compared to Pandora's decadent lifestyle, it made her angry.

Teddy always felt a sense of guilt at how lucky she was, but at least she recognized it and was trying to give back. Pandora hadn't a clue or a care about the lives the people in here were forced to live.

"How's your grandpa's garden?"

Teddy smiled. "It's doing well. I was just helping him with some planting. It's going to be a big crop this year."

"Tell him I was asking for him."

"I will," Teddy said.

Her grandpa had been a gardener all his working life, until he retired when his daughter married the Queen. It became too difficult to continue work then, and her mama wanted her parents close, so they moved to the Windsor Estate.

Andy had helped her grandpa with his garden while he was at college, and Grandpa had been a mentor for Andy's final garden design project. He had loved helping out and had even given Andy some of his old contacts for work.

"How's life? I got your wedding invitation," Teddy asked.

Andy looked uncomfortable. "Listen, I know you probably can't come. It's hard for you to go anywhere, but I didn't want to *not* ask you."

Teddy pulled an envelope from her back pocket and handed it to Andy. It was a traditional wedding invite RSVP.

"I'll be there. I've already cleared the day in my diary. I'll try to keep it secret. I don't want my presence overshadowing your day."

Andy had a big smile on his face and reached out to give her a hug. "It would mean so much to me to have you there. You were here with your mum, Queen Beatrice, the first day I came in here looking for food and help, and I've never looked back."

Teddy patted his shoulder. "I'm glad you still come here. You give the people hope that there is a future, a good future."

Jack appeared at her side, pulling on his jacket and then straightening his tie. "Excuse me, Andy—ma'am, we have to go. The press are encamped outside, stopping the people coming in. They've found out you come here."

Teddy closed her eyes as her stomach sank to her toes. *I knew this couldn't last forever.*

"We've got the car out at the back entrance."

She took a deep breath. "I better go, Andy. Can you finish up with the teas and coffees?"

"I will. Get yourself going."

"Can you tell Kath I'm sorry about the obstruction out front, but they'll soon go when they realize I'm gone."

"Yeah, on you go. See you soon, okay?" Andy said.

Teddy nodded but knew this was probably over. She followed Jack to the waiting car at the back alley where the bins were.

She got into the back of the car, pulled off her hat, and threw it across the seat. Teddy was so angry. This was her last haven of privacy, one where she could do some good. One where she felt like a normal person. And it was gone.

The car drove off, and when they got out on the road, some of the press pack noticed and set off after them.

Jack turned around in his seat. "Apparently your dinner the other night has gone completely viral, and someone talked about Street Kitchen."

"Fuck."

Teddy took out her phone and ran a quick search. She and Pandora were trending everywhere. There were stories about Pandora, delving into her family history, her influencer status, and implying she and Teddy were already engaged and about to announce it in days.

There were also more concerning stories about Pandora taking money to use her influencer status to talk about Teddy.

"Computer, play voicemail."

"Hey Teddy, I know you're at a homeless thing, but we hit the headlines in a big way. Did you see we're trending on social media? My phone is ringing constantly for interviews, but don't worry, I won't do anything without talking to you."

Pandora sounded excited, and not surprised in the slightest that she was at Street Kitchen. The thing was, Teddy never told her where she came twice a week. This wasn't good.

Someone had told Pandora. When she thought back to the restaurant debacle, Kurt and Pandora seemed to have planned it together. In fact, they appeared to be getting closer.

She had to tell Pandora it was over between them, but Teddy was worried what the fallout would be, what Pandora would share about her private life.

The car pulled into the gates of Kensington Palace, where Teddy's apartments were, and left the press cars behind them. Her heart sank when she saw the Rolls-Royce with the Sovereign's flag on it.

Teddy let out a sigh. *I'm in trouble.*

She walked into the palace and upstairs to her apartment. Standing outside her door was Major Cameron, the Queen's protection officer and dresser, and a male protection officer called Boothby.

"Cammy?"

Cammy and the other officer bowed their heads. "Your mother is inside waiting for you, ma'am."

Cammy had been close to Teddy all her life, but she was a stickler for protocol.

"I'm about to get a bollocking?" Teddy said.

"Just listen to your mum and be open-minded. She loves you."

Teddy nodded and took a breath. "Wish me luck, then."

Teddy walked into her apartment and made her way to the living room. She opened the door and saw her mum sitting in an armchair, typing away at her holo screen.

"Mum?"

When her mum looked up, Teddy bowed her head. It would seem

strange to an outsider, but she and Annie were brought up since birth to show her parents the respect that they were due, as others did to her.

They were bowing to the Crown rather than their mother, although her mother and the Crown were one.

"Teddy." Her mum stood and kissed her daughter on each cheek, then sat back down. "Why is this happening, Teddy?" Her mum pointed behind her to the screen on the wall.

Pictures and headlines flashed across the screen about her and Pandora.

"Yeah, I'm sorry about that. I—"

"You're sorry?" her mum said. "I am between visits today, and I've had to find the time to come and see you."

That pissed Teddy off. She wasn't a child. "There was no need to. It's just media stuff that we always have to deal with."

"No, this is attention that you have created for yourself. You have the press waiting for you at this restaurant and have a table right in the middle of said establishment, with cameras all around you."

Teddy walked up to her mum and said defensively, "That wasn't my fault. Someone leaked where I was going."

"It's never your fault, though, is it Teddy?"

Teddy squeezed her fist trying to control her anger.

Her mum continued, "I was touring a hospice this morning, and the press pack are trying to push their way closer to me, pushing the local schoolchildren out of the way, just to shout and ask me about your relationship. That is not fair to the hospice staff and local people, who had come out to see your mother and me."

Teddy closed her eyes. "I'm sorry about that."

"This is the worst it's been, but every relationship you enter into brings this unwanted attention. You are called the playgirl princess. Is that what you want to be known as?" her mum asked.

Teddy didn't answer and walked over to the living room window.

Her mum got up. "You and your sister are being launched as full-time royals this summer. You don't need this following you everywhere you go. Is this relationship with Ms. Priestly serious, or like the others where you get bored and move on?"

Teddy turned around fast and couldn't stop her anger spilling out. "I'm sorry we can't all be perfect like you, Mum. You waited patiently for your *one* to come along, and in walked Mama. Fairy-tale love story and wedding. The end."

Teddy could see from her mum's tightened jaw that she was trying to control her anger.

"Your mama and I just want you to be happy. We thought you had that with Summer—"

"Of course Summer is just perfect in your eyes. The perfect future Queen Consort. Well, no. She broke up with me at the first hint of scrutiny and stomped on my heart."

Her mum reached out to touch Teddy's shoulder, but she pulled away and walked back to the centre of the room.

"Pandora hasn't broken my heart, but you don't approve of her, or any other of my girlfriends." Teddy's body was almost shaking with frustration.

"We were always open to whoever you had in your life, but you never let us meet them," her mum said.

"I could see in your faces you didn't approve without ever meeting them. We can't all be perfect like you, Mum. Be the perfect Queen, the perfect army officer, the perfect naval officer, and meet the perfect wife."

Teddy couldn't stop her fears and resentments flowing out. This morning she'd lost the one activity that meant something to her, and her emotions were all over the place.

"Teddy," her mum said seriously, "I'm going to be completely honest and straight with you. For good or bad, you are not a normal person. Every move you make, every decision, good or bad, has an effect on the public's view of you, of us as a family. If you were a normal person, you could date as much or as little as you liked. You could have the freedom to work and play as you will, but you don't have that freedom. For that price you live a hugely privileged life and owe a duty of service."

"You don't think I know that? The one thing I loved doing was working at Street Kitchen, and now I can't do that privately. It was important to me that I had one place I was just Teddy."

"I understand that, but your dating lifestyle, especially this young woman Pandora, brings extra publicity. She is a social media influencer, and that creates drama around you and brings attention to things you don't want to get attention, like Street Kitchen. It creates newspaper speculation like this."

Her mum opened a file on the TV holo screen. "You get speculation like this."

Teddy saw a poll that was running on the biggest news channel:

Should Pampered Pandora be our next Lady of Wales?
  No 86%
  Yes 14%

Teddy didn't want anyone as her Lady of Wales. If only they knew. Teddy was resolved to break up with Pandora, but her parents' and the public's disapproval made her feel backed into a corner. Who were they to tell her who she should date?

"You see, Teddy? Your relationship is either serious or it's not, and you need to know because everyone on the outside sees the person on your arm as the next princess," her mum said.

Teddy's answer was out in seconds, simply through her stubbornness. "I'd like permission to bring Pandora to the Windsor Horse Trials and the family party at night."

Her mum's eyes opened wide. She was clearly surprised. "Of course you may bring your girlfriend, and we will look forward to meeting her."

"No, you won't, but thanks." *What have I said? Idiot.*

But she couldn't backtrack now. It looked like she would be dating Pandora for the longer term. In the end it wouldn't matter. She wasn't going to marry or have children. She'd decided when she and Summer broke up. She would serve out her time as Queen and hand the royal authority to Annie, if she was still living, and then to Annie's children.

The country would be far better served by her sister.

"Teddy, I wish—"

"I was more like Annie, I know."

"If you would let me finish, I was going to say I wish we were close as we used to be. You need to get this monumental chip off your shoulder, Teddy. You are very privileged." Her mum stood awkwardly, then looked at her watch. "I better go to my next appointment."

"I'll see you at the weekend." Teddy felt bad. She shouldn't have jumped to conclusions about what her mum was saying. She rubbed her face vigorously.

She was sad that she had drifted apart from her mum. But when you were constantly not meeting the standard set by your mum's high bar, it was easier just to stay away.

"Computer, call Pandora."

After a few rings she answered. "Hi Teddy."

"We're going to the Windsor Horse Trials," Teddy said.

"And the family drinks party?"

"Yes." Teddy sighed. "The whole thing."

"Thank you! What will I wear? Oh, I've got to go shopping."

Why did I get into this?

That night Bea and George lay in bed. Bea was trying to sleep off a migraine, trying too hard, but her mind was full of worry. George wasn't even trying to sleep, it was too early for her, but she was sitting up in bed reading, just keeping her company really, a heavy, leather-bound copy of Charles Dickens's *Hard Times*.

It was unusual for someone to read a real book, instead of a computer screen. But that was George—she banged her own drum. A few years ago George had committed to reading every book in the library at Windsor. She tried to read a book every week while they stayed at Buckingham Palace, and chose a new one at Windsor at the weekend. It didn't always work out, as George had little time of her own in her busy weekly diary.

Bea looked at the time. To her surprise it was half eleven, and she'd been trying to sleep since nine.

"Do you want a painkiller?" George said.

"Yes, I think I need one." Bea wasn't one for taking medications easily, but they had such a full day tomorrow. She needed sleep.

Bea pushed herself up so she was propped up on her pillows.

George laid her book down. "I'll get you some. Hang on."

George went to the bathroom and came back with a painkiller shot.

While Bea took it, George said, "I didn't expect Teddy to invite Ms. Priestly. She never normally lets us meet her girlfriends, except for Summer. Is she really serious about her?"

"I really can't see it. I think she chooses her girlfriends to avoid another serious relationship. It's my guess that she feels backed into a corner. She's under a lot of pressure. Becoming Princess of Wales, the scrutiny of the press, them finding out about her private work at Street Kitchen, then you going to see her…"

George sat on the edge of the bed. "Why is she angry with me? She could hardly contain her temper when I told her what she needed to hear."

Bea reached over and took George's hand. "Georgie, she has put you on so high a pedestal that she can't imagine ever getting close to you."

"I don't know why. I'm not special. I'm boring. I read old novels and make model ships."

"You are anything but boring, sweetheart. You are a great mum, the best partner, and the perfect Queen. Teddy has to live up to you wherever she goes," Bea said.

"I've never made her feel that way," George said.

Bea rubbed George's hand soothingly. "Of course you haven't. Remember, you told me you felt the same about your own father. You thought he was the perfect King, and you couldn't step into his shoes."

George took her hand and brought it to her lips. "I had you to help me through those first months. Remember I had panic attacks?"

"I do. It was a big change in your life, and you lacked confidence. Teddy isn't becoming Queen like you were, but she's taking the step up to become a full-time working royal, and becoming Princess of Wales. I think that and running the Duchy of Cornwall are so overwhelming, she's pushing against it instead of embracing it."

George sighed. "I don't want our relationship to be like this."

"It won't be. She needs confidence and reassurance," Bea said.

"It wasn't always like this. She used to come on long hikes with me, and all she could talk about were the plans she was making."

"That she was making with Summer. Summer was her confidence, her anchor when she felt pressure."

George lay back on the bed and put her arms around Bea, before kissing her head. "Just like I had you. I thought they were meant for each other."

"Me too. The break-up took so much out of her—that's why I don't believe Pandora or any of the others will stick," Bea said.

"But what if this one does? She doesn't take much interest in public service, if any, and likes the cameras around, and dropping Teddy's name for publicity. That's not good for a future Queen."

"If she does, then we welcome her into the family. We have to support our children's choices. Some of your family wouldn't have chosen me."

"No, the immediate family did, Mama and Granny loved you. I wish Granny was still here to talk to us all. Her advice was invaluable. I'm glad Teddy has your mum and dad, and my mama. I know Teddy confides in them all," George said.

"They love Teddy, Annie, and Roo so much."

"You know, Teddy said something when she was angry. That we thought Summer was perfect and could do no wrong. She said Summer broke her heart, and yet we love her, compared her to other girlfriends."

"I suppose we do," Bea said. "Teddy's not told us all the details, but the scrutiny from outside was too great for Summer, especially with her illness. I think they both hurt. But Summer is part of the family. We just need to be careful and try to treat Pandora in the same open way, if that's what Teddy wants."

"Parenting is hard, even when the children are not so little," George said.

"Just wait till Annie has her first serious boy or girlfriend, and then there's Roo."

George looked horrified. "Don't even say that."

There was a knock on the door. George called out, "Come in."

Roo's head popped round the door, and then he ran and jumped into the bed.

"Why are you still awake?" Bea said.

George moved so that Rupert could lie between them.

"I saw some things online, and I don't understand."

Bea exchanged a look with George, worried by what he'd seen. It was something that all the children had gone through.

Magazines and news sites needed new content every day, whether it was true or not. Bea remembered when Annie had come home from school crying, because her friends had shown her a story about Bea having an affair and leaving George.

It had taken them both the whole evening to comfort Annie and explain to her that people made things up to get views, followers, and people to buy their magazines.

This was a hard lesson in the world the royal family existed in. They needed to be seen to do their job, but that came at a cost.

"What did you see, Roo Roo," George said.

"It says that Ted is getting married, and I don't even know her, and that she's a playgirl princess. What does that mean?"

"It's just silliness," Bea said. "That is Teddy's girlfriend, but they are not getting married. Ted is bringing her to the Windsor Horse Trials so we can all meet her then."

"Do you think she'll like me?"

George kissed his head. "Who wouldn't like you, Roo Roo?"

Rupert idolized Teddy. So her girlfriend liking him was a big thing.

"Can I stay here till I feel sleepy?"

"Of course you can, sweetie. Get under the covers."

This happened quite often if Rupert had a nightmare or was feeling stressed about something. He would drift off in their bed, and George would carry him to his own bed when he fell asleep.

Bea put off the lights, and they lay quietly. Just as Bea thought he was drifting off to sleep, Rupert said, "I love Summer. I wish Ted and Summer were still best friends."

George and Bea looked at each other. Didn't they all.

Bea worried that was unfair, after what Teddy had said to George about any new girlfriend being judged against Summer. No matter how much Bea loved Summer, if it wasn't to be, it wasn't to be, and she would make a special effort to welcome and get to know Pandora.

CHAPTER FOUR

Summer heard the beep of a car outside. She checked the window and saw it was Annie, and she was waving and smiling from the driver's seat of her vintage green Aston Martin.

She looked at the time. Seven o'clock. *Punctual as ever, Annie.*

Annie had fallen in love with the vintage sports car because her uncle Theo had one, and she'd gotten one from her parents for her eighteenth birthday. In the passenger seat was the ever-faithful Laney. Annie was very independent and liked to drive if not on official business. Laney was never happy with that, but Annie knew her own mind.

Summer grabbed her backpack with her wellington boots hanging from it and made her way to the front door. The Windsor Horse Trials were for horse enthusiasts, and the dress code was about function, rather than dress to impress.

She would need something more formal for the family get-together later that evening, but she'd left a dress and other items in Annie's dressing room the night before.

She made her way down to the car. Laney took her bag and helped her into the small back seat. There was no way Laney could fit there comfortably, and so Summer always took the more uncomfortable ride.

"Morning, Sunshine," Annie said.

"Morning. You look bright and breezy as usual," Summer said.

"And why shouldn't I be? I get to spend the day with my beautiful horse Honey, and my good friends." Annie looked at both her and Laney.

"Her Royal Highness is happy any time she gets time to spend with her beloved horses," Laney said.

"And you don't?" Summer said.

"Point taken." Laney got in the car, and they set off on their way.

"Did you hear that my dear sister and heir to the throne is bringing Pandora today?"

That gave Summer a jolt. "Really? She never normally brings anyone."

"No, I know. Apparently Mum gave Teddy a talking-to after her recent date night was splashed across the world's media. She had to take things seriously or cut Pandora out of her life. Teddy chose to bring her," Annie said.

Summer didn't know how to react to that. Teddy had never had a serious relationship since they broke up.

"That's surprising," Summer said.

"More out of stubbornness, I think," Annie said. "Pandora's intentions are clear to me. She doesn't do anything if she isn't getting views or making money from product placement. You'll see her tonight. She's coming to the family drinks do."

"Maybe I shouldn't go. It might be awkward. Pandora meeting your parents is a big thing. I suppose Teddy won't want an ex-girlfriend hanging around," Summer said.

"You're not an ex-girlfriend, you are a family friend. You're my best friend, so this Pandora will have to get used to it. Okay?"

Summer couldn't think of anything worse, but Annie was her friend and if Annie insisted, what could she do?

"Why didn't you and Teddy work out? You were perfect together."

Summer consistently asked that question, and it was taxing trying to justify it. "Because fairy tales don't have happy endings in real life."

"I try to tell her that," Laney said, "but she has her head in the clouds."

"I can make you walk, you know," Annie said.

If Summer had known this, she would have used an excuse. Not because she still had feelings for Teddy, but because the truth would be awkward. She would try and just keep out of the way tonight.

❖

"You're not going to be able to walk in them," Teddy said to Pandora.

Teddy had picked up Pandora in her Land Rover. They were sitting in the back while Jack and Mark, their driver, sat up front.

Pandora was wearing a pink mini-dress with matching high heels and bag, while Teddy had on jeans and walking boots.

"Why? I have been to horse events before, you know."

"This isn't the Möet and Chandon VIP tent at the polo. It's competition events."

"Well, I never go anywhere underdressed."

They stopped to pick up Teddy's PA, Kurt. "Morning, happy people."

"Oh, Kurt, don't even try," Pandora said. "Teddy's unbearable today."

Teddy was in a bad mood. Had been ever since last night. She'd wanted to finish it with Pandora, but out of stubbornness, here she was. That on top of her Street Kitchen work being found out made everything worse. "Kurt? I want a file on the Duchy of Cornwall estate."

Kurt narrowed his eyes. "You have a board of trustees that manage it. You only have to watch the money rolling in."

She knew Sebastian or Summer would have responded to that request by producing a file in hours, and it would not be framed in terms of money and personal wealth. "I want it as soon as possible, okay? And not just about finances. I want to know all the farms that depend on the estate, small businesses, disued buildings that could be used for community projects. Everything like that."

Kurt wasn't used to her asking for things like this, but Teddy was getting fed up of the image of her underprepared and lurching from one engagement to another.

No one knew the real Teddy, apart from her family, and her mum was right about one thing—service was their most important duty. Working at Street Kitchen had taught her that, and if it was now going to be difficult for her to work there incognito, then maybe she had to find some other outlet.

"I'll get it together if you want. But you do have an estate manager."

"I want to know how everything works and how it can be used to help the community, all right?" Teddy said.

Kurt held his hands up. "Okay, okay. You're starting to sound like your sister."

That annoyed Teddy. He was getting way too familiar. She didn't mind for herself, but the rest of the family was different. "You mean *Princess Adrianna*?"

By the look on Kurt's face, he knew he was being reprimanded. She noticed Pandora give him a nudge.

"Sorry, ma'am. I got carried away. I'll get the report for you."

Why was Pandora nudging him? They hadn't met each other before Teddy met her, and yet there was something of an understanding between them, she felt. Teddy's mind cast back to their dinner date the other night.

The little worry she had was growing. Yet here she was, backed into a corner because of her own stubbornness. Stubbornness had played a big part in her life and happiness. After she and Summer broke up, Summer had come back to Teddy, but her hurt and anger made her walk away.

Teddy really couldn't wait to get this day over with. She normally looked forward to this event, even though she wasn't passionate about horses like some of her family.

What she did look forward to was spending time with her family. On the last day Annie would take part in the showjumping, and that was her passion, so Teddy always made sure she was there to help support her.

Her uncle Theo and his wife, Aziza—the Duke and Duchess of Clarence—had two children, Juliette who was ten, and two-year-old Benjamin. Juliette loved horses, and she and Roo would be taking part in the children's Shetland pony Grand National.

The rest of the close family would be there for the events, and in the evening for the drinks party. God knew what Granny Sofia, the Queen Mother, would make of her date. It didn't matter what background a person had, her granny wasn't a snob. She appreciated kindness and unselfishness, and people who helped serve their community.

Pandora had a rich daddy and a robust online profile. Service wasn't in her vocabulary.

"Teddy? Teddy? Are you listening?"

Teddy had been lost in her thoughts. "What?"

"Will she be there?" Pandora sounded annoyed.

"Who is she?"

"You know who. Your ex."

Teddy sighed. "Yes, Summer will be there."

"Why?" Pandora said angrily. "Why does she hang around your family? Everything you all do, she's there, hanging on to the limelight."

Teddy did not like that description of Summer, no matter how hurt she still felt about their break-up.

"Summer is there because she is my sister's PA and her best friend.

If you knew anything about her, you would know that Summer hates the limelight," Teddy said.

"The way you defend her sounds like you still have feelings for her."

Teddy let her head fall back on the headrest. "Oh, for God's sake. Summer and I were childhood sweethearts, and then we broke up. It was over then. We were kids."

"Okay, but it just annoys me she's here," Pandora said.

"Well I can't choose my sister's best friend, can I?"

The car came to a halt. Jack got out and opened her door. Teddy then stepped out and offered a hand to Pandora. Pandora stepped out of the car, and her high-heeled shoe went into the mud with a squelch.

"I told you wellingtons were more suitable."

Pandora looked at her with simmering fury.

George stood next to the fence at the showjumping arena with Bea, Rupert, and Reg, while her mama and Sarah sat in camping chairs nearby.

George turned to Bea when she saw Teddy walk towards them with Pandora. "Put on your best smiles, everyone. Teddy's here."

"Family!" Bea said. "Best smiles."

As soon as Rupert heard his sister's name, he ran off and jumped into her arms.

"Ted!"

Teddy lifted him and swung him around. "Hi little Roo bear."

"I missed you."

"Me too."

The dogs had followed, jumping up at Teddy excitedly. "I see you, guys."

Teddy ruffled Freya's and Bear's heads, and then lifted Ollie into her arms. "Hi little man."

The dogs loved Teddy and she them. She always had great fun playing with the family dogs.

Bear jumped up on Pandora excitedly, muddy paws getting on her dress. "Get down. Teddy, get this dog away."

George had to bite her tongue. They all had similar muddy splashes on them, but they were dressed for a muddy day in the country. There were dogs all over the place today, and everyone was happy as long as the dogs were having fun.

No, a bit of mud never harmed anyone, George thought.

The only quiet dogs were her mother's two toy poodles, Bramble and Amber, who sat on her knee or lay quietly by her feet. They were the princesses of the dog world.

"Dogs? All come." George issued the instruction, and they all went back to her heels, including Ollie who Teddy put down again.

Teddy bowed her head to her two mums and granny. "Family, this is Pandora."

Rupert held out his hand to shake, as he'd been trained to all his life. "Hi, Pandora, I'm Rupert."

George felt sorry for Pandora, whose high-heeled shoes were caked in mud. She looked miserable already.

Pandora changed her expression in a second to all smiles. "Hi Rupert. Your sister talks so much about you."

Teddy let Rupert down and bowed her head. Then she cleared her voice nervously. Was Teddy nervous about this introduction because she was anxious for it to go well, or something else?

"Pandora, may I present my two mums, my granny Queen Sofia, my grandma Sarah, and my grandpa Reg."

Pandora gave a very exaggerated curtsy. "I'm delighted to meet you all."

George shook her hand first. "Welcome, Ms. Priestly. We're glad to meet you."

Bea was next. "I'm sorry about your beautiful shoes. Teddy? Did you tell Pandora the kind of footwear she would need?"

"Yes." Teddy sighed. "But obviously I wasn't clear enough."

"Let me have some boots sent down for you, Pandora." Bea pointed to her own polka dot wellington boots. "You can't survive these events without boots."

"It's all right, Bea. I'll just be happy to find the drinks tent. A glass of champagne is all that you need in these situations."

George looked to her wife with wide eyes. Bea wasn't one for formalities of address, but addressing the Queen Consort by the family nickname on first meeting was taking it a bit far, not to mention turning down her offer of help.

She saw Teddy look up to the sky and shake her head. Teddy certainly didn't look like someone hopelessly in love.

"Perhaps I can show you to the refreshment tent, Ms. Priestly?" George said.

"No, no." Teddy jumped in quickly. "I'll take her. See you in a bit."

"Teddy"—Rupert held on to her hand—"you'll come back soon, won't you?"

Teddy winked at him. "I'll be back in no time, Roo Roo."

"Well, that was an experience," Bea said.

❖

Teddy picked up two glasses of orange juice and lemonade from the server. "Thanks."

The server bowed her head and said, "Thank you, ma'am."

She started to walk across the refreshment tent to where she had left Pandora and Kurt. Teddy was squirming with embarrassment at the first meeting with her family. To call her mum *Bea* as soon as she was introduced? It was so uncomfortable to watch.

It was all of her own doing. If she hadn't reacted so defensively to her mum, Pandora wouldn't even be there. What was happening to her life? She was dating someone she didn't want to, Street Kitchen had been taken away from her, and she was a constant disappointment to her family.

The thing was, Teddy had no idea how to get off this destructive path and do better. But there was one thing that was clear—she wanted to do better.

Pandora and Kurt weren't where she left them. Teddy looked around and finally spotted them with their heads together beside one of the poles that held up the tent. They looked as if they were having an intense conversation.

Kurt spotted her and whispered to Pandora before waving her over. "Teddy, we thought you had gotten lost," Kurt said.

"No, it was you two who moved."

Teddy handed them their drinks. Pandora looked at hers like she had handed her a snake.

"What is this?"

"Fresh orange and lemonade." Teddy pushed her hands into her pockets.

"I asked for champagne."

"And I told you there was none. No alcohol is served here," Teddy said firmly.

"I thought you were joking."

"No. Ever since my two mums' first year of hosting the event. My mama, Queen Beatrice, gave the order. She is involved in children's charities for youngsters affected by family violence and alcohol. She said that this is a family event. A good number of the attendees and those taking part are children. So she didn't want adults getting progressively worse for wear in the drinks tent. As I said, this isn't the polo."

Pandora said something she couldn't make out under her breath just before she took a drink.

"What?" Teddy asked.

Kurt was bouncing on his toes nervously. "That's understandable, isn't it, Pandora?"

Pandora put on a false smile and said quickly, "Of course, Teddy."

Kurt sounded like he was coaching Pandora through the conversation.

"What is going on here?" Teddy asked.

Kurt looked to Pandora with worry in his eyes. "What—"

"Just ignore Teddy, Kurt. She's all upset because I didn't bow and scrape enough to her mum."

"Nobody asked you to do that. My mama doesn't care about strict protocol, but even I bow to my parents. It's out of respect. You are bowing to the Crown, and you don't just call the Queen whom you've just met *Bea*."

Pandora sighed. "Your family is weird."

"Not to ourselves. If you think that, then why were you so insistent on coming today?"

"Because I'm your girlfriend, and I didn't expect it to be like a village fair. Anyway, what's the big deal? All your family call your mother Bea," Pandora said.

"Family do—you're not family."

Pandora gripped her glass so hard it looked like it might break. Just as Pandora was about to speak, Rupert came running towards them.

"Ted, Ted, Summer said to tell you that Annie is going out on the jumps in five minutes. Are you coming?"

Teddy smiled. "I'm coming."

"You're going to go and watch with your ex-girlfriend?" Pandora said with fury.

"No, I'm going to watch with my family."

Rupert's brow furrowed and he looked up at Pandora. "Why don't you like Summer?"

Before anything else was said, Teddy put her arm around his shoulders and they walked away together. She heard Pandora growl behind her, "You see, Kurt? She puts everything ahead of me."

Teddy was really paying for her stubbornness today. She couldn't wait for this day to be over.

As they walked over to the event area, Rupert said, "Are you going to marry Pandora, Ted?"

"What? Where did that come from?"

"I read it."

"Roo Roo, I can promise you I am not going to marry Pandora. You know not to believe things about us you see on TV or online," Teddy said.

"Mums said that you wouldn't do that without us getting to know her, but—"

"But what?"

"She's mean to the dogs, and I don't think she likes Summer. I love Summer," Rupert said.

"I know you do."

Teddy couldn't feel annoyed at her little brother liking Summer. She had always been a part of his family.

As they got closer to the event area, Teddy saw Summer leaning against the wooden fence, laughing with her cousin Lady Victoria, and Aunt Azi, Uncle Theo, and their kids. Summer had a way of laughing with her whole body and spirit. *Joy* was what she would describe it as.

No matter how hurt she'd been by Summer, she couldn't shake those deep, deep visceral reactions to her. More often than not Teddy's reactions turned to anger, which was why she liked to keep a distance when she could.

"Come and watch with Vicky, Aunt Azi, and Summer, Ted," Rupert said.

"Eh…no, I said I'd keep Granny company. Off you go. I'll see them later."

"Okay. Juls!"

He sped off to see his cousin Juliette. Teddy wished she could run away.

❖

Summer flopped onto her bed. *I wish I could run away.*

It had been an awkward day. Summer had told Annie this wasn't the right place for her. Not with Teddy's new girlfriend there.

She hadn't seen Teddy for a long stretch of the afternoon, but then she appeared after Annie's event finished. Summer offered to walk the Queen Mother's dogs, Bramble and Amber, around the area, to give the family and Teddy a break from her.

As much as she didn't like what Pandora stood for—making money as an influencer, gaining notoriety and fame through the same methods—she thought Pandora deserved some space for her and the royal family to get to know each other without an ex hanging around.

The looks she had caught Pandora giving her testified to that fact. Even if it wasn't Pandora, it would be someone else eventually, because Teddy would have to marry and create a gaggle of heirs for the succession.

Summer had to get out of the way.

There was a knock at the door. "Come in."

Summer jumped up when Bea walked into the room, dressed in her evening gown. "Your Majesty."

"Annie says you're not coming down tonight," Bea said.

Summer nodded. "I think it's best, ma'am."

"Bea in private, remember. We are celebrating Annie's and Juliette's wins. You have to be there."

Happily Annie had won her showjumping tournament and Juliette the children's pony Grand National, with Rupert getting bronze.

"Why is it best?" Bea asked.

"Because it's awkward for Teddy, me, and I suspect Pandora. As her girlfriend, Pandora deserves the right to get to know you without me being around."

Bea walked over and sat on the bed and indicated for Summer to do the same. "Oh, Summer, why couldn't you and Teddy have worked it out? We love you, you'd make the perfect partner and Queen for Teddy."

"I couldn't cope with the intrusion into my life, and then—well, it doesn't matter."

Summer wasn't going to tell her all the details. Best to let Teddy's mama think that it was all her doing.

Bea took her hand. "I know that there's a lot I don't know about the days the press chased you, and followed you at university, but I know the Queen and I could have done more."

"It's all in the past. What I do know is that this is a family night, and—"

Bea put her hand up to stop her. "You are family to us, and I would appreciate it if you would come tonight."

How could she say no to Queen Bea's direct request? "Okay, but you can tell me to push off at any point."

Bea smiled. "I doubt that will be happening. Now get your best dress on and come on down."

Summer didn't think she could say no to a request from Queen Bea.

"Okay, if you insist."

"I insist," Bea said. "Come on."

Bea left, and she went over to her wardrobe. Summer was nervous about going downstairs. She would be the last one to join, and she felt awkward about going in and making an entrance, eyed by Teddy and Pandora.

Summer's heart began to thump, and a familiar whooshing sound ran through her ears. She felt the wave of dizziness, and black dots appeared in front of her eyes until her medication swirled around her body, saving her from the symptoms that would engulf her without it.

She came back to normal quickly, but this was a good reminder. She was due for her check-up soon with the specialist. He had floated the idea of a new treatment he'd been researching, one that would dispense meds before the symptoms crashed. They would need to talk.

❖

By the time Summer got downstairs, the younger children had gone to bed, leaving just Rupert and Juliette.

They were playing a virtual board game on the card table with Theo and Max, Lady Victoria's brother and now Duke of Bransford. Both Max and Lady Victoria had children, but they were small and in bed long ago.

Max had been a career soldier until he inherited the title and lands from his father. Now he ran the estate with the help of his husband Khalid, whom he met on deployment to Egypt.

She took a big breath and walked into the room. Rupert spotted her and ran over. "Summer! Everyone, Summer's here."

She could have done without the huge announcement. Everyone either waved or said good evening.

Rupert quickly went back to his game, but Annie was close behind him. "You made it." She handed Summer a glass of champagne. "Non-alcoholic for you, and alcoholic bubbles for me."

Summer raised her glass. "Cheers."

After they clinked glasses, Annie said, "I knew you'd never be able to resist Mama."

"I knew it was you who sent her. This is really awkward, you know."

"Don't worry. Pandora was already making it awkward before you came down."

Summer couldn't resist looking up any more. Pandora was having an intense conversation with Teddy, then Teddy walked off. Her place was taken by Kurt. Pandora looked furious, and the fury was now looking in Summer's direction.

"If looks could kill, I'd be dead and buried," Summer said. "So, what's been happening?"

"She told Teddy, in front of Granny, to *get those dirty dogs off the couch.* Made a disparaging comment about the unemployed, and boasted about the free gifts she gets from designers if she promotes their products. It's not going down well."

"I can imagine," Summer said.

"Stay there," Annie said, "I just need to ask Vicky something really quickly."

Summer wandered over towards Bea's mum to say hi but stopped at the side of the room when she saw Pandora making a beeline for her.

"Summer Fisher, we meet at last," Pandora said as she slugged a glass of champagne.

"Ms. Priestly, nice to meet you."

Pandora held her empty glass out to the side as if she was expecting a lackey to whisk it out of her hand.

"You are so prim and proper, *Ms. Fisher.*"

Clearly Pandora was a little bit drunk. The quicker she got away from this conversation, the better.

Pandora turned around and glared at a passing footman with a tray of drinks. "Do you not see me waiting for a drink, idiot."

"Sorry," Tommy said. He took her empty glass and then handed her a new one.

"Thanks, Tommy," Summer said.

"Tommy? You know the servants' names? On first-name terms, are you?"

"They aren't servants, Ms. Priestly, they are staff, and you shouldn't be rude."

Pandora leaned in. "I'll call them whatever I please. You're not welcome here any more. I'm Teddy's girlfriend, not you, and tonight she'll be sleeping in my bed. Remember that, little sweet Summer."

Summer shook her head and walked out to the hallway. She needed a breath of air and made her way to the front entrance. Soon she heard footsteps behind her. Summer could sense who it was without turning around.

The air changed whenever Teddy was around. Her arm hairs stood on end, and she shivered when she felt Teddy's breath on her neck.

"What was that all about?"

Summer shivered and hugged herself. "Your girlfriend didn't approve of my presence and was extremely rude to Tommy. I told her that wasn't how the family treated staff."

Teddy walked around her and said, "What did she say to Tommy?"

"She expressed annoyance that her next glass of champagne wasn't at her fingertips and called Tommy an idiot. I couldn't stand for that rudeness."

Teddy pushed her hands into her pockets and said, "No, you must be mistaken."

Summer looked up at her and said simply, "Have I ever lied to you?" She turned around and walked back into the house.

CHAPTER FIVE

T eddy?" Granny Sofia said. "Will you help me with the stairs?"
"Of course, Granny." Teddy pulled Sofia up and offered her
arm.

"Goodnight, Sarah."

"Goodnight, ma'am. I won't be long behind you," Grandma Sarah
said.

Juliette ran over and gave her granny a hug. "Night, Granny."

Sofia kissed her head. "Goodnight, my darling. I'm very proud of
you today."

"Thanks, Granny."

Teddy loved to see how close Juliette, Rupert, and Benny were
with their grandmother. It gave Granny such joy to be with her
grandchildren.

Her mum and mama would be exactly the same, and since she
wouldn't have children herself, it made Teddy so glad that Annie would
give them that. Annie had always talked about having loads of kids.

There was a time when she'd planned a whole gaggle of kids, but
that dream had long gone, with so many other things.

Her granny clung to her arm as they walked up the wide staircase.
When they reached the top, Granny said, "I heard you were having a
rather intense conversation with Summer."

"Our conversations, if we have them, are always intense."

"What was wrong this time?"

Teddy could never keep things from her granny. "She accused my
girlfriend of being rude and disrespectful to the staff," Teddy said.

They continued along the long corridor towards Granny's room.
"I heard her being just that."

Teddy stopped and closed her eyes. Deep down she knew it was true, but Teddy hadn't been ready to hear that from Summer. From her Granny, there was no doubt it was true.

They made it to her bedroom and stopped at the door. Granny said, "Here's a piece of advice that my mother gave me, and it's foolproof. Never trust anyone who is rude to the waiter and perfectly nice to you. How they behave to the waiter is who they truly are."

Teddy looked down at her shoes. Why had she found herself in this situation?

"I don't know what to say, Granny."

"You don't have to say anything, darling. You have to work this out for yourself. I know you don't care for her in that way, and you feel lost in your life. You have to work out why you are with Ms. Priestly and find a path so you're not lost any more," Granny said.

But Teddy knew why. It was because she didn't want a serious relationship, but she would rather be alone than feel like this and bring people like Pandora into her family.

Teddy kissed her on the cheek and said, "Thank you, Granny. Goodnight."

"Teddy, have you read *Henry IV, Part 1*?"

Teddy shook her head. "No, Shakespeare was never really my thing."

"I think you'd get a great deal out of it. Goodnight."

Her mind was racing as she walked away. When Pandora wasn't with her, she was with Kurt. He must have heard the way Pandora was talking to people. What had started as a gnawing worry about Kurt had grown and grown. Her trust was gone.

Kurt had been a good friend to her at university, but the signs were all there. He liked to be associated with her and enjoyed the limelight. He encouraged Teddy's slack attitude towards duty and appointments, and now she'd had enough. Even though she was proud of her work at Street Kitchen, her way of life had brought failure to her door, and Teddy didn't want that.

As she neared the bottom of the stairs, her phone beeped. She opened up the notification and saw a selfie of Pandora sitting in her mum's study, in her armchair with her feet up on the table and a glass of brandy in her hand.

The picture was titled *Chilling at the Queen's Castle*. Teddy felt such a rush of anger. She had to find Pandora and headed towards the study. She heard laughter coming from inside.

A footman called Bill was standing in the corridor, at the drawing room door. "Bill," Teddy said, "please follow me."

"Yes, Your Royal Highness."

Teddy marched over to the study, her anger growing with every step. She opened the door to find Pandora and Kurt laughing, while Pandora took pictures.

They both turned around sharply when the door opened.

"What is this?" Teddy showed Pandora the picture on her phone.

"It's just a picture to show my followers."

"You have disrespected my family's privacy. This is not just a castle, it's a home. A home where my family guards its privacy. It's bad enough that you are sitting at the Queen's desk with your feet up, but you are sharing it with the world."

Pandora walked over and tried to put a hand on Teddy's chest, but Teddy took a step back. "I don't want to hear it. You've gone too far."

"You never took this silly royal life seriously before," Pandora said.

"I am now. You violated my privacy before—I know you told the paparazzi we were at the club. I also know that my so-called friend has been helping you." Teddy looked at Kurt. "You were supposed to be my friend."

Kurt put his head down.

Pandora said, "I only chatted to a friend who happened to be in the press—"

"Stop lying. You've gone too far. We are finished. Kurt, you too."

Pandora's pleading look turned to anger. "You don't mean this."

"Oh, I do. Go and pack your things. You are both leaving tonight. Bill, call Ms. Priestly and Kurt a taxi, and then have the protection officers make sure they leave quietly."

Pandora gave her a deathly stare. "You have no idea what I can do to you. Your name will be mud."

"I have no doubt you will try your best, but I will get over it."

An hour later Teddy watched Pandora and Kurt being ushered out the door. The drawing room door opened, and Summer came out. She stayed at the door while Pandora left. Once they were gone, Summer looked up at her and said, "Teddy?"

Teddy couldn't deal with Summer's *I told you so* right now, so she turned and walked upstairs to her room.

❖

Summer sat in the window of her room, her knees pulled up to her chest, trying hard not to worry about Teddy. She couldn't believe Teddy had finally seen through Pandora. Teddy had stubbornly defended her when Summer told her what she'd heard.

But after Teddy helped Queen Sofia upstairs, Pandora was being escorted out, and Kurt too.

In that moment after they left, Summer had looked up and caught Teddy's gaze.

She had seen that look once before, the day that she had come back to Teddy, hoping to have a second chance. Summer had watched Teddy slowly close up, burying her emotions deep inside. The same happened tonight, and it saddened her. Someone else had shown Teddy that relationships could never be long-lasting.

There was a knock at the door, and Summer wiped away her tears. "Come in."

Annie bounced into the room. "Did you hear about Teddy and Pandora?"

"I saw Pandora leaving, but I didn't know what was going on."

Annie sat cross-legged on her bed. "Granny told her that she'd heard Pandora being extremely rude to staff."

That was it. Teddy might doubt her, but there was no way she would doubt her beloved granny.

"Really?" Summer said.

"That's not all. Look at this." Annie showed her the picture of Pandora in the study.

"She put that on social media?"

Annie nodded. "Yeah, and Teddy caught her and Kurt taking more pictures. Private pictures. She ended it there and then and gave them an hour to pack and get out."

"I didn't think that would happen any time soon. It seems to me she likes to date women the family won't approve of."

"I don't know, but she hasn't taken dating seriously since you," Annie said.

Summer didn't want to dwell on that. "How did you find out?"

"Teddy asked to speak to Mama and Mum. She warned them that Pandora threatened to destroy her in the media."

"This isn't good. Not just when we're about to launch both of you to the public," Summer said.

"Mum and Mama said that she did the right thing, and whatever comes with this, we would all get through it. We've all made mistakes."

"Yes, we need to show the world that Teddy has so much more to her, that she cares about people and wants to help using her position in this family."

"Yeah, we'll get her through this."

Summer had to do this. No matter their personal feelings, Summer had to make this work. She would help Teddy be the best Princess of Wales she could be.

CHAPTER SIX

Teddy hid away at her Kensington Palace apartment for the next few days, while the hailstorm of bad publicity aimed at her crashed around outside.

She was off social media, and yet the trail of news still trickled in. To make it even more depressing, today she should have been at Street Kitchen, but there were banks of journalists outside there too.

Teddy texted her friends at Street Kitchen to apologize for the disruption. Of course they said they were supportive and gracious about it, but it hurt her to cause them and the people who relied on the kitchen this much trouble.

The last few days had given Teddy time to reflect on her relationships, both long-term and all the short-term ones she had. Neither had served her.

Teddy got up from the couch and walked to her bedroom. She sat on the edge of her bed dejectedly. She bowed her head.

She was utterly directionless. No PA, no plans for the future, and the ex-girlfriend who'd hurt her most would be running her life for the next six months.

Teddy looked up at her wardrobe. There was a plan up there on the shelf from many years ago. She hadn't looked at it in such a long time, but for some reason, Teddy wanted to look through its pages now.

She got up, opened the wardrobe, brought a dusty box down from the high shelf. Teddy opened the box and found different notebooks, most full of drawings that she had done of different life events, and an old-fashioned photo album that Summer had made up for her, with real physical photographs.

Teddy opened the album. Written on the front page was the inscription *To Prince Charming, love from Cinders.*

She looked at the first page of pictures. It was strange to see the look of innocence and optimism on her face as she held Summer in her arms.

Teddy slammed the album shut. She should throw it away. That Teddy was long gone. But there was one more notebook she knew was sitting there, and she couldn't stop herself from lifting it up.

The front cover had a hand-drawn forest scene, in a fairy-tale style. There was a knight with short dark hair in shining armour on top of a white steed, with a damsel at her side. The knight was her, and beside her the damsel was Summer, with her long blond hair and flowing dress.

But Teddy wasn't rescuing Summer. They were standing together, facing what the world had to offer them.

Underneath the picture was the title: *Prince Charming and Cinderella.*

Teddy had a talent for drawing, something she shared with her uncle Theo. He'd studied art and helped her hone the talent.

She flicked to the first page, with the heading: *The five-year plan of the Princess and Lady of Wales.*

What a joke that turned out to be.

There were pages of which charities they wanted to work with, what programs they wanted to start when they got married and inherited the Duchy of Cornwall and the Wales title, and how many children they were going to have.

The optimism was just too much for her, and Teddy threw the notebook across the room. She needed someone to talk to, someone who wasn't her family, but who she trusted implicitly.

"Computer, call Inspector Quincy."

❖

Quincy arrived at Kensington Palace as soon as she could get away. Luckily Queen Beatrice didn't have an official appointment today, so when Teddy called, Quincy could go to see her quickly.

Once up the stairs she was greeted by Jack. "Inspector. Good to see you."

"You too, Jack. How's everything here?"

"Security-wise, no problems, but I think Princess Teddy is suffering," Jack said.

"Yes, it's been a bad few weeks for her. Hopefully I can help."

When they arrived at Teddy's front door, Jack said, "If there's anything you need, let me know, Inspector."

Quincy patted Jack on the shoulder. "Thank you, Jack."

She pressed the doorbell and waited for the door to be opened. When it was, Quincy was saddened by the dejectedness on Teddy's face.

Quincy bowed her head. "You asked to see me, Your Royal Highness?"

"Thanks for coming. Come through to the kitchen. Tea, coffee?" Teddy asked her.

"Tea please, ma'am."

"It's just us, Quin. I need my friend, not Inspector Quincy, late of the Royal Marines," Teddy said.

"Very well. Tea please, Teddy, nice and strong."

"I know." Teddy managed a half smile.

Teddy brought the tea over and placed one in front of Quincy. Quincy stood until Teddy sat at the kitchen table. She might be calling her Teddy, but Quincy had rules and standards she'd never let up on.

They were drilled into her as a child, as her aunt, who took care of her, was in the Royal Navy, and then drilled into her even more in the Royal Marines.

"How are you, Teddy?"

Teddy curled her hands around the mug of tea. "Shit. I've let everyone down."

"You haven't."

"I have," Teddy said firmly. "Mum came to see me last week after the restaurant debacle. She has never been as angry—she gave me a bollocking. Told me I had to accept I was different and couldn't behave like other people. I'm such a disappointment to her."

"That's not true, Teddy," Quincy said.

Teddy stared over her shoulder absently and shook her head. "It's true. She must wish Annie was born first. Annie would be a fantastic Princess of Wales, and Queen when the time came."

Quincy couldn't just keep contradicting her—the message wouldn't get through to Teddy at the moment. So she tried something different.

"Do you remember as a child you always wanted to be a Royal Marine?" Quincy said.

"Yeah, something else I failed at."

Quincy decided to let that comment slide. "You had the little uniform, and your mum and me made you a small-scale assault course."

Teddy nodded. "I loved that."

"You used to ask me every question under the sun about being a commando. I taught you everything I could." Quincy chuckled. "You were so enthusiastic about it. You even memorized the four ethos of the commando spirit." These were the values every marine lived by. "Can you remember them?" Quincy asked.

Teddy looked her in the eye and said, "I can never forget them. Courage. Determination. Unselfishness. Cheerfulness in the face of adversity." Teddy's joy at the memory was clear to see.

"You see?" Quincy returned Teddy's smile. "I knew you couldn't have forgotten. I live by them, and they get me through most situations. But what about you? Have you internalized them? Or did you just learn them off by heart?"

"I'm not a marine, Quin," Teddy said angrily. She shot up and leaned against the sink, facing away from Quincy.

"Teddy—"

"No, I didn't have the guts to be a marine, and I'm lost. The world out there is going crazy about my life, and it's all my fault. I've brought all this onto my family. Now they have paps following them at their public events, disrupting everything, all because of my mistakes."

Quincy clasped her hands in front of her and said calmly, "You don't need to be a commando to live by those values."

Teddy screwed her eyes shut. Any mention of the marines made her feel failure inside.

"Do you think the world out there is crashing in on you? *Courage.* Think about it. You love your work at Street Kitchen. Go there and face the press, and face whatever Ms. Priestly says about you, with courage, and use the press pack to publicize the charity." Teddy slowly opened her eyes.

"*Determination.* If you make a misstep, you keep going and concentrate on your work to help places like Street Kitchen."

Teddy turned around and looked at Quincy's steady gaze. "*Unselfishness.* Your team is the family, the royal family. Think of it as your commando unit. Together you can do great things for the country."

It made sense. From that point of view, from that work ethic, she could make it through tough parts of life. Teddy pulled out the kitchen chair and sat down.

"When you feel at your worst, think about this. *Cheerfulness in the face of adversity.* If you repeat and repeat these ethos in your mind, you can face anything."

Teddy scrubbed her face with her hands. "Thank you, Quin, that helped. I'm going to try, but—"

"No buts. Trust everyone around you to help, and you'll get there. I know the pressure you've always felt."

"Wouldn't you? Following one of the greatest members of the royal family, in its long history?" Teddy said.

"You've always idolized your mum, but you can only be you."

But what if being herself wasn't good enough?

Quincy's gaze lingered on the kitchen counter. She rose and picked up the copy of *Henry IV, Part 1* Teddy had brought back from the Windsor library.

"Shakespeare? And a real leather-bound volume? I don't think I've seen you with anything like this before."

"Oh yeah, Granny recommended it to me. She said I would recognize some things about the character that would chime with me. I thought holding a real physical copy would help, so I got it from the Windsor library, but I haven't gotten past the first few pages, to be honest," Teddy admitted.

Quincy smiled. "The young, raucous Prince Hal. He transformed himself into Henry V by choosing to embody the role of king and cutting out the friends who got into trouble with him, like poor old Falstaff. It's a tough lesson. It would be well worth reading."

"I've ended it with Pandora and fired Kurt as my PA. He wasn't helping me be the best."

"Good start. Can I suggest something to you?" Quincy asked.

Teddy nodded.

"Since Summer is doing the PA scheduling work for you and Princess Anna, perhaps I could suggest an equerry for you?"

Teddy had always pushed against having an equerry. An equerry was a military post, an officer assigned to a member of the royal family, to be their dresser and attend them in personal and public life. It always seemed such an old-fashioned position to Teddy, even though she loved Cammy, who did the job for her mum.

"You think that would help?" Teddy asked.

"Yes, I know an exceptional officer who will support you. Commander Robinson. He was originally in the marines and then moved to special forces, Special Boat Service. I served with him. He was the best turned out, bravest officer I've ever known."

Teddy felt a small buzz of excitement at the thought of working with such an exceptional officer, the way she used to when she was young, looking up to Quincy and Major Cameron.

"Robbie will make everything run smoothly for you, if that's what you want, and it's an extra layer of protection for you. I can clear it with the Queen if you'd like to meet him," Quincy suggested.

"What about Jack? I wouldn't want him to feel like he was having his toes trodden on."

"Don't worry about that. I'll have a talk with him."

"Yes, I'd like that."

❖

Summer was standing at arrivals at Heathrow. Her mum and dad were coming back from their cruise, and she was here to pick them up. It was good to get out of the house. The last few days had been a blur.

She was inundated with calls from different news media about Teddy when she should be planning out her programme with Annie. Summer was glad Teddy had broken up with Pandora, with her new role at stake, but things were going to get worse the more Pandora talked.

One thing was certain. Pandora loved her publicity, and she was savouring the interviews, the social media posts, the likes, and general notoriety. How she and Annie were going to get Teddy through this, she didn't know.

She spotted her mum and dad coming through the arrivals gate. Her dad ran to her and spun her around. "We missed you, sweet pea."

Summer laughed. "You're making me dizzy, Daddy." That was something she didn't need at the moment.

He put her down, and her mum pulled her into a hug. "How have you been? Feeling okay?"

"Don't fuss, Mum. I'm always okay."

"I worry about you."

"I know, but don't. I'm fine. Let's get to the car."

They got the bags to the car and started to drive to her parents' house.

Her mum said, "I was reading about Teddy. I'm sure she will be unhappy about the publicity."

"She shouldn't give them any cause to write any stories," Summer said quietly.

"Are things going okay with Teddy?" her dad asked.

"It's awkward, but it's not forever," Summer said.

"I was reading about it on the plane," her mum said. "I don't believe half of what they say about her."

"That's because you love Teddy, Mum, no matter what we went through together."

"Well, you were perfect for each other. If it hadn't been for those bloody photographers…"

"Mum." Summer sighed. "It would have happened sometime. It wasn't meant to be."

They arrived at her mum and dad's house. Summer was staying over tonight to help them settle in.

Her dad started taking the bags out of the car and asked, "When's your next hospital appointment, honey?"

"Soon. I'll need to check the date and let you know."

Summer knew what was coming next. True to form, her mum said, "I'll come with you. I want to make sure you're okay and saying the right things to the doctor."

Summer didn't want to argue. It was easier to give in. "Okay, you win."

❖

After Quincy left, Teddy had a lot of thinking to do. She might not be her mum, but she had to become someone else. She had to create Edwina, Princess of Wales, because she couldn't let her family down.

Teddy went to her bedroom and got the old notebook, which earlier she couldn't look at, and a fresh new notebook.

She was going to make a new plan. A plan that would craft her into the heir to the throne that the public wanted, like Quincy had described Prince Hal had done to become King Henry V.

Teddy quickly turned over the childish page with the picture of Prince Charming and Cinderella. Now there would only be the Princess of Wales. She didn't know if she could do it well, but she was going to try.

It was time to step up and face the music. In the new notebook Teddy started to make notes about the charities and causes that were listed in her old plan. Some were causes that were put in the list by Summer and were more suited to her, so Teddy left them out.

Moving forward, her new focus would be her place in the family and fulfilling her duty. The only thing that would stay the same was her plan for the succession. Teddy vowed to herself again that she wouldn't marry, and would not have children, so that the crown would pass to Annie and her heirs.

They would be much more suitable. In the meantime, Teddy would do her part.

Teddy was also determined to silence her heart even more. There would be no more Pandoras, and certainly no Summers, and she would be all about business, distant from her feelings inside. That would be the only way Teddy could be the princess the country wanted because feelings had taken her down a bad path.

She wrote a header on the next page: *Edwina the Princess of Wales—who is she?*

"Time to build a character."

CHAPTER SEVEN

George was working at her desk signing some papers. There was a knock at the door, and Bea walked in. "Georgie? Quincy is here. She's just seen Teddy."

"Bring her in."

George hoped to God that Quincy had gotten through to her. When Quincy told her Teddy had been in touch, George thought it was a perfect opportunity to help her. Teddy had always looked up to Quincy and her love of the Royal Marines.

It pricked George's pride that she couldn't make it through to her firstborn herself, but as Bea explained, Teddy had her up on a pedestal, and it was easier for Teddy to push back against her. Somebody slightly removed from the family was sometimes more able to bridge that gap.

Quincy came in and bowed her head, before walking forward.

"Sit down, Quincy." George stood and gave her seat to her wife. Bea smiled at her for her politeness. "How was Teddy?" George asked.

"Quite low, to be honest. But we had a good conversation."

"What did she say?" Bea said.

"Teddy is feeling lost, just as you said. I reminded her of some of the things that were important to her when she was young. Her love of the Royal Marines, the ethos of a commando. She remembered them clearly but is focusing on her failures and is scared about the scrutiny outside her door."

"My poor baby." Bea grasped George's hand.

"I feel like I've failed," George said. "I should have protected her more."

"If I may, ma'am. She has to go through her own journey. The military helped me do that, but maybe it wasn't the right time for Teddy at army officer training."

After her break-up, Teddy's plans went out the window, especially the Royal Marines. She drifted around with no plan any more. In the end, Teddy reluctantly was shipped off to Sandhurst.

"I got Princess Teddy to start thinking about a way forward using the commando ethos," Quincy said.

"What about the equerry?" Bea asked.

"Yes, she agreed to meeting Commander Robinson. Appeared quite excited about it."

"Excellent," George said, "she needs someone like Cammy was for me at a young age, someone who is totally focused on her and what she needs. Someone on her side—who is not her family."

Bea leaned forward. "Will Orlando Robinson be that person for her?"

Quincy smiled. "I believe so, ma'am."

The next day Teddy was woken by the doorbell. She came to consciousness and felt pain in her neck. In fact she felt like shit. Teddy struggled to open her eyes and lifted her head. She soon realized that a piece of scrap paper was stuck to her cheek and a few bottles of lager were sitting by her side.

What a night.

The buzzer reminded her there was someone at the door. She got to her feet and moved as quickly as she could. She pulled open the door to find a very tall man, well over six feet, with a Royal Marine officer uniform.

He saluted her and said, "Commander Orlando Robinson, Your Royal Highness."

Teddy felt so caught on the hop. "Commander, yes, Inspector Quincy said you were coming. Come in, come in."

When she led him into the drawing room, Teddy was embarrassed by the mess on the table, and the lager bottles.

"Excuse the mess, Commander. I was making some new plans last night. Sit down."

Commander Robinson took off his cap and white gloves and stood at ease. "I'd much rather stand, ma'am."

Teddy wasn't quite sure how this was going to work, so she started with something simple. "Quincy said you worked together, during her time in the marines?"

"Yes, ma'am. Quincy was a good friend. I started off in the marines then moved into the SBS." Orlando Robinson was almost bouncing on the tips of his toes, full of energy. "Inspector Quincy is an incredible officer and leader, and as fit as anyone I know."

Teddy smiled. "She is. Quincy used to take me running, and I built my fitness with her. I wanted to take part in a triathlon and join the marines, but then life happened."

Teddy let her head drop.

"I take part in ultramarathons. Training is part of my everyday. I got a twenty miler in first thing this morning. It really clears your mind and helps you deal with any pain you're feeling and sets you up for the day."

That interested Teddy. "I've read and watched a lot about ultramarathoners. It's something that really appeals to me."

"Would you like to start training again? It helps you deal with the day ahead. I couldn't live without training. Whatever you face that day, you know that while everyone else was in their beds, you have already won the battle of the morning."

Teddy grinned. Commander Robinson's enthusiasm was infectious. "Yes. That would be excellent."

"If I can make a suggestion, why don't we have a run and talk. I find it's a good way to get to know one another."

Teddy was surprised and didn't know what to say. "Have you got running gear with you?"

"Yes, ma'am. My kitbag is in my car as always."

"Okay…Commander."

Orlando gave her the biggest smile. "Call me Robbie, ma'am."

Running was the last thing she felt like doing, but Robbie's enthusiasm was sweeping her along.

Once he left for his kitbag, Teddy held her head in her hands. "What am I fucking doing?"

Eventually she made herself get changed. Robbie came back in and placed his bag on her couch. He looked her over with his hands on his hips. "You have good musculature on your upper body."

"It's the only part of working out I've really kept up with."

"What height are you, ma'am?"

Teddy felt like she was on the first day of training here. "Six feet, like my mother. About the only thing we share."

"It's a good height for a combat position. Shall we go, ma'am?"

"Okay."

As they walked down the stairs, they passed some staff who were surprised to see her in her training gear. It had been a while since she'd been down to the gym and pool in Kensington Palace.

When they walked outside, Teddy felt the chill of the morning hitting her tired, weak body and thought this was a bad idea.

"We'll walk for a brief warm-up, then get into a run. Where's the best direction to head?" Robbie asked.

"If we go to the grounds at the back, then there's a big wooded area to run through."

"Excellent. Let's start a fast walk."

The bright morning sun was dazzling her eyes. *Why am I doing this?*

"Is this not too much for you? You've already completed a long run," Teddy said, still hoping to delay this activity.

"I work till the job's done, ma'am. Can you tell me about your training history?" Robbie asked.

"I was always fit. I went out running with my mum and Quincy. They were so fit, still are. As I got to my middle teens, I started seriously training for the marines. Then in my early twenties, some personal issues made me question what I wanted."

"Okay, then you went to university?" Robbie asked.

"Yeah, then"—Teddy looked down at her feet and realized they had gone into a run without her realizing it—"I went to Sandhurst officer training."

Robbie ran in front of her and began running backward to talk to her. "You changed your mind about the marines?"

Teddy never talked about this or admitted it out loud, but with Robbie, the truth started tumbling out. "I had a bad break-up, and I wasn't interested in anything any more. The Queen told me that if it wasn't the Royal Marines, then I had to go to Sandhurst. She said if I was going to be Queen and Head of the Armed Forces, then I had to do some military service."

Robbie fell back in by her side. "Let's pick up the pace."

Teddy was starting to feel the bad night's sleep and the bottles of lager, but she did pick up the pace.

They passed some staff in the gardens who looked bemused at Princess Teddy running in the early morning. She had lived at home with her parents when this kind of activity was normal for her.

As they approached the wooded area, Robbie said, "Will we find out where this takes us?"

Teddy nodded. The thought of getting lost in the woods was appealing right now. "When do you run?"

"I get up at five, out the door at half past five. You have to win the morning before the real day starts," Robbie said with confidence.

It wasn't just the exercise that was pumping Teddy's heart, it was the strength and enthusiasm. Robbie wasn't criticizing her or expecting too much from her. Robbie was a breath of fresh air.

"Just keep one foot in front of each other, ma'am."

"Can you call me Teddy?"

Robbie answered with a question. "How was Sandhurst?"

"Disappointing for everyone."

"Were you fit?" Robbie asked.

"In body, yes," Teddy said, "but everyone was expecting my mother. Her picture was everywhere, all the officers told stories about the records she broke, that she topped her class, and I thought, what's the point?"

"You passed out into the Welsh Guards?"

"By the skin of my teeth. I wouldn't have if I was anyone else. But the future Princess of Wales had to pass out into the Welsh Guards."

Teddy was expecting some sort of negative reaction from Robbie, but it did not come.

They jumped over a big log in their path and landed in a puddle of mud. Robbie exclaimed, "Woo-hoo! Let's keep grinding."

Teddy went further than she could have imagined. Five miles later, she came to a halt, doubled over, trying to catch her breath.

"Take deep breaths. We'll have you doing twenty milers in no time. If that's what you want?"

Last night's alcohol was rolling around in her stomach, making her feel sick. She threw up and felt a little better.

"Ma'am, follow me. I see there's a stream down there. We can get a drink."

They walked down, and Teddy scooped the cold fresh water into her hands and splashed it on her face before having a long drink.

She took a seat on a large rock. "My granny and great-granny used to bring me down here to play."

"Queen Sofia and Queen Adrianna?" Robbie said.

Teddy nodded.

Robbie sat beside her. "What do you want from an equerry, ma'am? From me."

"I didn't know before we started running. I never wanted one, but

I think, now, I maybe do. Someone to help me bring discipline to my day, my life. Can I be honest with you?"

"Always, ma'am."

"Life has been difficult recently, but I want to do better. I want to be the Princess of Wales that my family and the people want. I want to make my body better, my mind better."

"You have those things inside you, ma'am," Robbie said.

"You don't know me well enough to say that. I'm not my mum, so I need to craft a new person. Someone who can at least act in the right way." *Even if I'm really not good enough*, Teddy added silently.

"I held a similar role when I was a young officer, for my commanding officer. I'll take care of your uniforms, your wardrobe—everything will be perfect, so your life can run seamlessly."

"That will help. I need to craft this new person out of the pieces of me. I started that job last night, planning out what was important to me, but most of all I need someone who is on my side."

"You can count on that, ma'am." Robbie held out his hand.

Teddy shook his hand. "Let's get started."

❖

"Did you get Teddy's email last night?" Annie asked.

Summer sat at the dressing table in Annie's bedroom, while she got ready for today's event. The whole family was due to take part in a thanksgiving service at Westminster Abbey for the National Health Service's anniversary. "Yes, I was surprised. Shocked, even."

Annie looked at herself up and down in the wardrobe mirror. "I know, I phoned her to make sure she wasn't some sort of imposter. She said that it was time to take things seriously. My sister? Teddy? This recent incident with Pandora must have affected her."

Summer remembered the look on Teddy's face as she watched Pandora leaving while threatening her. It had haunted her since. Teddy was lost, but now this? Was Teddy *so* lost?

"If I'm to take full control of both of your calendars for the next year, I'll need help, a deputy," Summer said.

"You need to concentrate on Teddy. She's the most important one here. I could ask Demi to help me, to help us both."

Lady Abidemi's father was the Earl of Handsworth. Even though her father was an earl, he expected his children to make their way in life. She worked in the art world part-time, and also as a companion to Princess Anna.

Summer got on well with her, and the professional skills Demi had would help enormously. "That would be perfect, Annie."

Annie walked over to her. "Are you sure working with Teddy is going to be okay with you?"

"Why wouldn't it be? We've talked about it before."

Annie held out her hands and took Summer's. "This is more than you anticipated, and you know what I mean. Teddy and you—"

"Teddy and I were a long time ago. We were children."

"You were childhood sweethearts, and you haven't exactly dated since, have you?"

"Some," Summer said defensively, but her dates had consisted of a drink and no second date. She thought on her feet and told a white lie. "I've joined a dating app. I'm ready to move on."

Annie gave her a questioning look. "Really?"

"Yes, really." Summer felt bad about lying, but it would stop this questioning about Teddy.

"You need to be careful on those sorts of apps," Annie said.

"I know." Summer stood. "Now stop worrying about me. You'd better get going."

"If you say so."

"I do. Now get going, Princess Anna."

CHAPTER EIGHT

Sitting in a meeting room at Kensington Palace was a new experience for Summer. She and Lady Demi had come to a planning meeting called by Teddy, which was unusual enough, but when they arrived, Teddy was already waiting.

"Good morning, sit down," Teddy said. "Sebastian is busy today, so I said I'd chair this informal meeting myself."

Teddy sounded businesslike and blunt. There was something different for sure. When Summer watched the thanksgiving ceremony a few days ago, she could tell Teddy had changed. Shut down, even. *Cold*, that was the word she would use.

"I'm going to take you through some of the ideas and plans I have, and then you can come back to me with ideas for events we could do. Lady Demi, you can let Annie know about the plans."

"Yes, ma'am."

Demi looked at Summer questioningly. This Teddy, who was taking them through things that were important to her, was changed.

"Housing insecurity, and the mental health issues associated with that, are important to me. I want to make something lasting, something that can help people with all aspects of having no permanent address. We are in a difficult time. More people are struggling with rent, heating, and food bills. Food banks are needed, more and more. I want to help all over the country and have events in all parts of the kingdom. Mark my inauguration with something meaningful. Think about that, and come back to me with ideas."

With that, Teddy shut down the computer screen and began to pack up.

"Is that it?" Summer asked.

"Yes, thank you for attending, Demi and Summer," Teddy said firmly.

Demi looked at her and shrugged. "I'll get off, then. I have another appointment. Bye, Summer. Goodbye, ma'am."

"Thanks, Demi."

Summer waited for Demi to leave, then said, "Teddy, if I'm helping you, you can't just send me ideas and expect me to get it done."

"That's what a PA does, I thought," Teddy said.

"You can't go from doing the minimal amount as a part-time royal to a full-time calendar without proper planning. You have family events that come around every year to fit in too—Trooping the Colour, Ascot, Wimbledon, amongst others—between the events you want us to come up with."

"Surely someone of your obvious organization skills can arrange it."

Summer felt that as the barb that was intended. "*I can*, but we need open communication. This was meant to be organized last year, but because you weren't interested, everything is being done at the last minute."

Teddy leaned forward, "I'm sure you enjoyed that remark, but I'm interested now, so we need to make it happen." Teddy stood up. "If you excuse me, I have other things to do."

"Don't you think I recognize it?"

Teddy turned back. "Recognize what?"

"The plan. Our plan."

Teddy looked at her silently, but there was anger there.

Their plan for a series of events in Wales, Scotland, Ireland, and England was made with laughter, love, and excitement. Summer recognized it. Only the causes that she had made part of it weren't there.

"This is the Princess of Wales plan, *my* plan," Teddy replied. "I went back to the passions that used to be important to me, and I revised it. I built my dreams on you, and you left me with nothing. Now my dreams are only for me and those I can help."

Teddy walked out, and Summer was left stunned. Tears welled up in her eyes. She thought she had left all that pain behind. Normally her and Teddy's encounters were sarcastic jokes, digs here and there, but this?

Something had changed about Teddy. She was cold, hard, and the anger that lay in Teddy's words was a shock to Summer.

Could this really work?

❖

Summer gathered herself and her things, angry and surprisingly hurt. Surprising because she thought all those hurt feelings and pain were in the past, part of her young adult life, but that exchange with Teddy exposed some buried emotions.

She packed her things and made her way down to the main entrance and outside to the gravel driveway. She was about to call for a car when she felt a wave of weakness, then an instant answering relief from her medical implant.

Summer rubbed her forearm. Her illness was a reminder that her reason for breaking up with Teddy was justified. Stress would have made her illness worse. At least that's what she told herself.

Something made her look up to Teddy's windows, and she saw a flash of someone moving away. She was unsure of what to do. If Summer left it like this, the next six months to a year were going to be miserable.

She would keep getting stressed, and Teddy's chip on her shoulder would keep getting bigger and heavier. In that instant Summer decided to face the mess that they had created so many years ago.

She took a breath and walked back inside. She saw Jack walking downstairs and asked, "Jack, can I talk to Teddy?"

"Sure, head on up, Summer."

Jack had known Summer since she was a child. She had their trust to a level that those outside the family would never have.

When she arrived at the front door, Summer hesitated. Could she shove the hurt feelings deep down inside, bury them, just to help Teddy for the greater good?

Just do it.

She knocked before she could think about it too much. A few moments later Commander Orlando Robinson answered the door.

"Ms. Fisher?" he said with the biggest smile.

Summer liked him, based on their brief interactions. "Could I speak to Princess Teddy, please?"

"Come in, and I'll let Her Royal Highness know you are here."

In the hallway of the apartment, suits in covers and a few military uniforms hung from clothes rails.

"Excuse the clothes everywhere, Ms. Fisher. I'm putting Princess Teddy's wardrobe in order and cleaning her uniforms."

Summer smiled at him and nodded. Teddy had always been untidy, and when she moved out into her own apartment here, she had obviously gotten worse.

She sat at the table in the living room and tapped her fingers. This was going to be a hard conversation.

Teddy walked into the room with the same cold air about her. Summer stood and bowed her head quickly. She noticed Teddy tense up even more.

"What do you want?" Teddy asked.

"We need to sort this out. You can't just walk out of the meeting in anger and expect everything to work out well."

"I'm not angry. I'm trying to do my job, like everyone has always wanted me to."

Teddy was full of anger, but she was pushing it deep down, just like Summer was doing.

"To make this work you can't just give me a brief plan and expect me to organize a diary of events."

"I never asked you to help me," Teddy said.

"No, I know you never would, but your mums did, and I'm not going to let them down. Since you don't have a PA, and you can't get one at short notice that will understand the way this family works, we are stuck with it," Summer said.

"That's the truest thing you've said. We are stuck."

What had happened to Teddy? She was distant and detached. Where were the gibes, the bad jokes to annoy her?

"We're stuck, and we can't have arguments or bad feelings every day we work together. It's going to be six months. Six months and it'll be all over. We won't need to see each other again, unless I'm with Annie, so let's put everything to the side, and just get through it."

Teddy sighed. "That plan is all I've got."

"Sit down, and I can show you what I need from you for the diary," Summer said.

"Fine."

Summer took out her notepad. She always got things clearer in her head if she made handwritten notes.

"Okay, as well as the things that are important to you, we have the royal court events that happen every year. They are the backbone of your calendar, and now you're working as a team with Annie, so there's even more."

"So what am I expected to do?"

"There was the Windsor Horse Trials, that's done. Next up at the end of the month is the Chelsea Flower Show."

Teddy looked at her as if she had lost her mind. "The flower show? My mums, Granny, and Aunt Grace deal with that event."

"Not this year. Annie has been working with a group of young gardeners to produce a mental health garden, something to help people and publicize the national mental health trust, Peace of Mind. The Queen thinks the two of you together can bring much more focus on the charity."

"Because my life is a soap opera?" Teddy said.

"I think because maybe you can understand and empathize with people who are feeling that way, with your work at Street Kitchen."

Teddy looked her straight in the eye and said, "And I've had my share of painful episodes in my life."

Now that was a gibe, but to get through this, Summer had to bite her tongue. "After Chelsea, there's Trooping the Colour, and Royal Ascot in June, and then Wimbledon, and that's just up to July."

"And in between all that there's the events to launch me as Princess of Wales?" Teddy said with exasperation.

"That's what being a full-time royal is all about," Summer said.

Teddy forcibly kept her mouth shut. That wasn't how life was meant to pan out, and she couldn't help but reply, "Is it? I suppose you know how it feels to have your life mapped out for you? Being followed around constantly, and not having the luxury of running away from it?"

Summer didn't say a word.

Of course, Summer did have the luxury of running away from her and this life, and yet Summer was lecturing her on what being a full-time royal was all about.

"Clearly my help and my presence aren't serving you." Summer stood. "Add what you need to this list, and I'll organize it. If we need to discuss something or you have any ideas, just message me. That way we won't need to talk more than is necessary."

"That sounds like the best idea you've ever had," Teddy said sharply.

Summer stared at her silently, then marched out of the room.

Robbie came into the room holding the boots and belts from her uniforms. "Ms. Fisher didn't stay long."

That last comment might have been hard, but the pain inside was still real. "No, she's good at that."

Teddy couldn't live with this weakness. She had to become the person that didn't care, that didn't hurt, and just concentrate on her mission—being the best heir to the throne Teddy could possibly be, for her family, for her country.

"Robbie, let's go for a run."

"If you'd like to, ma'am. Let's get after it." Robbie smiled.

Teddy was learning that tough exercise every day was a way to cope with her mental health, and cope with her life.

❖

"Are you sure you've been feeling okay? I told your dad we shouldn't have gone on that last cruise."

Summer and her mum were waiting to be seen by her specialist at hospital. It was her six monthly check-up. Usually it went like clockwork, but this time her mum had insisted on coming.

"Mum, I'm fine. I just need my levels checked," Summer said.

"You haven't looked well." Her mum touched her cheek. "You look pale."

Her parents panicked and worried. Summer knew why they were overprotective. It wasn't surprising. They had been under stress about her physical health since Summer was a toddler. So whenever Summer had the slightest sniffle or cold, she tried her best to cover it up, so they didn't worry unnecessarily.

She had managed to get her dad to stay at home today and to go to work, but Mum was insistent.

"I'm just tired, Mum. I have so much work to do at the moment, and I'm not sleeping well." That was true. At night when the lights were off and it was dark, it was all should could do not to replay every memory that she had of Teddy.

"Can I come in with you?" her mum asked.

"No, Mum, I'm an adult. I'll tell you what Dr. Dickenson says."

Her mum let out a long breath. "How are things going with Teddy?"

"Tense communications. It's making things difficult," Summer said.

"I don't understand. Why can't you both be friends?"

"Have you seen the playgirl she's become?"

Her mum shook her head. "It's just gossip. That's not the Teddy I knew."

"Because she's not the Teddy you knew. She's changed, Mum."

Summer's parents had always loved Teddy. When they were together, Teddy and often Annie would spend the weekend with them, come to dinner. Teddy loved the family dynamic the Fishers had.

There were no footmen waiting to tend to your every need, no security officers opening doors and clearing a path for you.

"People don't change that much, Summer. You need to have patience with each other and try to build a friendship again. I don't know why you broke up. You had such plans."

"Mum—"

"Summer?"

Summer was just about to tell her mum some home truths about Teddy when she heard someone call her name. She looked up and saw a face from her past, smiling. The woman in green scrubs was walking over to her.

"Doc?"

Summer met Dr. Mel Henry at an NHS charity event a few years ago. The children in the children's unit they were fundraising for called her *Doc*, and so she had joined in.

They'd dated for two months before Summer brought it to an end. It had been her first dating relationship since Teddy.

"Hi, Summer, good to see you again."

"You work here?" Summer asked.

"Yeah, I came here about six months ago," Mel said.

Mel looked to her mum, and Summer said, "I'm sorry, Doc, this is my mum, Diana."

They shook hands, but her mum wasn't as open and smiley as she usually was.

"Pleased to meet you, Mrs. Fisher."

"You too," her mum said.

Summer expected her mum to say *Call me Diana*, as she normally would. She just kept quiet.

"Is everything okay with you?" Mel asked.

"Yes, it's just a check-up. Are you still working in paediatrics?"

"Yes, it's my calling, I guess." Mel smiled. "It is rewarding."

This was one of the reasons she had dated Doc. After Teddy, people had asked her out, but Summer was never ready to move on. But Doc was such a good person, driven by a calling to help children with life threatening and life limiting conditions, like she had been.

But when Doc wanted their dating to become more serious,

Summer ended it. She wasn't ready, she told herself. The truth was she just couldn't get Teddy out of her head.

But she needed to, and maybe Mel could help her.

"Could I give you a call sometime?" Summer asked.

Mel's face lit up. "Yes, that would be nice. Do you still have my number?"

"I've got it. I'll call you soon."

Mel smiled. "Nice to meet you, Mrs. Fisher. Hope everything goes well with your check-up today, Summer."

"Thanks. I'll talk to you soon."

Once Doc turned the corner, Summer said, "What was that about, Mum? You weren't exactly friendly."

"I was polite," her mum said.

"You are the most friendly person you could meet. You're never just polite."

Her mum was silent for a second or two. "I never liked her when you dated her."

"You never met her when we dated. You don't know her," Summer said.

"You never brought her home. Why was that? Because you weren't that serious about her."

"Maybe I wasn't then, but I think I am now." Summer had a sneaking suspicion why her mum wasn't the warmest towards Mel. "Doc is a dedicated children's doctor. What could be better than someone like that?"

"She's not Teddy."

"Oh, for God's sake. I knew it." Summer raised her voice, and she saw some people in the waiting room looking. She lowered her voice. "Teddy, going from woman to woman, living life on her privilege, and fighting against her duty? Doc is not as good as that?"

"That's not the real Teddy. I watched her grow up with you, I was like a third mum to her, and I know she's not changed that fundamentally."

Summer was about to argue back but a nurse called her name. "Summer Fisher?"

She raised her hand.

"The doctor will see you now."

❖

Summer was sitting at the doctor's desk as he showed her test results in a 3D image.

"Your levels are up and down all throughout the day. They've been like that for the last year. Your implant isn't working as quickly as it should."

"Can you adjust my medication?" Summer asked.

Dr. Dickenson pursed his lips. "We have a few different combinations we can try, but we might have to try a more invasive treatment eventually. The implant ought to work seamlessly with your blood levels, working in the background, so you don't notice any momentary symptoms."

She had been with Dr. Dickenson since she was young. The doctor ran a pioneering study on Dawson Syndrome.

"Gene editing?"

He nodded. "I know you have a fear of that, but it is a relatively safe treatment now."

"Relatively?" Summer said.

"All treatments have an element of risk, Summer. I know you have heard some horror stories, but they are mostly unlicensed practitioners, selling people a treatment to cheat death, become superhero strong and indestructible. In your case, we are talking about an experienced medical staff who aren't trying to sell a dream."

Summer became part of Dr. Dickenson's research program at seven years old, and his treatment had helped her get back a normal life. She did trust him, but the little fear inside her head was stopping her.

She'd made the fatal mistake of doing a general search on the internet for the pioneering treatment. That was always a mistake. For some reason internet searches always led you to the worst diagnoses.

"But can we try to adjust the meds first, give my implant a tune-up?" Summer asked.

"We'll try. Come back in a few months and see if anything has changed. If not, then we really have to look at gene editing."

Summer didn't like the sound of that, so she prayed the new meds could make the difference. She stood up. "Okay, Doctor. I'll see you in a few months, then."

"Remember, keep your life as stress-free as you can, and think about the new treatment. I'll email you a patient information pack. You can trust the information there."

If he only knew the stress that was in her life at the moment…She walked out of the office door, and her mum stood and came over to her quickly.

"What did he say?" her mum asked.

"Just a little tweak to my meds. Everything is fine."

Her mother hugged her tightly. "I was so worried."

Summer closed her eyes and absorbed the love from her mum. "It's going to be okay."

She didn't want to discuss the gene editing with her parents as yet. The last time it was brought up as a possibility, they were all for it. But her lifelong battles with her health had left Summer with anxiety issues, and she wanted to think about the treatment with no pressure from them.

CHAPTER NINE

Teddy knocked on the door of her aunt and uncle's Chelsea town house. Jack stood at the bottom of the steps surveying the street.

She was so glad that she had this evening to look forward to. This afternoon Teddy'd had a video conference with the trust of the Duchy of Cornwall. It was so frustrating. They had been running things for a long time, and having a younger person asking about new ways of doing things didn't go down well.

The door opened and Princess Juliette jumped into her arms. "Teddy!"

Teddy did well to catch her in her arms as she had a bottle of wine in one hand and flowers in the other.

"Hiya, beautiful girl," Teddy said.

"Juls," Teddy heard Aunt Azi shouting.

One of Theo's security officers arrived at the door with exasperation on his face.

"It's okay, Mike. It's just me."

He bowed his head. "Your Royal Highness."

Azi arrived and took her daughter's hand. "What have we told you about not answering the door? You have to let Mike or one of the other officers answer the door, Juls. It could be anyone."

"But I was watching for Teddy."

"It was just me." Teddy smiled and offered her gifts to Azi.

Azi kissed her on both cheeks. "Come in, Teddy. Your uncle is watching Benny."

"For you." Teddy handed over the bottle of wine and flowers.

Azi smiled and inhaled the scent of the blooms. "They're beautiful, thank you. We're downstairs in the kitchen."

Juliette clasped her hand and they walked downstairs. Theo was sitting on the floor with Benny. When Benny saw Teddy, he toddled over to her.

"Hi, Benny boy." Teddy picked Benny up and gave him a kiss.

Theo walked over to her and bowed his head quickly, then kissed her. There was no need for Theo to bow his head to her. Theo was someone she looked up to. But it was just a reflex of how Theo and George were brought up.

"How are you, Teddy?"

"Better, I think," Teddy said.

"Sit down, everyone. Dinner is ready," Azi said.

"Mum's made your favourite dishes," Juls said.

Teddy loved Azi's cooking, the Middle Eastern dishes that Azi had grown up with and learned from her mother.

"Let's eat, Juls. I'm starving."

Once the children went to bed, Teddy, Azi, and Theo sat in the conservatory that looked out onto the garden.

"It's so nice out here."

"We practically live out of here and the kitchen," Theo said.

Azi cradled her glass of wine. "We heard you have an equerry now."

Teddy gave her a small smile. "Yeah, I bowed to pressure—no, that's not right. I needed some structure in my life, and Quincy suggested Robbie."

"How are you getting along with him?"

"It's the best decision I've made. He's a great man. I started running again, the way I used to with Mum."

"Teddy running?" Theo said. "You have turned over a new leaf."

"I felt it was time to face who I am and what I am. Robbie has been great, looking after my clothes and uniforms. Anticipates what I need before I do, somehow."

"How was today?" Theo asked. "You said you had your first meeting with the Duchy of Cornwall board."

Teddy rolled her eyes. "Yes, a video call. I think if I'd been there, I would have thrown a chair out the window or something. A bunch of stuck-up, old-fashioned men and women, more concerned to tell me about the profit the land and buildings were making than what could be used for something productive for society. I know that it's meant to fund the Prince or Princess of Wales's expenses, but there's more than enough money. I wanted them to tell me how we could use the land for charitable projects. You'd think I had grown horns the way they reacted."

"I can imagine. They are set in their ways, I'm sure." Theo laughed.

"I told them to do a survey and find out what land and buildings are sitting vacant. I want to do something with it, I just don't know what yet."

"Have things been difficult since the break-up?" Azi asked.

"Summer was a long time ago." Teddy was surprised by that question.

"No, no, I meant Pandora."

"Oh, oh, okay. Yes, my reputation as the playgirl princess has now been cemented in the public's mind."

Why had she assumed Azi meant Summer? Was Summer the only one she considered as a relationship?

Theo poured out some more wine. "Believe me, Teddy, I know how that feels. That's how people thought about me. I put fun above my duty. Then I realized that George needed my support. The pressure on her, on the crown, was made heavier the more I didn't support her. I changed, took my duty seriously, and then met the perfect woman to keep me on the right track."

Azi squeezed his leg. "I judged him on his reputation, but he showed me who he really was, and he was persistent, so I couldn't help falling in love."

It was so nice to see the love Theo and Azi had for each other, just like her two mums.

"There won't be any more Pandoras in my life. I'll live for my duty. I've let too many people down," Teddy said.

"To change the subject completely," Azi said, "how are you getting along with Summer as your PA?"

Teddy sighed. "We find it difficult to communicate, but we are trying to draw a line in the sand and move forward."

Teddy didn't tell them that they communicated in text messages. That would be awkward.

"How're the plans going for your Princess of Wales investiture?" Theo asked.

"Slowly. I know what I don't want—a big ancient ceremony. But what instead? I'm not sure."

Azi said, "Summer must have some ideas. She's very good at her job."

Teddy took a sip of wine. "That's where the bad communication comes in."

"What's important to you, Teddy? As in, charities you feel most strongly about."

Teddy answered without hesitation. "Housing insecurity. My charity, Street Kitchen. It's important to Annie too. I told Summer that at our last meeting."

"That sounds like the perfect kind of charity. Bea took you and Annie there as kids, didn't she?"

Teddy nodded. "I've been working two days a week there since I was a teenager. Then someone broke my cover, and it's over."

"It doesn't have to be," Azi said. "You need to learn to use the media to your own advantage. Invite the news cameras into Street Kitchen with you."

"Take them with me?"

Azi nodded. "Yes. You are always going to be followed by cameras, and stories will fill up newspapers and websites, so take the chance to leverage that publicity."

Theo agreed. "That's something I had to learn. Give them a little, and you get your charity or cause promoted everywhere."

"You mean make an *official* visit to Street Kitchen?"

Theo said, "Uh-huh. Your mums used to do that if they were on a state visit to another country. You invite the cameras to one set-up picture or event, and then they leave you alone for the rest of your private time."

Teddy was intrigued by this idea. "What makes them stay away?"

"Because if they don't," Theo said, "they don't get invites to the next new photo call."

"Summer will have good connections with the TV media. Ask her to set something up," Azi added.

"You've given me a lot to think about."

It always came back to Summer Fisher.

❖

The next morning, Summer was working in her office at Windsor Castle, trying to brainstorm some ideas for Teddy and Annie. It was a challenge, especially when Teddy was such hard work.

Summer heard an alert from her phone and put it up on her computer screen. It was from Teddy.

She was more than surprised, even more so when she read the text.

Summer, could you organize an official visit to Street Kitchen and invite some news media to come on with us?

Wow. This was new. At least by text they couldn't clash too much.

Great idea. I'll get back to you with the details.

"Okay, this can work," Summer said. Taking their personalities out of the equation helped it become a detached, businesslike relationship.

She stood up and walked to the window. It was a nice day out there. Annie was out riding with Laney. Summer hated to be on the back foot with her diary. She had Annie's diary up to date until Christmas next year.

The problem was the six months blocked out *this* year for Annie to support her sister's launch as Princess of Wales. That gaping hole in the diary made Summer uncomfortable, but hopefully this first message was a sign that they could fill that hole.

Who was she going to contact about the Street Kitchen event? Her first thought was the BBC. They traditionally were sympathetic towards the royal family, but it had an older audience.

They wanted Teddy and Annie to be relevant. Summer would have the social media team post the footage afterwards on all the apps, but maybe if they used a small independent film company, she could then share the footage with all the national news organizations.

"Perfect." A name came to mind immediately. "Computer, Giovanni Rossi."

Twenty minutes later a proposed deal was in place. Summer felt positive about this situation for the first time. Was something good actually coming?

Don't jinx it, Summer. This was just a first step, and who knew if that would be acceptable to Teddy or not.

She quickly messaged Teddy and moved on with her day. Summer walked into the town of Windsor to get lunch. She stopped at a nice little pub with outdoor seating. Summer had eaten here many times before, often with Annie. Usually they could fly under the radar in the town if Annie wore jeans, a T-shirt, and a baseball cap.

She ordered a vegan sandwich and a salad, and fizzy lime water. Summer looked at her messages. Nothing. Well, obviously, there was nothing or she would have heard an alert tone. It didn't stop her looking, though.

Her lunch arrived and there was still no return message. *Stop looking. I'm sure she's busy.*

Summer finished her food, then looked around a couple of shops before walking back up to the castle.

She finally heard an alert and opened her phone to find a text from Doc. She was hoping it was Teddy. She put the slight disappointment she felt down to the urgency of getting the calendar in order.

Hi Summer. It was good to see you again. Would you like to go for a drink when you're free?

She had forgotten she was to phone Doc. What would she say?

Summer typed out the message. *Hi Doc, good to see you too. Can I give you a call in a few weeks' time? Work is really busy.*

She didn't want to put Doc off or insult her, but she was so busy at the moment. She was, wasn't she? Summer was home most nights, pouring herself into her new project. Trying to lose herself, in all honestly.

But when Summer thought about going out with Doc, she could feel her stomach tightening and images of Teddy floated across her mind. Summer held on to so much baggage from their relationship that she thought she had gotten over, but working so closely with Teddy had shown her that she hadn't.

She massaged her forehead with her fingers. *Why can't I get her out of my head?*

But it wasn't right to fob Doc off, so she decided to be brave and call her. "Voice call Doc, please."

Doc answered very quickly. "Hi Summer."

"Doc, hi. I didn't just want to text you back. I'm sorry, I did mean to call you sooner."

"That's okay. Would you like to go out for that drink?"

Now came the hard part. "Doc, you are an amazing person and I'm so drawn to you, but I'm carrying a lot of baggage from a previous relationship. I don't think it would be fair on either of us to take it further," Summer said.

She heard Doc sigh. "Princess Teddy?"

"You know about our past?" Summer said with surprise.

"I see stories and rumours in the media about you both, from time to time."

"We're not together, but I have some issues to work out within myself going forward before I'm ready to date again. I hope you understand."

"Yeah, I do. Princess Teddy was always there in the background, though, wasn't she? Thanks for your honesty. Goodbye, Summer."

"Bye Doc. Take care."

Summer felt terrible, but she just couldn't deal with romance at the moment. Doc was right. Teddy was always there. Now she had to think about letting her go, for both their sakes.

When Summer arrived back at her office, a message announced itself. It was Teddy. She read it on her holo screen.

That sounds perfect. I'm sorry I took so long getting back to you. I was out on a run with Robbie.

Teddy was running? She hadn't heard about Teddy running since they split up. She used to go out with the Queen and Quincy. It was partly a bonding thing Teddy took part in with her mum, and partly training for Royal Marine officer selection.

It had been Teddy's dream to be a Royal Marine. Something went downhill when they split. Why Teddy let her dream go, Summer didn't know. She knew Teddy had it within her to pass selection.

It shouldn't have mattered that they weren't together. Teddy had been super fit and strong like her mum, but Annie said Teddy lost interest in her fitness when they broke up and starting going out to clubs and bars.

Summer had to reply. "Computer, send reply. *Running? Teddy running? That's a new thing.*"

And so a message conversation started. *Yeah, sounds crazy, doesn't it? Maybe I'm turning over a new leaf. What do you think?*

Wow. This kind of communication worked. Teddy was being more real than she had been in years.

You always had it in you, you just took a break. I'm sure your mum would like it if you went out running with her again.

There was silence in return. Uh-oh. She'd said too much. Been too familiar. Had she ruined this?

But a few minutes later, Teddy replied. *Maybe when I get my fitness up. Thanks for organizing the Street Kitchen event.*

Summer could feel the tension in that last message. She had pushed it too far, too fast.

Annie came bounding into the office. "I had a great ride. Laney thinks I could qualify for the next Olympics."

"That would be amazing, Annie."

"What have you been up to?"

"Just organizing a joint event for you and your sister."

Annie sat on the edge of the desk. "Really?"

"Yep, Teddy messaged me and asked if I could organize a TV crew to follow you both at an official visit to Street Kitchen."

"Wow. She asked for that?" Annie asked.

Summer nodded. "Kind of inviting the media in to publicize Street Kitchen, and hopefully raise more funds."

"I can't believe Teddy wants to work with the press. She went to dinner with Aunt Azi and Uncle Theo last night. They probably talked to her about things."

"Did you know Teddy was running again?" Summer asked.

"Oh yeah. Her new equerry got her back into it. I think it's great. Teddy was always super fit, super strong. It'll be so good for her mental health too."

"You're right. And it was so much easier communicating via message. It created a distance so we couldn't aggravate each other."

"I'm glad it's working, but you will have to see each other on the day of the visits," Annie said.

"I know. I know, but it can help ease us into working together again."

"Anything that helps. I think things are going to turn out well now. I hope, anyway," Annie said.

"I maybe pushed it a little far. I said she should run with her mum again."

Annie pursed her lips together. "Ooh, that's a sore spot."

"I shouldn't have been so super confident, but things were going so well," Summer said.

"Don't worry about it. I say the wrong thing most of the time."

"But you can get away with it. You're still her little baby sister," Summer said.

Annie walked around behind her and hugged her. "Everything's going to work out great. I have faith."

CHAPTER TEN

For the next two weeks, Teddy continued to train with Robbie, on runs and in the gym. She loved working out with the weights and pushing herself on the runs. The fitness bug was beginning to bite her once again.

Today was Sunday, and she and Annie were expected for lunch at Windsor. It was the one time in the week when the immediate family got together. But in the last six months Teddy had missed quite a few Sundays, and even when she came, Teddy would clash with her mum.

Something Summer had said to her had been bothering Teddy. She'd said Teddy should go running with her mum like she used to. That comment made her feel guilty. These days, Teddy didn't spend time with her mum unless they were arguing.

So last night, Teddy had messaged her mum and asked if she wanted to go for a run on Sunday morning. And Teddy was so glad she had. Her mum was so positive and surprised.

Her guilt ran a bit deeper. Her mum had obviously really missed this time together. It took Summer to suggest this. Summer did understand her family dynamic.

When she arrived at the castle, Teddy went first to the bedroom she used when she stayed, and then headed to the kitchen, as she knew that's where her family would be. It was their tradition to give the chef Sundays off, and Bea would cook her traditional roast dinner with the help from everyone who came.

It was important to her mama to make a big family meal, and not rely on staff, as they did the rest of the week. The other difference was that they ate in the kitchen, not in one of the castle dining rooms.

Teddy remembered her mum saying that had been an adjustment

for her Granny. Queen Sofia never ventured into the kitchen, not because she thought it was beneath her, just because that was her chef's domain and that was how things were done in Sofia's time as lady of the house.

Teddy and Robbie walked to the stairs that took them down to the kitchen.

Robbie said, "I'm just going to security to talk with Inspector Quincy and Cammy. Send a message when you're ready to go."

"Will do. We'll probably be thirty minutes."

Teddy bounced downstairs. She had more energy than she'd had in a long, long time.

She found Annie peeling, chopping, and preparing vegetables with help from Rupert, her mama was preparing the beef for the oven, and her mum was taping up an old ankle injury.

"Hey Buckinghams!"

Her mama rushed over and threw her arms around Teddy. "My Teddy bear."

Teddy bowed her head, lifted her smaller mother, and spun her around. "Hi Mama."

"I missed you." She placed lots of tiny kisses all over her Teddy's face.

"Mama." Teddy pretended she was embarrassed about the hugs and kisses, but she loved her mama's attention. She used to have the same tactile relationship with her mum, but it had changed in the last few years.

Rupert ran over and hugged her. "Hi Ted. Annie's making me peel vegetables."

Teddy hugged him right back. "I would help, Roo Roo, but I'm going running."

"Can't I go running?"

Her mama wrapped her arms around Rupert from behind. "No, it's for adults. You'll be grown up enough soon."

She kissed Rupert on the head.

Teddy went over to her mum, bowed her head, then kissed her on the cheek.

"Hi Mum, ready to run today?"

Her mum smiled. "I'm always ready."

"Robbie has gone to speak to Quincy and Cammy. We have to message them when we're ready."

Her mum nodded. "I'm just taping my ankle."

Teddy walked over to Annie and said, "Good morning, pipsqueak."

"Don't think I don't know this is your way to get out of peeling the vegetables."

Teddy laughed and took a raw piece of carrot to munch. "Never."

"Can you lift this meat into the oven for me, Teddy," her mama asked.

"Delighted, Mama."

When she'd put it in the oven, her mama asked, "How's your new equerry working out for you?"

"Great. I never, ever wanted one before, but Robbie has really motivated me, and he anticipates exactly what I need," Teddy said.

"I'm glad you're happy with him," her mum said. "Shall we go?"

Teddy could sense a little bit of hurt in that comment.

Cammy, Quincy, and Robbie ran together as a group, a few metres behind George and Teddy.

George ran every day. It was a discipline that kept her body and mind in check. "Thank you for coming out running with me."

"I'm sorry it's taken so long, but I wasn't ready to get back into my fitness routine. It's going to take a while to get my fitness back up," Teddy said.

"You're young, Teddy. It won't take long."

"I'd like to aim towards doing a marathon, then an ultramarathon. It used to be one of my ambitions," Teddy said.

"I remember, and I have every faith in you."

George was loving this. They talked intermittently, but they didn't need to. It was quality time they were spending together. George didn't know if it was a good idea but she had to bring up her plans.

"So, how are you, Annie, and Summer getting along with your launch plans?" George asked.

"We've made a start. Summer's organized a visit with my Street Kitchen charity. We're going to invite the cameras in, instead of fighting against them."

"Good plan. It's really important to you, that charity, isn't it?" George said.

"It is. I've been with them for years. I've got to know everyone and understand the reasons why they're unhoused. I just want to help." Teddy jumped a log that had fallen to the forest floor.

"You know I supported Timmy's, your mama's charity, in my first year as Queen. It will be good for you."

"It's only one thing, though. I've wasted so much time. I'm sorry I haven't been pulling my weight—with the family."

"Your life's been filtered through a camera lens, just like it was for me. But we all react to it differently. I tried to make myself perfect because I never thought I'd live up to your grandfather."

"You didn't?" Teddy said.

"No, I was quiet, didn't have much confidence, and no charisma with people. I had to train myself to be more open. Your mama helped. When she walked into the room, it lit up, and that allowed me to be who I needed to be."

Teddy knew she wasn't going to have that support. She was going to have to tackle this herself. How could she do it? She imagined walking into a room full of people. They expected a graceful, charismatic Princess of Wales, and instead they got her.

What did she know about anything?

After five miles Teddy was starting to struggle. Her body hurt, and the dark thoughts were dragging her down. How would she be able to stand in front of the general public and expect them to respect her, her passions, if they'd only seen her in gossip columns or in pictures of her out at clubs?

"I don't think I can go any further, Mum." Teddy stopped running.

George slowed down to a stop. "That's okay. We'll walk back."

Imagine being in your twenties and being outrun by your middle-aged mother. *I'm tired of not being good enough.*

Teddy stopped talking on the way back. She was falling down into the dark hole of pity again.

Her mum kept trying to talk to her. "What about your plan for your investiture?"

"No plans yet, nothing," Teddy said sharply.

"Teddy, you don't have time to wait much longer. This should have been sorted out last year. I've given you leeway, but it's getting to be the point of no return."

"I'm sorry I disappointed you," Teddy said.

"Have I ever said that?"

"You don't have to, I can see it in your eyes," Teddy said angrily as she strode ahead.

"Teddy—"

"Look, forget it. Postpone it to next year, postpone it altogether, for all I care."

Teddy started to run and didn't look back.

❖

Annie walked into her parents' living room, followed by Freya, Bear, and Ollie.

"Did Granny, Grandma, and Grandpa get off okay?" Her mama lifted Ollie onto her lap.

"Yes. Teddy will make sure they get home okay." Annie flopped onto the couch next to her mama. "Well, that was a tense lunch."

Her mum was in the armchair across the room, thinking deeply to herself. Freya and Bear lay down at her feet.

Her mama pulled Annie's legs onto her lap. "Your mum is a bit upset."

"Everything was fine, we were running together and she was really open, talking about inviting the cameras into her Street Kitchen, and then…I don't know what happened. Suddenly Teddy doesn't want to run any more and is shouting at me to leave her alone or cancel her investiture."

"It's not going to be perfect straightaway," her mama said. "Like I said, she puts you up on a pedestal, sweetheart."

"She can talk to Robbie, apparently."

"Mum," Annie said, "it's sometimes easier to talk to an outsider than to your parents."

"You talk to me."

"That's because we have a different energy, Mum," Annie said.

Her mama smiled and nodded. "Exactly. You and Teddy are like two bulls locking horns. The older Bully"—she winked—"and the younger bull trying to show how strong she is and feeling like she's losing."

"This isn't a competition," her mum said.

"You need to be patient, Georgie," her mama said. "She's made major strides in the last few weeks. She's broken up with a girlfriend that was making her life, and the family's, difficult."

"Yeah, Mum. Teddy's working well enough with Summer and me, she's exercising and getting healthy, and she's got an equerry to help her."

Her mum smiled at her. "That's true, little bug. I just want my Super Ted back."

Annie had heard the story behind the nickname as far back as she could remember. Super Ted was what their mum called the toddler Teddy, as she whizzed her around above her head.

Her mum was so sweet. The world out there saw a small part of Queen Georgina, but this side of her was only shown to her close family.

"She'll find her way," her mama said. "She's making the first steps to being the Teddy we once knew. Remember how happy she used to be? Think about how she could reinvent the title of Princess of Wales."

Her mum frowned. "I wasn't exactly an old-fashioned Princess of Wales."

Her mama shook her head. "No one's saying that, George. It's just that every generation modernizes the way things are done."

"Hmm." She was silent and then said, "I'm taking the dogs out. Come, boys and girls."

Annie watched her mum leave the room. "Uh-oh. Mum is not happy."

"Neither is Teddy," her mama replied.

CHAPTER ELEVEN

Summer lay on her mum's couch working on her computer, while her mum watched her favourite soap opera. She always came to her mum and dad's on Sunday, to spend some quality time with them.

Most of the time she stayed over in her old bedroom. Her parents loved that.

Summer's eyes were getting heavy. After a large meal, the comfy, warm living room was sleep inducing.

Just as her eyes were closing, a message beeped on her phone. She saw it was Teddy and her stomach clenched. She ignored the reaction and read the message.

Summer. Cancel the media event at Street Kitchen.

"Bloody hell."

Her mum turned around and said, "What's wrong?"

"Teddy wants to cancel her first joint event with Annie. I can't believe she would do this. It's Wednesday this week."

"Maybe she's ill or something," Diana said.

"Mum, I know you always think the best of Teddy, but she can't do this."

Summer quickly typed out a reply. *You can't do that, Teddy. It's been announced. You'd be letting down a lot of people.*

Teddy replied, *Yeah, that's what I do. I let people down.*

What's wrong with you? Your charity is banking on getting national exposure and donations from this publicity. I thought you cared about this organization? You are letting them down.

Almost immediately the phone signalled a voice call. Teddy.

"Is that Teddy?" her mum asked.

Summer sighed. "Yes, I'll go to my bedroom."

She hurried upstairs, the phone ringing and ringing. Summer shut the bedroom door and said, "Answer call."

"You took your time."

Summer sat cross-legged on the bed and made the holo screen big in front of her. "What can I do for you?"

"I'm letting my charity down? How could you say that? I've worked for them since I was a teenager."

"You will be if you cancel this. Everything is set, the staff are excited, they've had the building cleaned from top to bottom, and you want to cancel?" Summer said.

Teddy looked at her with a mixture of emotions in her eyes. Hurt, panic, fear, inadequacy.

Summer had seen this look in Teddy's eyes once before. Once when they were young, when Teddy was eighteen, when they'd only been dating for six months…

Summer looked all over for Teddy. Everyone was looking for her. Teddy was giving her first speech. It was on behalf of her great-grandmother, Queen Adrianna, who was ill. Queen Adrianna was due to tour a Royal Marine base in Arbroath, Scotland, and give a speech. Queen Georgina thought it would be a good first public appearance for Teddy on her own.

There was one place where no one else knew to look—the attic rooms of Windsor Castle. They were always told the rooms were haunted, but Teddy persuaded her to come up to the attics as a young girl.

They weren't frightened. In fact they made dens to play in and passed their time using the many items up there as part of the game. It was a place that was their own. A place where they could be on their own.

Summer went through the doors to the back stairs area and climbed the small wooden steps until she got to the ladders. They were down, so someone was up there.

She wiped some worrying cobwebs from the ladders and began to climb. When she reached the top, she pushed up and over onto the wooden floor.

Summer brushed herself down and looked around for Teddy. She couldn't see her. She started to walk around. Summer recognized so many of the old chairs, paintings, toys, fishing rods, ornaments, all that had been part of their play.

She saw a foot sticking out from the side of a wooden box. "Ted?"
Teddy didn't reply. So she walked around and stood in front of her.
"Ted, I've been looking everywhere for you."
"I didn't want to be found," Teddy said.
"You can't hide from me, Charming."
"I suppose not, Cinders."
Despite being in a nice dress, Summer sat down on the dusty floor and pulled her legs to her chest.
"What's wrong, Ted?"
Teddy's head was bowed down. "I can't do this."
"What can't you do?" Summer asked.
"This stupid speech." Teddy held up paper from a notebook where she had copied it.
Summer looked in her eyes when Teddy raised her head. She saw fear, trepidation, inadequacy, raw emotion. What most people didn't understand about Teddy was that she had low confidence in herself.
They saw the cocky but good-natured princess who played every sport, was full of fun, had lots of friends. That was only the surface. Beneath that was the Teddy that only a few people saw.
The sweetly unconfident, not so sure of herself teenager who struggled to feel worthy of her mum's legacy.
"I can't do this," Teddy said.
"Of course you can, Ted, we've practised and practised the speech. You have got it."
Teddy lifted her hand and it was shaking. "Why am I like this, then?"
"Because it's a big deal. Your first time attending an event on your own and representing your great-granny. It's only natural to be nervous."
"The speech is bad enough, but I have to walk into the room and make small talk. When Great-granny walks into a room, people automatically respect her for all she has done. She's perfected talking to people."
"Everyone has to start somewhere. There was a first time your great-granny did this too."
Teddy shook her head. "I can't do it."
Summer took her hand and kissed it. "You can. I believe in you."
"I wish you could be there with me."
Summer laughed softly. "I think the world would find I'm your girlfriend, and the media would go crazy."

Teddy pulled her into her lap. "They won't find out until you're ready. I promised you."

"You can do this, Teddy," Summer said. "Just imagine you have me with you. Okay?"

Teddy gave a weak smile. "Okay, Cinders."

Now the years made them look older, and what they were to each other was different, but Summer had to get the same result. She had to get Teddy to her appointment. It was her job.

"Okay, okay. You don't have to do it. Nobody can force you, and I'm sorry to put it this way, but you would be letting them down. They've spent money on decorating just so they can look their best for the cameras, and you know how important expenditure is to Street Kitchen."

Teddy clasped her hands around the back of her neck and pulled her head in frustration.

The woman that had once been her girlfriend hadn't changed as much as she assumed she had, going by Teddy's life and relationships while living in the glare of the media.

This was pure emotion and fear. Teddy had been putting on a mask. A mask of *I don't care, nothing fazes me, I just want to party and have a good time.*

There was still a semblance of the old Teddy lurking in there.

"Teddy, you can do this. The people love you there."

Teddy covered her face in her hands. And shook her head.

Summer couldn't understand it. Teddy had been doing so well, and now she had fallen so far back.

"Teddy? What happened? You were so enthusiastic about this."

Teddy moved her hands and clasped them in front of her. "Do you know Shakespeare's *Henry IV, Part 1?*"

"Um yes. We read it at school."

"Granny told me to read it. Prince Hal cast away his drinking buddies and raucous friends and became King Henry V."

Summer smiled. "I can see what she was trying to say."

"Then Quincy told me to attack life according to the Royal Marine ethos. Remember that?"

Summer did remember. She'd helped Teddy learn the values as a teenager when her dream was to be a marine.

"Yeah, I remember."

"I thought I was doing it, but then one run with my mum, and I just want to hide away," Teddy said.

"Why? What happened?" Summer asked.

Teddy's eyes darted to the side. She was hiding something, Summer realized.

"I don't know," Teddy lied. She knew exactly why she'd lost all her confidence. Her mum reminded her she was alone, and that she would have to face these visits all alone. She wouldn't have her own Queen Consort like Mama.

When she imagined walking into Street Kitchen, she saw herself becoming tongue-tied. They were waiting for her to talk, to speak and uplift them, and it scared her. This was someplace she knew well, so how was she going to do this at places she didn't know for the rest of these six months?

"Teddy? Look at us talking without shouting at each other. That's something neither of us would have believed, and if you can do this with your ex that you dislike, then you can do anything," Summer said.

Teddy didn't like Summer describing them as exes that disliked each other. They had a different dynamic. It was a one-to-one relationship with a lot of hurt.

Summer didn't really dislike her, did she?

She probably did. The things Summer said about Teddy's relationship with Pandora were a testament to that fact.

"If you go to this one, Teddy, I'll walk right by your side and fill in any gaps in the conversation with the cameras and the clients," Summer said.

"For years I went there two or three times a week," Teddy said, "dressed down, my hat on, nobody batted an eyelid. Now that it's an official visit—it's awkward. I just don't feel I can do it."

"You can, you're just out of practice. Do this one, and then see how you get on. Will you?"

It felt strange having Summer encouraging her again. But could she trust her? Summer was doing this for the two Queens. But if that helped her get through this, so that she didn't let Andy and everyone down, maybe it was worth it.

"Okay, I'll try."

"You're making the right decision, Teddy."

"I hope so."

❖

The car pulled up outside Kensington Palace. Summer was in the back of the car, ready to pick up Teddy. Then they were meeting Annie at Street Kitchen. Summer was nervous, but she couldn't show it as she was supposed to be getting Teddy through this, not be nervous herself.

But this was the first time in years they'd be alone together for a prolonged time. She kept telling herself that she had to be professional. Their former private life had no place here, and if Summer was to be successful, it had to be that way.

She watched Jack and Robbie leading the way. Behind them a tense looking Teddy walked down the steps.

Please let this work.

Jack held open the door for Teddy, and she got in. It was a dressed-down visit, meant to look as natural as possible. So Teddy was wearing jeans but with a fashionable navy blazer. Teddy didn't look at her. She looked so tense.

"Good morning Your Royal Highness."

"Don't say that," Teddy said in a low voice.

"What?"

"Your Royal Highness."

"That's what you are," Summer said firmly. "Anyway, I only have to say it once, when I meet you."

Teddy didn't respond and stared out of her window.

Great, this is going to be fun.

Jack got in, then the other guards, and Robbie went into a car behind.

They set off, and the tension in the back seat was so intense you could cut it with a knife.

Summer had to be professional and do her job, no matter how difficult. She opened the computer file containing the plan for the day.

"Ma'am?"

Summer saw Teddy's fist tense. She seriously didn't like to be reminded of who she was, so Summer gave in.

"Teddy? Can we do a once-over of the plan?"

Teddy did turn round this time. "I did go over it a million times last night."

"I find it always helps when I'm working with Annie."

Teddy sighed. "Fine."

Summer pointed at the screen. "The camera and production people will film us arriving, then we get out and will be met by the centre manager, Gabby, then the cameras follow us inside where we'll be met by Andy and the catering manager Kath—"

"These people are my friends. What am I meant to do? Act all formal and shake their hands?" Teddy asked.

"No, try to be yourself. I know the cameras make it difficult, but try to be as natural as possible. We want the public to see you when you're not out—"

Summer was going to say *out clubbing and enjoying a rich social life* but thought that sounded bad. So she simply said, "Out and about. We want them to see the other side, working hard for your charities."

"You think I have another side? I thought you believed I was the cause of my bad reputation. You said that I put myself in the position to invite the bad publicity into my life."

Summer sighed. "Teddy..."

But the car stopped, and Summer thought there was little use in answering that.

Jack got out to open the door. Teddy sat forward, ready to get out, and said, "Funny, isn't it. You left me because of the cameras and media in my life, and now you're directing those very same cameras."

Summer didn't know what to say to that. It took her by surprise. What could she say?

CHAPTER TWELVE

It wasn't normal. Not by any means, but Teddy was coping okay so far. After greeting everyone, Teddy went to the kitchen with Kath and Marco, to help with the teas and coffees, while Annie stayed in the dining room talking to the people that came in for help today.

Kath and Teddy's interactions were stilted. They weren't quite sure how to react with the little buzzing drones that videoed them.

Teddy looked at Kath, then at Summer. If they were there on their own, Teddy would have no problem. Luckily Summer stepped in and said, "The tea urn is Princess Teddy's specialty, I've heard."

Kath laughed, and it broke the tension. "Yes, ma'am. If you get the tea, I'll get the coffee."

"No problem."

Teddy heard Summer whisper, "Just make the tea like we're not here."

Teddy swallowed hard. *I can do this.*

She concentrated on filling the urn with water and tea bags. Having a task was certainly making it easier. It was just so different than coming here on her own and enjoying spending time with Andy and her friends.

This was weird, but if it was going to help her charity, then she would pretend it was normal.

"Tea's ready, Kath."

"I'm with you," Kath said. "Let's go."

Summer whispered, "You're doing well. Smile and serve tea."

Teddy shivered. *Tea. Get the tea out. Nothing else.*

When she pushed through the kitchen door, all the faces turned to her, and the cameras turned to her, directed by their human operators.

Smile and serve tea, Teddy told herself.

Annie was at the first table and said loudly, "Tea at last. I thought you were never going to brew it."

Teddy poured out the tea and chatted as normally as she could, as she made her way around the tables. In the reception hall another production team and a journalist were interviewing some of the staff and clients about Annie, Teddy, and Street Kitchen, and its association with them both and how their becoming official patrons would help.

As the morning calmed down, Teddy was finally able to chat to Andy in private.

"It's gone well today, Teddy. Thanks for doing this for us— officially, I mean."

"I'll do anything to help. I was so disappointed the day the press found out about me," Teddy said.

"It's turned out to be good in a way. We'll get national exposure now. Raise some good money, I think."

"I hope so. Anything I can do, I will."

"Who is the woman that was with you today? She's very efficient, handled the day well," Andy asked.

Teddy looked over at Summer talking to one of the production people. "That's Summer. My sister's PA. She's helping us both for a while. I'm supposed to be created the Princess of Wales this year."

"Wow, are you going to have a big medieval type of ceremony?"

"The Queen wanted me to, but I think that's outdated. I'm trying to work that out. A new modern way of doing things."

"Is Summer helping with that?" Andy asked.

"Between me, Annie, and Summer, we're trying to come up with something."

"Well, you're doing so much for us. Your patronage is going to help donations. We've already had supermarkets, clothing suppliers, restaurants, all contact us and ask if they can donate food and clothing to us regularly. That's with having Princess Edwina and Princess Adrianna as our patrons. Imagine having the Princess of Wales on our letterhead?"

That really brought home to Teddy the value of the title she was fighting against. Maybe it was worthwhile.

❖

Summer went into her bedroom to get changed, but she was so tired she flopped down on her bed. It wasn't the physical activity, it was the mental tension. Trying to walk Teddy through the day without anything going wrong in front of the cameras was like doing the high wire.

She rubbed her temples as she felt a headache building. Summer reached for her handbag for a painkiller shot, but before she got the opportunity the meds under her skin whooshed and kicked in.

Summer rubbed her arm. The doctor said she shouldn't be aware of the device, but she had been for quite a while now. She had read over the patient information that the doctor sent her, but she couldn't help have anxiety over all the gene editing horror stories out there. Summer trusted her doctor, but there was always a little voice in her head saying that she would be in that five percent that had life-changing side effects.

Summer couldn't deal with this just now. She had too much on her plate. She decided to file that decision away for later.

She pressed the painkiller shot against her skin for her headache and closed her eyes. She was exhausted. It had been a strange day. It didn't start well in the car. Teddy was nervous, and Summer was her target.

What Teddy had said about her leaving Teddy because of the cameras had cut deep. There was so much more to their break-up, and she hadn't *left*. She went away to take some time to sort out her head, and Summer did come back for Teddy. But by then the closed-off Teddy wasn't interested.

Summer played the images of the day over in her mind. She wished Teddy could see what she did, and how worthwhile days like today were, and how much royal patronage helped. But after a stiff formal start, and some direction from herself, Teddy had relaxed into the day.

Teddy's friend Andy was a real asset. He'd come into Street Kitchen with nothing, and they'd helped him back onto his feet. The country needed success stories like Andy's, and Summer would have to tell Teddy that at their next meeting.

Teddy had surprised Summer. There was a lot more of the Teddy she remembered in the princess than she'd realized. Maybe it had been easier all this time for her to deal with the heartbreak to see Teddy as having lost all of herself down a bad road.

❖

When Teddy arrived home, she was full of energy. "Robbie? Do you want to head down to the gym?"

"Always, ma'am. Let's go."

The Kensington Palace gym wasn't currently occupied. There was usually just staff there, as mainly older members of the extended royal family lived there.

Empty was perfect. It allowed Teddy to think and burn off the tension of the day.

"Let's hit your legs and chest. We want to push before we run and get after it in the morning. Start with the leg press," Robbie said.

Even though Teddy had been immersed in this world since birth, she hadn't appreciated the power that someone like her could hold. She'd questioned her role so many times, even questioned the monarchy. She still wasn't sure what she thought.

Imagine being a future monarch and being unsure of the monarchy's value? There were too many thoughts in her head. She could go for advice to her mama, the former antimonarchist, and her grandmothers, but she knew what their replies would be.

Pushing her body at least gave her something to fight against.

"Push it, ma'am," Robbie said. "You're strong, come on."

Teddy felt the lactic acid in her muscles and wanted to stop, but she wanted to push and do more. Push her body to its limits.

As she kept attacking her body, it became clear what she needed to do, who to talk to.

CHAPTER THIRTEEN

A few days later Summer was spending her Sunday morning on the couch, catching up with her emails. It was meant to be a day of rest, but Summer's job didn't stick to a schedule, and she felt anxious knowing there was work to be done.

The doorbell rang, and Summer looked at the camera on the door. It was Teddy. That was the last person she expected to see. She was just in her pyjama shorts and T-shirt, so Summer hurried to get her dressing gown.

She opened the door, and Teddy's eyes took in every inch of her. "I'm sorry if I'm disturbing you."

Summer was tongue-tied. She was so used to their antagonistic, gibing relationship that it was hard to react to a kind remark.

"No, it's fine. Just a lazy Sunday morning. Come in." Summer led her into her living room.

"You're working on a Sunday morning?" Teddy pointed at the computer.

"Yes, a royal diary is a lot to organize. I don't like leaving things to the last minute. Coffee? Tea?"

"Coffee, please."

"I'll just be a second."

Summer went into the kitchen and started to make coffee at the espresso machine. *What is she doing here?*

She made a double espresso for Teddy and placed one cube of sugar on the saucer, and a latte for herself.

Summer took the coffees through. Teddy looked at hers silently.

"Is there something wrong?" Summer asked.

"You remembered. Double espresso and one cube of sugar."

"I have known you a long time."

"Our whole lives," Teddy murmured. "That's why I wanted to speak to you."

"Sit down," Summer said. "What's on your mind?"

"Our engagement at Street Kitchen. Andy was so grateful for the media exposure for just one day. They have supermarkets, restaurants, and food suppliers offering to donate money and food."

"That's wonderful."

"Is it? Just because of who I am? I'm struggling to understand it. The power of the monarchy. I knew you'd tell me the truth. Do you believe in the monarchy?"

Summer snorted with laughter. "I have the heir to the throne sitting next to me, asking if I believe in the monarchy."

"Yes, you're about the only one who won't tell me what they think I want to hear. I'm here by an accident of birth. Not only to be Princess of Wales, but to inherit the Duchy of Cornwall land and the revenues it brings—it's more money than I can imagine. I've been handed all this privilege because of this accident of birth. Why should I have it?"

Teddy waited on Summer's response, hoping that it would clear her mixed-up mind.

"You have power, Teddy, soft power. You can turn up somewhere to unveil a plaque and have a million eyes on you, your cause. That's priceless. I know exactly how much the Duchy of Cornwall lands generate. If you remember, it was part of *our* plans that we made when we were first dating. Yes, it might be an accident of birth, and off-the-scale privilege, but what matters is what you do with that privilege. It seems to me that you've lost that along the way."

That made Teddy's hackles rise. She put her cup on the coffee table and stood up. "If I have such a special gift, this soft power to do so much good, then why did you run away from it?"

Summer stood too. "Look, I thought we agreed not to talk about personal matters again?"

"Personal matters?" Teddy took a step towards Summer. "Two people who have known each other their whole lives, and you call it personal matters?"

"Teddy, don't."

"Don't what?"

"Stop blaming your whole life on me. We keep coming back to it over and over. Why can't we just be adults about it? Look, I made a decision for my health and—"

Teddy took another step and was inches from Summer. It was the closest she'd been to her since their break-up. Summer was pulling her in. Her eyes, her lips. Teddy's body was shaking inside. "And *you* need to stop blaming your health for breaking up with me. Just admit you were scared, admit that you didn't love me enough."

Summer's eyes went wide. "You want me to say I didn't love you? Why? You've had more girlfriends than I can count since we broke up. Why does it matter to you?"

Because none of them made her feel in one second what she felt now, gazing into Summer's eyes, being drawn into her soul.

Teddy licked her own lips, hungering to kiss the lips in front of her now. Summer opened her lips slightly and gazed at her with soft eyes.

Summer was still at first and then put a hand on Teddy's chest. That was enough to break her out of this emotional moment, and she walked over to the window.

A tension hung in the air, and Teddy wished Summer would fill it. *Why does this matter to you?* Teddy didn't want to answer that.

"Teddy, I know you care about the causes you represent. I saw you at Street Kitchen. You really care about it."

"I do. It's the one thing in my life that I'm proud of. Housing insecurity is something that I feel really can be tackled and changed. Not just feeding and housing people, but tackling the causes."

"Sounds like you've written a part of your first speech." Summer smiled. "Teddy, if you recognize the privilege you have, don't waste it. Many people would give anything for the platform you have."

Teddy nodded and walked back to Summer. "I don't want to waste it. I just need help. These past few years I've lost focus on what's important."

"Do you want to talk things through and see how we can move forward?"

Teddy had the response out before she could even think about it. "Yes. I would love that."

"Let me go and get dressed, and we'll go through some ideas."

"Shall I go and get us some lunch? I saw a nice sandwich bar around the corner."

"Okay, great. I'll have—"

"I remember what you like too. A wrap with falafel, salad, and sweet chilli sauce?"

That brought about the biggest smile from Summer that Teddy'd seen for years. "You do remember."

I remember everything. You broke my heart, and I've ached for you every day.

❖

"A cheese sandwich?" Summer laughed.

"What's so funny?" Teddy asked.

"You'd think after all these years since we've been together, you'd have broadened your tastes from just cheese on white bread."

Teddy unwrapped her sandwich on the coffee table. "What's wrong with cheese? It's a classic. You don't mess with a classic. That's the one thing people don't realize about the royal family."

"What's that?" Summer said, then took a bite of her wrap.

"That everywhere we go to eat, we don't want quail's eggs, caviar, pheasant, and peacocks."

Summer chuckled. "When you'd rather just have a cheese sandwich."

"Or a bacon sandwich. Although I need to start being serious about my nutrition, now I'm back to training in the gym and running. I did ten miles with Robbie this morning," Teddy said proudly.

"Wow, well done. You used to love training. I'm glad you have it back in your life."

Teddy looked different this morning. The coldness that she had seen had gone, and in its place was a smouldering warmth. When Teddy stepped close to her earlier, she thought she was going to kiss her. Summer's body had reacted, but her brain engaged and she put a hand on Teddy's chest.

A kiss couldn't happen. Nope, no way. It was just the high emotion of the argument. Now that the undercurrent of their past relationship was dealt with, everything was back to normal.

As normal as they could ever be with each other.

"Are Jack and your guards going to be all right out there? They can come in."

"It's okay. They got food from the sandwich bar."

Summer nodded. "So, do you think we can move on from texts?"

Teddy smiled. "I want to. I mean, I want to leave all the past in the past and try to work together. I know how good you are at your job. Organization is easy for you. And—"

"And what?" Summer asked.

"You are my most honest critic and will have no trouble telling me the truth, not what I want to hear."

"Okay, let's get to it."

"I thought we could use the plan we both came up with when—"

Summer thought Teddy would say in love, so jumped in quickly with, "We were both idealists and wanted to save the world?"

"Exactly." Teddy smiled. "Obviously adjusted to suit me and not a couple."

"Yes," Summer said awkwardly.

They'd made a five-year plan for what they wanted to achieve. The ending was a wedding, after which they'd agreed they'd make another five-year plan.

"I wish I had brought it with me," Teddy said.

"It's okay, I have a copy in my files."

Why did she say that? It begged the question: Why did she keep it?

Luckily Teddy said nothing.

"Computer, open file—" Uh-oh, this was going to be awkward. "Charming and Cinderella."

"Charming and Cinderella..." Teddy laughed. "That takes me back."

Summer said nothing and opened up the file.

Teddy's laugh faltered. "This is going to work, isn't it? I mean things *can* be all right between us."

Summer didn't know, but it was her job to try hard and make things work. "I think it will as long as we don't talk about the past."

"Agreed."

"After all," Summer said, "we're adults now. We've both changed and grown."

"I suppose." Teddy sounded unsure.

CHAPTER FOURTEEN

Queen Beatrice and Annie were being driven to Battersea Dog and Cat Home for an engagement. Battersea and other dog charities had been the domain of Queen Adrianna, George's grandmother. After she died, Bea was the natural choice because of her love of the family dogs. Then Annie asked if she could represent some dog charities too and support her mama.

Bea hadn't grown up with dogs, but then she met George and her three dogs at the time, Shadow, Baxter, and Rex. Rex had been the late King's dog. But when the King died, Rex was lost and attached himself to George, then stuck like glue to Bea when she met him.

They'd had many dogs over the years, and Bea had loved them all, but Rex was her soul dog. Ollie, however, was her little baby, now that her human babies were all grown up.

Bea straightened Ollie's little dog jacket, a green jacket with a fake-fur collar and the Battersea logo, one of a range of dog wear and apparel that generated income for the dog and cat shelter.

"Doesn't he look gorgeous?" Bea asked.

Lali, Bea's PA and best friend, ruffled his head. "He's a handsome little man. You landed on your paws when Queen Georgina picked you out for your mama."

Annie leaned forward and almost whispered, "Guess who spent Sunday together?"

"Who?" Bea asked.

"Teddy and…Summer."

Bea and Lali said, "Really?" at the same time.

"Yep, Summer told me." Annie grinned.

"Were they fighting?" Bea asked.

"No, trying to come up with a plan going forward but, crucially, together. They shared lunch."

"That is a big change," Lali said.

Bea scratched behind little Ollie's ear. "Why are you grinning? Is it friends or *friends*?"

"I wouldn't say anything as strong as *friends*, but it's a step forward, don't you think?"

"It is," Bea said. "I wish things had turned out differently. If I were to pick anyone to be Teddy's wife and future Queen, it would be Summer."

"Do you think they still care about each other?" Lali asked.

"Annie? What do you think?" Bea asked.

"I'm certain that Teddy still loves her, but the hurt runs deeply between them, and Summer cares, no matter what she says, but this life—"

"Frightens her?" Bea answered for her.

Annie nodded.

"No matter what," Bea said, "at least Summer can be a good influence on her. Keep me posted, Annie."

The car pulled up at their destination. Bea could see a red carpet and dogs, in the same kind of jacket that Ollie had on, lining each side of the red carpet, in a guard of honour.

"Aww, they look so precious," Bea said.

"Remember what Mum said, Mama? Don't fall in love and bring more dogs home," Annie said.

"I don't remember her saying that. Do you, Lali?"

Lali smiled. "No, certainly not when I was around."

Bea kissed Ollie. "Now, best behaviour, Ollie. We're going to see all your friends."

Quincy opened the door of the car and the cameras buzzed around and started flashing. "Let's go, Annie."

❖

The next day George stood by the window of the main drawing room, Freya and Bear sleeping by her feet. It was her weekly meeting with the prime minister, and she didn't much enjoy it since Crawford Blackmore became the leader.

She saw the official car come through the gates, but it would take some time to get up to her.

George had always looked forward to her meetings with the prime minister of the day. Whether she agreed with their politics or not, she loved to hear about how the country was doing and its place in world events, but with the election of Crawford Blackmore things changed.

The new political party that Crawford Blackmore led was right wing. Dangerously right wing. Crawford's Alliance Party came into being as a very small, fringe party, but rather quickly attracted the worst kind of right wing politicians.

Crawford promised extreme rules on immigration, the welfare state, the NHS, and environmental factors and protection of wildlife.

That really worried George because there was something dangerous about the Alliance Party. Most right-wing or right-of-centre parties wrapped themselves up in the Union Jack and took patriotism to the extreme, which included huge support of the monarchy.

The Alliance Party was different. They found the monarchy a hindrance to their power, and Crawford in particular came across as being annoyed that this meeting was taking up vital time in his day.

In fact, when they were sitting across from each other, George had a distinct feeling of sitting with Oliver Cromwell, the Puritan politician who beheaded King Charles I and became Lord Protector of England.

George rubbed her neck and smiled. *I'm too attached to my neck to lose it.*

She walked over to stand by her chair. The dogs started to follow, but George said, "No, Freya, take your brother and sleep over there."

The dogs trundled back to the window. She felt bad as her dogs were always close, wherever she went, but the prime minister had made it clear, when he came to the palace to be sworn in, that he disliked dogs, or pets of any kind. Another reason to dislike the man.

George had had many prime ministers over the years, some more pleasant than others. Her very first, Bo Dixon, was a chameleon who changed her beliefs depending on who she was speaking to or what the situation was, but her views were nothing like Crawford Blackmore's.

There was a knock at the door. George clasped her hands behind her back as Cammy led in the prime minister. They both bowed their heads, but Crawford looked like it was done with resentment.

George would rather he didn't bow at all. It wasn't something she insisted on, if someone was uncomfortable, but he appeared to keep up the pretence out of obligation.

"Prime Minister. Please sit down."

He sat, crossed his legs and clasped his palms together, and said nothing. Talking to Crawford was like pulling teeth. He didn't volunteer any information that he was prompted to share.

"So, Prime Minister, how was your week?"

Crawford looked at her with the faintest of smirks on his face. "Busy. Busy writing the speech that you'll be giving for me very soon."

He was talking about the Queen's Speech that she gave to announce the government's policies and agenda for the coming session of parliament. Crawford was ensuring she was reminded that it was him and his government that made the law, not her.

George had read many Queen's Speeches over the years, with lots of policies and agendas that she fundamentally disagreed with, but it was her job and duty as Queen to remain neutral, in their constitutional monarchy.

That was something her father had drilled into her, and it needed to be drilled because it was a very hard thing to do.

"Yes, indeed. What is your government focusing on this year?" George asked.

"Cutting the welfare budget, dealing with illegal immigrants, and making Britain a force to be reckoned with on the world stage again."

"When you say cutting the welfare budget, what do you mean?" George asked.

"Cutting the amount of unemployment payments. It's too comfortable for people to sit idle on unemployment. We want to make it less attractive."

"Attractive?" George was shocked but she used everything in her power to sound neutral and reasonable. "I understood it was quite hard to qualify for benefits under the new rules you had already brought into being."

"We feel it needs further tightening up," Crawford said.

"But with AI automation in industry it's very difficult to find a job, I understand."

Crawford leaned forward. "There are jobs out there that require a real human. I passed many members of staff while walking through the palace, for example."

George felt this was a dig at how she lived her life. "That's right. I believe in human interaction. In fact, we pay well over the minimum wage that your government set."

"That's up to you, ma'am, but we find it necessary to keep the country's finances under control. That means ending benefits and getting people working and putting an end to homelessness on the streets," Crawford said.

"I'm pleased to hear you want to tackle housing insecurity, Prime Minister."

"No civilized country should have people living on the streets. We want to do something about that."

That sounded good, but that didn't ring true to the Alliance Party goals, and it worried her.

His next statement proved her right. "Especially with the NATO conference being held here. We have to get them off the streets."

"I hope by that you mean that they will be given good accommodation."

"Our plans aren't fixed at the moment. I will let you know."

It was Crawford's turn to ask a question. "I understand our new Princess of Wales has decided against a lavish ceremony."

George had no idea how he knew that. "Yes, she is making plans for a more simple investiture. I will let you know about it as soon as I know."

"I think economy within the monarchy is extremely important."

Again with the smirk. George stood and pressed the bell and held out her hand to Blackmore. "Thank you, Prime Minister. I'll see you next week. Major Cameron will see you out."

Bloody man, George thought.

❖

Teddy was nervous. After speaking to Summer and reflecting on her behaviour, she wanted to apologize to her mum for her behaviour on their run. Teddy knew she was pushing her mum away, and she didn't deserve it.

Cammy had shown her into the office, and Teddy stood at ease with her hands behind her back while the Queen finished signing some of her papers.

"All finished." Her mum put the top on her fountain pen and looked up at Teddy. "You wanted to see me?"

"Yes, Your Majesty. I want to apologize for the last time we were together. My behaviour was out of order. I'm deeply sorry, ma'am, Mum."

Her mum immediately stood and smiled. She walked over to Teddy and pulled her into a hug.

"I love you, Teddy. I know things have been hard for you, everything outside the palace walls, but you can always come to me."

Teddy felt tears roll down her face as she held her mum tight. "I didn't want to let you down."

Her mum pulled back and cupped her cheeks. "You will never disappoint me. You're my daughter, my heir, and I will do anything to help you."

Teddy wiped her eyes quickly, embarrassed to be crying in front of her mum.

"Let's forget this ever happened. Tell me about working with Summer. Is it helping?"

"It's been down and then up. I resisted her help—there's so much hurt between us."

Her mum sat down on the edge of her desk. "So, has it gotten better?"

"Yes. I worked out that Summer is the only one who will tell me I'm being an idiot to my face, and she has good ideas."

"Good. Annie is so close to Summer, and it would be better if you could all be friends."

Teddy cleared her throat. "We can be cordial and professional."

Teddy knew it was more than that. There was an underlying understanding between them that had never gone away. She'd realized that when she visited Summer at her flat. They knew instinctively what the other needed and wanted, whether it was coffee, a sandwich, or more important matters for her new engagements.

There was also the raw heat in her anger that almost made her kiss Summer, and she didn't know if she would have if Summer hadn't placed her hand on Teddy's chest to put her back.

The moment of passion had never left her mind. Why could she not get over this? It was just the adrenaline of the anger, Teddy was almost sure.

Her mum patted her on the shoulder. "Good. I'm glad she's helping."

Teddy looked over to the side table by the window, where there stood a half-constructed model ship. Model building had been her mum's hobby since she was a child, as it had been for the late King before her.

"What ship are you working on, Mum?"

"HMS *Ark Royal*. A World War II aircraft carrier."

"Nice. Remember I used to help you with the building and usually messed them up?" Teddy laughed.

"You never did. I was more proud of the ships with broken sails or missing pieces than any of the ones I did alone. Because it was about spending time with you, not building the perfect ship," her mum said.

Teddy was so touched by that, and it made her feel more guilty about the distance that had grown in their relationship.

"Come on," her mum said.

As they walked down the corridor, Teddy said, "Have you met with the prime minister this week?"

"Yes, yes. Tuesday as usual."

"I hope you told him that moving the unhoused out for the NATO conference was out of the question."

"You know that's not how it works, Teddy, and I couldn't tell you even if I did."

"The Alliance Party are really showing their true colours. Attacks on the unhoused and unemployed are despicable. I don't know how you keep your true feelings to yourself with these people," Teddy said.

"That's my job, Teddy. Over the time I've been Queen, I've met some saintly, kind-hearted, public-spirited people. But I've also met dictators, racists, homophobes, people who have turned out to be murderers on a national scale, and simply those who are morally bankrupt. At the time my government have wanted me to meet them."

"How do you do that?"

"I make my feelings clear in the private audiences with the prime minister, but outside of that I have to keep my feelings to myself. It's what our constitutional monarchy and government system is all about. You have to put your faith in the British people that they will do the right thing at the next election. My father taught me this, and I hope I'll help you."

"It must be so frustrating," Teddy said.

"It is, but the Princess of Wales has more leeway within these rules. So take advantage of that and add to the national conversation on the issues that matter. Make the government uncomfortable."

Teddy smiled. "That sounds like a good idea. Summer and I have come up with a plan that I hope will do that."

"Great, is Summer with you today?"

"Yes, she's in with Mama just now."

❖

Teddy was praying this idea went over well, and her mums approved. Teddy wanted to make them proud. But this presentation was put together so fast, that maybe her mums would think it rushed and overreaching. But both she and Summer felt passionately about it.

Teddy looked over to Summer, who was readying the presentation. She couldn't have done this without her. Where Teddy was messy and had jumbled-up thinking, Summer was calm, methodical, and a compulsive organizer.

A large holo screen was projected in the air. Summer and Teddy stood either side of it, while her mums and Annie were sitting on the sofa, with the dogs curled up beside them.

Summer whispered, "Are you ready?"

Teddy nodded. Was she really? Probably not, but it was now or never. They had rehearsed that Teddy would start and then Summer would take over.

Just as Teddy was about to speak, Annie clapped loudly. "Yay, big sis. Show us what you got."

"The dogs are better behaved than you, pipsqueak."

Annie stuck her tongue out.

"Okay, enough," their mama warned her.

Teddy placed her palms together and rested them against her mouth. She took a deep breath and began.

"I know I haven't prepared for becoming Princess of Wales well, and I've resisted any help, but I apologize about that. I wasn't ready to hear what everyone was telling me. But with Summer's help, I think we've come up with a plan that will work for everything. Summer?"

Teddy handed things over to Summer. The screen read: *A new Princess of Wales for a new age.*

"Thank you, Princess Teddy. Your Majesties and Your Royal Highness, as you know, Teddy wants this to be a much more slimmed down version of the ceremony that Queen Georgina had. We want to focus on Teddy's personality and her determination to help with housing insecurity, food banks, and helping people find new skills and training. What we propose is this—Teddy has had Street Kitchen in her life since she was a teenager. The cause of housing insecurity has been at the core of her life, and we want to make it the sole issue of Teddy's purpose as Princess of Wales."

Teddy joined in the presentation again. "I don't just want to raise money for groups like Street Kitchen. I want to do something that will give those who want it skills, and a way out of poverty."

Her mama smiled warmly. "Sounds wonderful so far, Teddy."

Teddy felt a warm glow of confidence. "I would like to take a large parcel of land from the Duchy of Cornwall and create a place where people can learn gardening, farming skills, learn about farm to table, and learn traditional country skills. I want to get my friend Andy at Street Kitchen involved as a teacher. He's a landscaper and has been through the whole process of having no home, getting help at Street Kitchen, and moving on to a good job and better life."

Summer seamlessly took over. "Teddy would like to use old farmhouse buildings to give the students a home while they are there. Of course there would be a care team to offer counselling, help with any issues back home, addiction treatment, or emotional support."

"I've told the Duchy board of trustees of my plans, and they are resistant," Teddy said, "but I'm not taking no for an answer."

Her mum spoke after taking everything in. "They will not be a problem, Teddy. I'll give the chairman a call."

Teddy's knee-jerk reaction was she should be resisting her mum coming to her rescue. She should be dealing with this herself. But she had made a breakthrough in her relationship with her mum, and so she took the intervention with grace instead of being prideful about it.

"Thanks, Mum. We hope in time that the program will be self-sustaining, by selling the produce."

"But in the meantime…" Summer talked the two Queens and Annie through funding that could be funnelled from the Duchy. Summer moved on to a picture of Caernarfon Castle. "We'll hold a launch at Caernarfon, with local dignitaries, schoolchildren, and local charities. What happens after that is Teddy's great idea."

Teddy could feel her cheeks blush slightly. "I thought Annie and I could go to each of the home nations, and I would pledge myself to their service, one by one. I don't want to seem remote to the other parts of the United Kingdom by only going to Wales and maybe London."

"That sounds fantastic, Teddy bear," her mama said.

Teddy gave her a look for using her childhood nickname.

"It's a huge opportunity to generate publicity for housing insecurity, introduce myself as Princess of Wales. I'd like to do a marathon or ultramarathon in each nation and have companies as well as members of the public pledge money for the cause."

"A marathon?" Annie squealed. "Brilliant."

Summer unveiled a logo for the charity endeavour. It was the Princess of Wales crest surrounded by footprints, with a mountain in the background. Underneath it read: *Race Across Britain.*

"We thought that we'd take our own cameras to follow and document the journey and make it into a documentary. Then everyone can get to know me, the real me, that way. And when people donate money, it will go to projects in that nation."

Summer smiled at Teddy, and Teddy's heart thumped out of her chest. *Shit. Still there.* The complicated feelings.

First she'd nearly kissed Summer the other day, and now her heart was beating like a drum. *Shit.*

Her mama walked over to her with her arms out. "That's perfect, Teddy bear. Give your mama a hug."

Teddy put her arms around her mama and lifted her up a few inches.

"I'm so proud of you," she said.

Teddy had to gulp hard. She couldn't remember the last time she felt that she'd really earned her mama's pride in her.

Annie hugged Summer and thanked her. "You are awesome, Summer. If anyone can kick my big sister's butt into shape, it's you."

Summer gave a nervous laugh. "It's all Teddy's work, believe me."

"No, it isn't," Teddy said as her mama moved over to hug Summer. "Summer has really helped, and Robbie. He's going to train and run with me."

Her mum smacked her on the arm. "I'm proud of you. Now go out and show the country what an amazing person you are."

"I'll try."

Summer was packing up her things when Mama said, "Do you want to stay for dinner?"

"Sorry, ma'am. I'm due at my mum's for dinner tonight."

Her mama kissed Summer's cheek. "Tell your mum and dad hello from us. We must have them over for dinner again like we used to."

Summer looked nervous to Teddy, as if she felt this was too much. Too much like the old days.

Summer said goodbye to everyone, and Teddy took her chance. "I'll walk you out."

Teddy grasped Summer's bag and held the door for her. A passing footman stopped and bowed his head to her.

"I'm sorry if my family got too excited there. I understand why you wouldn't want to have dinner here with your mum and dad."

"I appreciate it, believe me. But we are supposed to be keeping our personal lives out of our new arrangement," Summer said.

"Yes, we are. Will you say hi to your mum and dad from me too? They are lovely people, and your mum's roast chicken dinner is something I won't forget."

Summer hesitated, and Teddy felt the awkward silence loudly.

"I will. Have a good night, Teddy."

"Hey, thanks for today."

As Summer walked away, Teddy's eyes drank in her bouncy blond hair and the skip she had to her walk.

Teddy clenched her fists. Summer had never truly left her heart, but she'd controlled the ache through turning it to anger and papering over the cracks in her heart behind a new persona. The playgirl princess who didn't care about her role in the royal family, the playgirl princess who partied all night and dated women that didn't care about good causes, good works, only about their profile.

Now there was nothing to hide behind, and here in the cold light of day, she was the same Teddy who had adored Summer her whole life.

Teddy pressed her forehead against the doorframe. "Fuck."

A passing footman discreetly moved past her.

Teddy didn't know how to deal with this except one way. "Call Robbie."

"Ma'am?"

"I need to go for a run tonight. My body needs it."

"As soon as we get back home, we'll get after it, ma'am."

"Thanks, Robbie."

Teddy walked over to the window that looked onto the courtyard. In her mind she heard the squeal of children's laughter, then saw a young Summer running across the courtyard. Coming up fast behind her was Teddy racing after her.

She caught up easily. Those were the days Teddy was really fit. The younger Teddy caught Summer around the waist and spun her around.

Teddy smiled at the memory that played out across her mind.

Her younger self lifted Summer and twisted her around.

"Ted, no, let me down." Summer laughed.

Teddy looked up at the entrance of the courtyard, knowing what was about to happen.

The prime minister's car swept into the courtyard and had to make an emergency stop.

Young Teddy held her hands up. "Sorry, so sorry, Prime Minister."

Summer grasped her, and they ran off together, away from the trouble.

Then the scene disappeared. Their love was all in the past, and she couldn't afford to let it disturb their new, fragile working relationship.

Summer certainly didn't have the lingering feelings that she had. The only option open to Teddy was to work her way through it in the gym, in her runs, and by pushing her body through hell in the marathons she had committed herself to.

❖

"You were right, Mrs. Buckingham," George said while holding Bea in her arms.

"I was perfectly right."

"Mums, stop the lovey-dovey stuff."

Annie was sitting on the couch with her feet pulled up to her chest.

"Would you rather your parents weren't in love?" Bea asked.

"No, but is there any need for so much expression of your love?"

Bea laughed and walked over to sit beside Annie. "Just wait till you fall in love."

"Let's stick to Teddy," George said. "It's truly astonishing that they have put together this project so quickly."

"Summer is very talented. She's a super organizer," Annie said. "I'm surprised they could get it done without falling out. Teddy would hardly speak to her, let alone planning."

Bea grasped Annie's hand. "Georgie, did you see the way they were presenting as a team?"

"I know. Summer gives Teddy something, confidence and clarity, but Bea, you told me that we couldn't pick our daughter's girlfriend," George said.

Bea sighed. "I know, but seeing them together like they used to be, working so well. I mean, we always agreed that she'd be the perfect future Queen."

Annie sat forward. "I'm sorry, but don't get excited. Summer won't go back there, I don't think. When the world found out about them, she went through so much. Summer was scared, and Teddy and you both don't know some of the things that happened to her during that time."

"She told you?" Bea asked.

Annie nodded. "She didn't tell her own mum and dad some of what went on. It was scary for her."

George started to pace furiously. "That was my fault. I should have had control of the situation, given her a protection officer, put pressure on the news editors."

"It wasn't your fault, Mum. It all happened too fast."

"I promise you, Annie. This will not happen to you or whoever you choose," George promised.

❖

Pandora was sitting on a couch in the middle of a photography studio. There were lots of staff busy with drone cameras, preparing to make her look perfect. It was a powerful feeling.

Everyone was here for her. She had hair and make-up done for her and had designer clothes ready just for her, hanging on a rail. This magazine had paid a fortune for her interview and exclusive pictures.

"You were saying, Pandora?" Cath the interviewer asked.

"Sorry, Cath. Yes, I met Princess Teddy at a party, and from then on she pursued me all over London."

"And were you attracted to the princess?" Cath asked.

"She is exceptionally good-looking, but I didn't know if I wanted to be part of the royal circus."

That royal circus had added a million more subscribers since the news of their break-up happened. She was going to make so much money on this, and hopefully embarrass Teddy.

Teddy wasn't going to walk away from her without any repercussions.

Kurt appeared at her side. "Can I have five minutes with Pandora, please?"

"Of course." Cath got up and walked away.

Kurt took her place on the seat. He was angry after being dismissed from Teddy's service. They had been friends since university, and he had loved his position with her.

But he knew how Teddy was. She was hopeless and unorganized without his guidance.

Teddy was going to fail miserably, and Kurt would be there to watch it and take half of the money Pandora made. That was their deal. Kurt would bring her the media deals, then she would give him half the money earned.

"What is it?"

Kurt leaned forward. "My source at the palace has told me that Princess Teddy is going ahead with her inauguration in Wales."

"Really?" Pandora said. "She must have bowed to pressure from her parents."

"Apparently she has turned over a new leaf and wants to make things right with her family," Kurt said.

Pandora laughed. "Teddy turning over a new leaf? Hilarious. I suppose it'll be all the more funny that I share my story of who their future Queen is. More media deals, more followers, more fame."

"Princess Teddy isn't doing this alone. The Queen has ordered Summer Fisher to be her and Annie's PA to organize her investiture."

"Fucking Summer Fisher," Pandora spat. "Her presence hangs around Teddy and her family like a bad smell. The royals treat her like one of the *family*. A PA from a suburban family, and I wasn't good enough for her? My father is a director of this country's top banking group. What was wrong with me?"

"It wasn't just you. Her mothers wanted Teddy to get rid of me all the time. Said I was a bad influence. Me? I was too good for that job. Pandora, we need to drip-feed info to my contacts. She isn't getting away that easy."

Pandora smiled. "No, neither Teddy nor the perfect Summer Fisher."

CHAPTER FIFTEEN

"That's ten miles, ma'am," Robbie said.

"Keep going, Robbie."

"Ma'am." Robbie dropped back to the police protection officers behind and said, "We're keeping going," and then shouted to the two up front.

Now that they were training seriously for the first marathon, and taking to the streets of London, they needed more people on the security detail.

It was five a.m. and dark on this June morning. Teddy inhaled a big lungful of air and let it out. This felt so good. The buzz of challenging herself again, getting up as early as she had as a teenager when she'd been running with her mum, and prepping for the Royal Marines.

It amazed her how quickly her body fitness had improved and how much she looked forward to running. Even in the rain she loved it. Getting up before everyone else and getting her miles in before the official day started made her day go better.

"This was supposed to be an easier day, ma'am. You do have a lot on today."

"I know. I just want to keep going," Teddy said.

Pushing herself, her body, was helping Teddy deal with the swirling emotions that were struggling to burst into the light of day. The feelings that Summer was evoking in her.

It was so much easier to pretend her emotions were anger. Anger was easy, but keeping her anger fuelled was difficult when Summer was trying to help her. It reminded Teddy too much of the days when they would sit and plan her future.

And so she wanted to push her body and squeeze every last piece of raging emotion out of her. At least it wasn't destructive. Teddy was helping herself train for the biggest few months of her life.

After a few more miles Robbie said, "I think we'd better get back now, ma'am. The streets are getting busier, and we don't want you to get injured on such a special day. I need time to get your uniform to perfection as well."

"Okay then."

They turned around and took a shortcut through the grounds of Kensington Palace. It would only take about twenty minutes to get back. Today was Trooping the Colour, the Queen's official birthday celebration in June.

It was a big royal event, shown live on TV, where the Household Division trooped their colour flag in front of Queen George, using intricate drill formations. It was a custom that dated back to the eighteenth century.

Over two thousand soldiers, horses, and musicians took part. It was a big showpiece event, and ever since Teddy was old enough she'd ridden just behind the Queen. When she was younger, Teddy went in a carriage with her mama.

"Robbie, my uniform has been perfect for days. Why the rush?" Teddy asked.

"Dust and hairs on your tunic can accumulate in an hour, the brass buttons and medals will need to be shined one last time, and the bearskin must be combed right before you put it on."

"I'll be frightened to put it on. Last year a soldier from the uniform store was sent over to help me."

Robbie remained silent just a bit too long.

Teddy laughed. "I suppose that silence means I should have been written up for bad turn out?"

Robbie allowed a small smile to break out. "All I can say is you will be perfect this year, as is befitting a royal princess."

Things were going to be quite different this year. She had Robbie to help her, and she also had Azi filming her getting her uniform on and leaving on her horse.

Summer had the idea to take some official behind-the-scenes footage and release it on Teddy's social accounts as a slick video. It was a way of controlling the narrative without the media getting involved.

By bringing the public into her world, they could have a one-on-one relationship, princess to public. That would better reveal more of who Teddy was, as opposed to who news headlines said she was.

The filming would be a trial run for her Race Across Britain, as it had been dubbed, which Azi planned to turn into a documentary. The documentary would highlight housing insecurity and mental health, two of the things Teddy cared most about.

It was amazing how all these things had come together so quickly and naturally. Teddy's aunt was an award-winning documentary film-maker, and she didn't even hesitate at the chance to help.

Teddy couldn't have got this together as quickly or at all without Summer.

Summer believed they could because she was brilliant. Teddy's stomach tightened and her heart pounded again as she thought about her ex again.

Not ex, just Summer, or Cinders. Teddy never thought of Summer as her ex, but now was not the time to be thinking about her heart. They had important work to do.

Just concentrate on one step in front of the other.

Teddy could see the courtyard up ahead.

"Let's push it and set a new PB," Robbie said.

There were some mornings Teddy felt sick by the time she got to this point. Now in short order she was running more miles and not near collapse. In fact Teddy could have kept going longer, but duty called her home.

This was the first day to show the public who she really was.

A good impression was essential for another reason. They'd got word that Pandora was selling her story to the media. Teddy'd already been embarrassed by comments and video on socials, but now the break-up was going to be the main talking point and embarrass her family.

Summer told her to stick to her path regardless and she would come through this. She trusted Summer to know what was best.

❖

Summer was checking her notes for the day while Annie got dressed for the day's event.

They and other members of the family participating in the parade had set up for the day at Buckingham Palace, so they could all leave from here and come back afterwards for lunchtime drinks.

"How do I look, Demi?" Annie said.

"Simply delightful," Lady Abidemi said.

Summer looked up and smiled. "You do, Annie. You are effort-lessly beautiful."

"Oh, shut up," Annie said.

Annie didn't take compliments easily. But the truth was, she *was*. Annie wore a navy-blue dress, a matching fascinator on top of her golden blond hair.

"Listen to your friend," Summer said, "You've done a great job, Demi."

"Thank you, Summer. At least someone appreciates me."

"I just can't breathe out for the next five hours," Annie joked.

"Nonsense, maybe three hours," Summer replied with a grin.

They laughed and joked until there was a knock at the door.

"Are you all decent?" Summer knew the voice immediately. It was Holly, Quincy's wife and Queen Bea's dresser.

"Perfectly," Annie said.

Holly walked in and gasped. "You look gorgeous, little Annie."

"That's what we've been trying to tell her," Demi said.

Holly walked up to Annie and took her hands. "You look like your mama."

This softened Annie and made her smile. "Thanks, Aunt Holly."

"Now to business," Holly said turning to Summer. "Queen Bea wants you to go and talk to Teddy. Apparently, she's causing a fuss about wearing a uniform."

"Shouldn't the Queen or Queen Bea talk to her? I don't know why she'll listen to me."

There was an awkward silence as everyone looked anywhere but at her.

"Queen Bea says you've made such a difference to Teddy already. Could you please talk to her? For Bea?"

Summer sighed. "Okay. I'll try."

Summer left the room and walked along the corridor with trepidation. It wasn't so long ago that Teddy was someone she mentally fenced with, someone she shot witty barbs back and forth with, as Summer tried to bury the hurt.

Now she had to be there for Teddy, to be close to her, to help her along. At first she was afraid of how hard it would be, but now she was afraid of how easy it was. Protecting her heart was easier when Teddy was that media caricature. Summer could deal with that. Not this vulnerable, sensitive Teddy that she thought had been left behind in her youth.

Outside Teddy's dressing room, Robbie and Azi's assistant director, Blair, were standing waiting.

"Robbie? Is she—"

"Her Royal Highness is inside. The Duchess of Clarence has gone back to her room to help get the children ready."

Theo and Azi were taking part in the parade by following along the route in a horse drawn carriage, as a few others in the family would too. Juliette was going with them, but Benjamin was staying here with his nanny as he was too young to keep still for so long in public.

"Queen Bea wants me to talk to Teddy."

"If you would, ma'am. That would be good of you. A sudden crisis of confidence, you understand."

Robbie opened the door for her, and Summer took a step into the room. Her breath caught as she got her first look at Teddy.

She was dressed only in her black dress uniform trousers, boots, and a tight white vest, with braces over her shoulders that held her trousers in place.

Teddy was leaning with one arm against the windowsill looking out onto the front of the palace.

Summer's breath was stolen from her by Teddy's strong upper body, the braces over her shoulders emphasizing her strong muscles there. Summer had known every inch of Teddy's body, but since she last saw it, when Teddy was twenty, she had matured into this tall, strong body.

All of her senses reacted to Teddy strongly. Summer didn't know what to say or do. The feeling of longing, of passion shocked Summer.

Teddy turned around when she sensed someone in the room. "Have they sent you in to talk me down?"

"No. I'm more concerned with the video getting made. Our team are waiting for it as soon as it's shot and edited."

With Teddy's blessing, Summer had hired a social media team to monitor all the platforms and to handle publishing any videos, like today's.

Summer pushed away her feelings and walked over to the classic red tunic that was hanging on the door of the wardrobe. Robbie had made it look immaculate.

"So why are you not fully dressed yet?"

"It's a farce. Look at that tunic. Colonel of the Welsh Guards."

"And? What's wrong with it? You were commissioned into the Welsh Guards after officer training," Summer said.

"I scraped a pass, and I'm sure that was because of who I am. They couldn't fail the heir to the throne."

"Teddy—"

"No. That red tunic represents men and women who've given the ultimate sacrifice or come home with life-changing injuries. I was passed and sent to Vospya for six months to train with their military."

Queen Olga of Vospya, or Kat as she was known to family and friends, was close to the Buckinghams. In fact Queen Olga's partner Clay had been the young Teddy's protection officer.

Summer knew how much Teddy loved Clay and Kat, and so sending her there would have been a good idea, but if Teddy didn't believe who she was or what she was representing, it clearly hadn't been a happy posting, career-wise anyway.

"You've been preparing for this event for the last few weeks. Why are you having an issue now? Your mum made you colonel of the Welsh Guards." Summer said.

"Yeah, because I was going to be Princess of Wales. No other reason."

"Your granny, Queen Sofia, is colonel of the Royal Corps of Signals. I don't think she's ever done active service."

"That's different," Teddy said. "Granny is the Queen Mother. The men and women under her respect her for all she has done, and her great support for the regiment. Even Aunt Grace did a year in the Royal Navy. She, my mum, and Uncle Max are the only ones in the family, on parade today, who have active service under their belts."

Max and his sister Vicky were in fact Queen George's cousins, but Teddy, Annie, and Roo called them aunt and uncle.

Teddy was a bundle of insecurities. That's why they were so well-suited as partners the first time round. Teddy felt all the pressure in the world on top of her, and Summer talked her through it.

Summer ran her hand over the red dress tunic. "Not going to Royal Marine officer training left a big hole in your life. And when the Queen wanted you to go to Sandhurst, you felt disappointed in yourself for not achieving your dream. Now you don't feel you deserve medals and an honorary rank. Am I right?"

Teddy looked down at her shoes.

"Teddy, when you wear this, the men and woman who salute you are giving respect to the uniform, the rank, and by extension, the Queen, through you. It's a symbol of respect. Do you get it?"

Teddy nodded.

Summer continued, "If your ambition to be a marine is hampering you, you have two choices. Learn to live with it, or go back and sign up."

"I can't do that. I'd fail."

If Teddy went into it with positive intentions, then Summer had no doubt she could do it. Teddy had been talking about the marines since they were children. But without the belief she could do it, then it would be a failure.

"So can you wear this uniform to honour all those servicemen and women, and those who've fallen and those who've had injuries?"

Teddy sighed and walked over to touch the fabric. "Yes, you're right."

"Excellent."

Summer took the tunic off the hanger and held it open for Teddy to slip into. Once she did, Summer started to fasten the brass buttons. When her hands got to Teddy's chest, Teddy covered Summer's hands.

"You're always talking me down from ledges. I'm sorry for the way I treated you when you first came to help me and Annie. You've made everything better."

"I've just done what any good PA would do."

Teddy shook her head. "No, you haven't. You've stepped up and organized my life, helped me accept my duty, and hopefully you'll help me help my charity."

Summer gazed into Teddy's eyes and felt drawn into them. Just like the day at her flat. They both inched towards each other, then thankfully a bang on the door made Summer jump back.

"Ma'am?" Robbie said through the door. "We're well behind time."

"Just a minute, Robbie," Teddy said.

Summer helped her finish buttoning the tunic and took a big step back. Just as Teddy was about to reach for her hand, Summer said, "Come in now, Robbie." She turned to Teddy. "I'll leave you to get ready."

"I'll see you after for drinks?" Teddy asked.

When the family returned to the palace for the balcony appearance, all the extended family came for drinks in the balcony room.

Summer was invited. She was supposed to go but in this moment made a decision not to. Things were getting too close, too personal. They were slipping into old habits, and Summer couldn't allow those feelings to take hold again.

Not after what she went through as a young woman. It was too much.

Instead of saying yes or no, Summer simply said, "I'll see you later. Good luck."

❖

Teddy stood in the corner of the balcony room nursing a non-alcoholic fruit drink. Everything had gone perfectly today. Teddy played her role and didn't let the side down.

But she was hugely disappointed when she got back, high on the excitement of the day, and found Summer had gone home. Teddy sensed Summer was giving her a message after they almost kissed again today.

It was clear that they both still had that energy, that intensity that pulled them together. Summer was distancing herself from Teddy, and she would need to deal with it in her own way.

She moved over to Robbie and said, "I'd like to get a strength workout in. We'll leave as soon as I get the balcony appearance out of the way."

"As you wish, ma'am."

"Teddy," her mum said, "we're going out now."

She went to her granny Sofia and helped her up. Sofia took her arm. "You did so well today, my darling."

"Thank you, Granny."

They walked over to the balcony windows and stood behind the two Queens. They would all go out in order of rank. Teddy behind her mothers, Granny in the middle, and Annie taking their granny's other arm.

Teddy kissed her. "Shall we, Granny?"

She brushed the shoulders of Teddy's uniform. "Let's go and show the people of Britain how glamourous we are."

❖

That evening Summer was at home alone. The social media team had just sent the raw footage from the video that was taken today. It looked really good. Once it went through post-production, it would be perfect.

The TV news played in the background, showing parts of Trooping the Colour. Teddy had done so well. She looked confident, regal, all the things she was expected to look like, and her position next to the Queen sent a powerful message, that the future of the monarchy was strong.

When Summer looked more closely at the raw footage, there was a difference in Teddy. She had looked unsure and far from confident earlier, unlike the way she appeared in the footage of Trooping the Colour.

Summer realized it must have been the talk they'd had that made the change. In one way she was happy to help, but it was clear that they both still had deep-rooted feelings for each other.

Summer traced her finger down the side of Teddy's face on the screen. She felt a deep yearning to nurture her, take care of her.

Would it really be so wrong to act on her feelings? They were both older and wiser now. She closed her eyes and started to imagine what it would feel like to kiss, to touch Teddy again, and her body felt a hunger that had long been suppressed.

Summer remembered one time they'd made love, hidden away from the world in one of the guest rooms at Balmoral in Scotland. Summer came to spend a week with the family and somehow everything was romantic. The long walks in the Scottish countryside, Teddy teaching her to fish, going sailing on a gorgeous loch. They felt free and insulated from the world up there.

When most of the family went out riding, Summer and Teddy stayed back at the house, so they could be alone.

They both were each other's first and had no idea what to do or expect, but every touch from Teddy seemed to burn her skin with fire. Soon they were moving together quite naturally, and youthful passion burst forth with a fury.

Summer's heart and sex pulsed with the memory of that time. It was special and it was theirs. Everything changed from that day. They talked about getting married after university and Teddy's Royal Marine Commando school.

That momentary burst of passion had sealed their hearts forever. Until they were caught out.

Whenever Teddy and Summer went out in public, they went with a group of friends, so that no one could tell who was with whom. But this particular time, the lights in the cinema had come on earlier than they expected.

Summer's head was leaning on Teddy's shoulder, while Teddy had her arm around Summer's neck. They were clearly two lovers together.

Some of the audience recognized Teddy and took pictures, then posted them on social media. The cinema staff had to let them leave by the back door, and Jack drove them back to Summer's house.

After that, Summer's life wasn't her own. She was pursued every time she left the house, she was being talked about everywhere. It was as if the media was weighing up whether she was good enough to be their future Lady of Wales.

Summer couldn't eat, she couldn't sleep, it was affecting her already compromised health. One event was the last straw and made her walk away. She was out shopping with a friend and had just said goodbye to her, when suddenly she spotted a camera drone filming her.

She started to walk faster to get away, but Summer could never outpace a drone. Suddenly people appeared at her side tossing questions at her.

"Are you and Teddy serious?"

"Are you already engaged as the rumours tell us?"

"Will you be the future Queen?"

Summer started a slow run and tried to evade them, going down an alleyway at the back of a shop. She grabbed her phone and tried to call Teddy. The drones were in her face, people crowding her.

There was only one way out, so she pushed through the crowd. Some people were simply members of the public wanting pictures with her, but no one was respecting her space. Summer felt suffocated and more than a little woozy.

Her health hadn't been at its best then. It was frightening. Eventually two police officers pulled her through the crowd. She learnt later from Annie that Teddy had called Quincy, and she had sent the police.

When she got home, Summer was physically sick. It was then she knew that she couldn't cope with Teddy's life or her future. When Teddy came to see her, Summer told her that she couldn't cope with the demands of royal life.

That day brought home the way her life would be, and she was well aware of how some members of the royal family, historically, had been hounded, and that was scary.

The devastation of breaking up with Teddy and the anxiety she had about what had happened made her miss the first six months of university. Summer was afraid to go out.

But with time and some therapy, she managed to get her life going again. Teddy had started dating a model by then, and she would turn her heartbreak into anger.

Summer told herself she was right to get out.

But was she? These feelings had never gone away. No, this couldn't happen again.

Summer cleared her throat and said, "Computer, send Teddy a message—No, forget about it."

Summer had to move on. She knew that logically, but in her heart, her love for Teddy was desperate to burst out.

CHAPTER SIXTEEN

The first engagement of Teddy's Race Across Britain had finally arrived. She, Annie, and the team were now en route to Wales. Annie had an appointment with a trust that sponsored horse riding for disabled people and would join them later tonight.

Robbie, Laney, and several others from the back room team had already travelled to their hotel in Wales, where they were setting up for the visit.

Azi's assistant, Blair, would be leading a team to take video for the documentary footage. Azi would join them in Scotland and England.

Teddy had been anxious for this day for more than one reason. Her body was ready to be tested in her first race, and she was finally ready to face her destiny as Princess of Wales, to meet the people of Wales, and especially those who gave their time to social causes.

The other big reason she was anxious was getting to see Summer. She hadn't seen her since Trooping the Colour. They'd texted each other about the project and had a couple of calls, but they weren't as relaxed and friendly as they had been. Teddy didn't know why.

Teddy looked over and drank in Summer. She'd missed her more than she'd ever imagined she would, but she had her captive attention now.

"What have you been up to since I last saw you?" Teddy said.

Summer looked up from her computer screen. "Nothing really. Just working."

"How's your mum and dad?"

"They're okay. They're going on a cruise soon. The second this year," Summer said.

"They're enjoying their early retirement, then?"

"Yes. I encouraged them to do it and go on as many holidays as they can. They missed out on so much when I was ill as a child."

"But you're well now?" Teddy asked.

Summer rubbed her forearm. "Yes, I'm well. Do you want to go over the day's events one more time?"

"If you want." Teddy felt like Summer was purposely changing the subject.

"Once we arrive at the hotel, you can get changed and ready for your visit to Caernarfon Castle. Schoolchildren from the area and many groups that work with the unhoused will be there to meet you and listen to your speech," Summer said.

"Did you see the minister for housing on TV this morning?" Teddy asked.

The prime minister's lackey had been sent on every breakfast news show to talk about the controversy of his government's new policy to make rough sleeping illegal.

"It's disgusting," Summer said. "He's going to open what he's calling Homeless Hotels outside of the city centre and cut people's benefits if they are caught twice."

"Uh-huh, and any rough sleepers in the city would, in this new policy, be offered jail time or removal to these hotels. I've seen the kind of buildings they are proposing. Disused buildings, with cheap facilities," Teddy said.

"It's simply to appeal to the extreme right wing of the party and electorate. Crawford Blackmore is terrified he's going to lose the next election. It's a classic tactic to get people blaming another group of people for their ills. No doubt the government won't appreciate your charitable causes."

Teddy sat forward in her seat. A plan was starting to form. "No, they won't want me shining a light on the people they are trying to demonize." She smiled. "How about we make some last minute changes to my speech?"

"You don't—" Summer's eyes went wide. "But your speech has been approved by the Palace. You're not meant to be political, Teddy."

"You said earlier that the Palace would send out the press release about mine and Annie's new titles at lunchtime," Teddy said.

"Yes, two hours before your speech and meet-and-greet."

"Okay, well, I think this first speech will be the most anticipated and widely watched."

Summer nodded. "All the news channels will be showing it live."

"That's perfect." Teddy grinned. "I do know my family's history, and that the Sovereign, my mum, can never be anything but neutral, but princes and princesses have always had some wriggle room in that department. My mum reminded me of that recently."

"There's nothing I'd like more than to do that, but I could get in big trouble for not running any changes past Bastian and the Queen's office."

"Come on, Summer. You know this is the right thing to do."

Summer smiled. "Let's do it."

❖

At lunchtime the announcement came from the Palace. Annie was sitting in the living room area of Teddy's suite. She had her feet up on the coffee table and looked through her social media apps while Teddy and Summer were locked in conference at the dining table.

Summer reread a paragraph of the speech they were working on. "Do you like this? Is it too strong? I mean, the language might be…?"

Teddy frowned. "No, in fact I think we are showing great restraint in what we are trying to say. We need to make a splash, set the tone for my tour."

"It's been announced," Annie shouted over to them.

"What?" Teddy asked.

Annie stood up and gave her a medieval flourishing bow. "You are now officially the Princess of Wales, and I your lowly servant, the Duchess of Edinburgh."

"Well. That's that, then," Teddy said with almost sadness.

Annie skipped to the door and said, "I'm going to get ready, you two. See you later."

"Bye, Annie," Summer said.

Summer could see the tension on Teddy's face. "Are you all right?

Teddy gulped hard and nodded. "Yes. I've known this was coming all my life. Especially since we began working on this project. But I wasn't expecting it to feel this way when it was official."

"What way?"

"Final. Like I've finally been locked in my box, ready for the next phase of my life."

Summer acted quite naturally by covering Teddy's hand with her own.

"You are going to be a fantastic Princess of Wales, Teddy. You care about people. You have energy and a need to make people feel better."

"You think so?"

Summer nodded. "And there'll be lots more firsts to come. You'll get married, have little heirs of your own, you'll find joy. I know you will."

Summer's voice shook as she said that last bit.

Teddy shut the conversation down. "Let's practise the speech again."

Later that day, when they got back from the opening speech at Caernarfon Castle, Teddy, Annie, and Summer rushed up to the room so they could watch the news reports of their day. Social media had been sending notification after notification, but they all wanted to see the full news report.

Annie, Demi, Summer, and Teddy made their way to Teddy's room.

Teddy took off her suit jacket and undid her tie, allowing it to hang loose. Annie and Demi were already sitting on the two seater couch. "Hurry up, Teddy."

"I'll just be a minute," Summer said. Summer walked through to the small kitchen, rummaging in her handbag.

"Hang on, Annie," Teddy said, following Summer.

When Teddy entered the kitchen, she saw Summer with a pain shot. She was holding it against her arm.

"Are you okay?"

Summer jumped. "You gave me a fright."

"It's just me. What's wrong?" Teddy asked.

"A headache, that's all. It's been a busy day."

Teddy went to the fridge and got her a cold bottle of water. "Here. Take a minute."

"Annie and Demi are waiting for us."

"They can wait a few minutes." Summer took a mouthful of water. "Is this too much for you? This project? I'd never want you to risk your health for this."

Summer shook her head. "No, I'm fine, Teddy. Let's go through."

When they settled on the couch facing Annie and Demi, Summer's phone pinged a message.

"And so it begins," Summer said as she read.

"What is it?" Annie asked.

"It's Bastian. The Queen wants you to phone her as soon as possible."

"Uh-oh," Demi said.

"It'll be fine. Let's just watch the news first," Teddy said. "Computer, play six o'clock news."

The voice-over began...

"Today the newly created Princess of Wales and Duchess of Edinburgh took to meeting the people of Wales in and around Caernarfon Castle."

The picture changed to the streets surrounding the castle.

"Hundreds of people lined the streets to get a glimpse of the two royal sisters who have long fascinated the public."

Annie laughed. "We're not fascinating, we're boring."

"Shh," Teddy said.

"This wasn't to be the serious, solemn ceremony that Queen Georgina had here many years ago. It was to be a simple visit for the princess to declare her gratitude to the people of Wales for allowing her to represent them.

"The princess gave a speech in Welsh and English where she thanked those who'd come, and dedicated herself to the Welsh people. In a tour that will take her all over the country, named the Race Across Britain, Princess Edwina will be raising money for charities that support the unhoused and food banks in every area."

It then cut to a portion of Teddy's speech.

"I dedicate myself to your service for the whole of my life. I will listen to you and hope to bring great focus to charities that mean so much to me and help with the worries and causes in your community."

Then the voice-over continued as they saw Teddy and Annie going on walkabout amongst those who were waiting behind steel barriers. Schoolchildren and trust workers were nearest the castle, but Teddy and Annie both continued walking down the barrier of well-wishers, shaking hands and talking.

Annie said, "This part was so much fun."

"The sisters moved down the line of people on either side of the road, getting gifts and shaking hands. One little girl got more than a quick glimpse of the two royals. Abby Johnstone dressed up in her princess costume and had a gift of a model of a princess on a horse for the new Duchess of Edinburgh. When Abby asked if Princess Edwina would give it to her sister, the princess lifted her from her mother's arms and over the barrier. She then took her over to meet Princess Anna.

"The crowd loved the sweet moment of kindness, as the Duchess knelt down and hugged little Abby and asked her all about the model. It was safe to say that the crowd absolutely loved the interaction."

"She was so sweet," Summer said.

"It was just lovely. The thoughtfulness of the gift," Annie said. "I got Demi to get me her address, and I'll send her pictures and maybe invite her down to one of the Horse and Pony charity days."

"That's a great idea," Demi said.

Summer held up her hand. "Wait, here's the bit that might be more difficult."

The newsreader and a guest were now onscreen.

"Our royal correspondent, Christine Faber, is here with us."

"Chris, this new approach to being the Princess of Wales was quite evident today."

"Yes, sources say that this is a Princess of Wales who wants to do things differently. In the economic climate we are in, Princess Edwina felt a large ceremony wouldn't be appropriate."

"Fess up," Annie said. "Who is the source?"

Summer lifted her hand and they all laughed.

"But there was some controversy. On the day when the government are briefing about their new homelessness strategy, the Princess of Wales had this to say."

"The fact that our people have no choice but to live on the street should bring sadness to us all, and especially our leaders whom we charge with looking after the most vulnerable in our society. The

demonizing of those who have nowhere to go is shameful and tells us a lot about the values of those who would make their lives harder. I hope I can help those who feel they are not listened to and allow them to be heard."

The royal correspondent returned to the screen.

"The whole theme of the princess's tour is about raising money for charities that combat housing insecurity and support the unhoused, so it's hardly surprising that anything she says is going to contrast with the government's policy. We approached Number 10 for comment, but they had nothing to say at this time."

"I bet they didn't," Annie said. She jumped up and said, "We'll go to my room and order some room service."

Annie kissed her sister's head as she went by. "Good luck with Mum."

"I think she secretly likes me getting into trouble," Teddy joked.

Summer grasped Teddy's hand lightly. "What you did today, for the little girl? That was so nice."

Teddy looked down at their hands. She wanted to grasp Summer's tightly but didn't want to scare her off.

"It wasn't planned. She wanted the girly princess, not the butch one in the suit and tie."

Summer chuckled. "You seemed much more relaxed meeting people today. You always worried about walkabouts."

"To be honest, I've felt better since I've gotten back to the Teddy that wanted to eat well, exercise, and be positive about life," Teddy said.

"I've seen such a big difference in you. I thought that Teddy was long gone," Summer said.

Teddy shook her head. "No, to be honest, having you behind me, guiding me and taking the gifts and flowers for me, gave me confidence. The Teddy you knew was just buried under a lot of sadness and pain."

Summer pulled her hand from Teddy. "You'd better call the Queen."

Summer obviously wasn't ready to talk about this, but Teddy felt they had to.

Teddy stood up and said, "Call Sebastian, please."

"Hello, Your Royal Highness."

"Hi, the Queen wanted me to call."

"I'll put you right through."

"Bastian, am I in big trouble?" Teddy asked.

"Let's say some feathers have been ruffled. I'll put you through, ma'am."

The next thing she saw was her mother out walking in the grounds of Buckingham Palace. She saw Cammy behind her and heard the dogs in the background.

"Hello, Mum."

"Teddy, Teddy. You've been making some waves today," her mum said.

"Have I?" Teddy said.

She could see her mum had a slight smile on her face. Hopefully at the situation and not about her private feelings.

"Indeed. I had the prime minister on the phone. He had great concerns over your speech and its timing and reminded me of my constitutional position."

Oh shit. "Sorry if it's caused you trouble, Mum. I was horrified when I saw the housing minister's comments on the news this morning, so I decided to change my speech a little. It wasn't Summer, it was all me."

"I told the prime minister that I was unable to inform you in advance about their new policy, as our meetings are secret, and you had no idea what the government was announcing before you wrote your speech."

Teddy smiled. "You did?"

"Mmm. Yes, and I also reminded him that as Sovereign I am completely neutral, but that the role of Princess or Prince of Wales had a tradition of engaging the public in discussion about social and ecological issues, a tradition that has been around a lot longer than he has, but that I would talk to you."

"Thanks for sticking up for me—"

Her mum brought a finger to her lips. "Consider this a firm reprimand from your Queen…but a well done from your mother. I'm so happy to see you find a cause you feel so passionately about. I'm proud of you, Teddy, and your mama thought you were brilliant."

"I won't let you down, Mum. Not any more."

Her mum smiled. "Say hi to Summer for me and tell her, good speech. Bye Teddy."

"That went well," Summer said, smiling.

Teddy stuffed her hands in her pockets and looked down at the ground. "Yeah."

Summer took a step to Teddy. "What's wrong? This couldn't have gone better today."

"I know. It feels good to make my mums proud, but it makes me feel guilty about all the times I haven't pulled my weight or I've made some bad news headlines."

Summer took Teddy's hands. "You mums love you and are proud of you, don't ever doubt that. Don't look to the past, look to the future, and all the amazing things you are going to do."

Teddy looked at her eyes and said, "I couldn't do all this without you."

"No, Teddy. Stop thinking like that. I'm just a planner. You, Teddy, have an unbelievable amount of power, without even opening your mouth. So much so you scare the government. Always think about that and use what you have for the betterment of people."

Just like in Summer's flat, Summer was falling into gorgeous green eyes. Teddy reached out to caress her cheek, and Summer's alarm bells went off.

"I better get to my room and catch up with my work. You need to get prepared for tomorrow, Ted."

Teddy nodded. "You want to have dinner together? Robbie's given the hotel kitchen a meal plan to set me up for the race."

"Ah, I think I'll get on with some work."

"Okay, no problem. I probably need the rest."

Summer could see the hurt covered by bravado. She hated hurting her, but she had to say no.

"Get a good night's sleep, then," Summer said.

"Yes, goodnight."

Summer walked back to her room and could think of nothing but Teddy gazing into her eyes.

She opened the door to her room and walked in. Summer threw her bag on the bed and sat down. Why did she have to be the Teddy she knew? Summer thought that Teddy was gone, but here she was, slipping back into caring and looking after Teddy as she always had.

It was frightening.

CHAPTER SEVENTEEN

The next morning, Teddy woke up energized and ready for her first challenge—that was until she saw the big news story of the morning. Pandora's bare-all magazine interview.

After reading the headlines she sat on the floor with her head in her hands. She was suddenly tired, depressed, and filled with self-doubt.

Annie hurried along to her room as soon as she woke up.

"Teddy, it's okay. It will be all right."

"How will it be all right? People will turn up today to either mock me or be angry with me."

There was a knock at the door. Annie let Summer in.

"Summer, thank God. Talk to her. She's afraid about what people are going to say today."

Teddy stood up quickly. "Do you blame me? Let me read the salient points."

From the holo screen on the table Teddy read, *"Princess Teddy doesn't believe in the monarchy. She doesn't want to be Queen. The princess only turns up at events when she is forced to. All she cares about is the money she gets from the civil list. Now that she is Princess of Wales, Teddy is sitting on a fortune and can't wait to spend it on holidays, drinking, and having a good time with her friends. Tomorrow, learn about what goes on behind Teddy's bedroom door."*

Teddy was furious mostly with herself for bringing Pandora near her family.

"Teddy," Summer said in a calm reassuring voice, "this is just gossip. It will be forgotten in time."

"Will it? I haven't worked as hard as Annie and the rest of my family, that's true. People know this. And what she said about money is ridiculous. You know the money and income I've gotten is going to help others."

"You are working hard, today, and all round the country," Summer said. "You are disproving what she is saying, and when we get your new Garden Kitchen programme set up in Cornwall, the people will see it's nonsense again. Pretend nothing is wrong, brazen it out, and it will die away."

Teddy started to pace. "I know you're an exceptional PA, but even you don't believe that. Especially not when she goes behind my bedroom door for the next embarrassment. It says she's going to write a book. I need to call her, or she'll be dogging my life for evermore." Teddy was feeling so overwhelmed. "I can't go out there."

Summer looked around at Annie and gave her a nod. Annie gave them some privacy. "What is the first ethos of the commando spirit?"

Teddy stopped pacing. "What?"

"You should know. I helped you learn them, Quincy helped you too. What is it?"

Teddy said in a low voice, "Courage. Get out front and do what's right."

"Exactly. That's what you need to do. Would a marine shirk this physical task?"

Teddy sighed, looked at the ceiling and then at Summer again. "But I'm embarrassed. What are the people going to think? If anyone comes, that is."

"That's what the courage is for. Don't let Pandora have power over you. If you don't go ahead with this, then she has won."

Teddy tried to remember the passion she had for those four marine ethos. That's what she needed to channel into these races.

She said them out loud to Summer. "Determination. Unselfishness."

"Yes, that's it." Summer smiled. "Think of all the effort everyone has gone to. The people setting up the course, security, the runners from the local charities. They are all relying on you."

To keep things as secure as possible, she was going to run with Robbie, Jack, and five more members of the security services, plus a few people nominated by the charity they were running for and the food bank.

"I know. You're right."

"Thank God," Annie said. "If you had just listened to me, we would have been at this point an hour ago. I'll go and get ready."

Teddy crossed her arms. "I suppose this situation calls for the last ethos. Cheerfulness in the face of adversity."

Summer smiled. "Now you're getting it."

"I'll need that, especially when the magazine goes behind my bedroom door."

Summer was taken aback when Teddy leaned forward and whispered, "But you've been behind my bedroom door. You know how I share my passion for someone I care about. Pandora knows nothing real."

Teddy walked away to get ready, and Summer was immediately plunged into a memory that burned inside her. It wasn't long before they broke up.

Summer held on to Teddy's neck as Teddy eased her strap-on inside her. They had both been eager to try one as they explored their sexuality. Teddy especially had hungered to use one as she connected with the male part of her expression.

"Is this okay?" Teddy asked. "It doesn't hurt, baby?"

"No." Summer moved her legs around Teddy's hips, allowing Teddy to go much deeper. "It feels good, so deep, Ted."

Teddy groaned as the full length of the strap-on moved in and out, slowly, until they were completely together.

The sound of Robbie's voice pulled Summer out of her memory. "We're good to go. Let's get after it, ma'am."

Summer was throbbing inside at the mere memory. She could almost feel the fullness that Teddy gave her. It wasn't something she had done again. She tried to shake off the heat that gripped her body, but that was hard. She and Teddy were always on the same wavelength. It was so easy, but hot and burning. She'd never felt anything approaching that since.

She'd dated a couple of people. One of them was Doc, and she couldn't have been more attractive, plus kind and thoughtful. But that burning fire was not there.

Why did Teddy have this power over her?

"Summer," Annie said, "we're leaving."

"Okay, good. Let's go."

❖

They were driven to the marathon start line. Azi's cameras with her assistant controlling them would be taping them as soon as they opened the car door.

"How do you feel, Teddy?" Summer asked.

Teddy rubbed her hands together. "Nervous, to be honest with you. Robbie's helped train me to fifteen miles. This is twenty-six. We just didn't have the time to train longer."

"Think of this as your first test at commando school. What is the test?" Summer asked.

"Ten mile endurance march in full kit, through tunnels and underwater tunnels."

"You have no heavy kit. Be confident. I know you can do it."

"Ma'am?" Jack said from the front seat. "We're just hearing, the crowds are huge."

"Great, they're either here to laugh or to jeer because of that magazine story," Teddy said.

"I know that's not true, and even it was—brazen it out, remember?"

"Okay," Teddy said.

"You remember your speech?" Summer asked.

Teddy nodded. "I just want to get on with it now."

The car stopped and Teddy could hear the noise of the crowd. Her knee was bouncing with nerves.

"Teddy, calm. Now, once you set off, Annie and I will look out for you at halfway. Then at the finish. Don't forget, be confident, Teddy. I'm proud of you for doing this."

Teddy was astonished when Summer leaned over and placed a kiss on her cheek.

"Thanks."

Jack opened the door at her side then, and the noise came crashing in the car. To Teddy's surprise, it was cheering and shouting for her.

She got out and was overwhelmed by the noise. Maybe Summer was right. She looked to her side where Summer was and smiled.

"I told you," Summer mouthed.

Teddy walked towards the start line, flanked by Jack and Tommy. The metal barriers at the side of the road strained to hold the crowd back.

The documentary cameras buzzed around her and up to the starting line, trying to get some good shots.

"Ma'am?" Jack said. "Just to go over it again. Robbie and I will flank you, then some of the protection service people will be in the group of runners, and there are some dressed as police, along the way."

"Is this necessary? All these security people? No one is going to attack me."

"The Queen thinks it's necessary. Remember, someone made an attempt on Queen Bea's life, not to mention Queen Rozala's father and brother."

"Listen to your protection team, Teddy," Summer said.

"Fine, okay. I'll go and do the speech, and then we can get going."

"Azi's assistant director asked for a few words before you go."

"Sure." Teddy turned to the familiar face. "Blair?"

"Princess Teddy, you're just about to leave and begin your race. How do you feel?"

"I'm nervous, but this cause means the world to me, so I'm ready."

"Thanks, ma'am. We'll catch up with you further around the course," Blair said. She took a step back and looked at her footage on a small screen.

"Okay?" Teddy asked.

"Yeah, thanks, ma'am."

"Right, let's go to it."

Those that were waiting to run clapped their hands as Teddy walked up a step onto the platform, while the crowd cheered and clapped too.

"Good morning, folks. I'm so glad you could make it, and an even greater thank you to those who are willing to run with me for their charities."

The crowd cheered even louder.

"All the money raised in Wales will stay in Wales. Those who donate will help food banks and shelters for those that most need it. If you're in the crowd or watching live online, I'd ask those who can afford to, to message the number posted all around the racetrack, and let's make some lives better. Let's get moving."

There was a huge cheer, and it charged Teddy up. She was ready. She pulled off her jumper and was left in her shorts and vest.

She walked over to Summer and Annie.

"I'm proud of you, big sis. Now go and smash it," Annie said with passion.

"Summer?" Teddy asked.

"I know you can do it. Now go."

Teddy grinned. The thought of that kiss on the cheek Summer had given her would sustain her mood for a long time on her run.

She went to the start line and shook hands with her fellow runners.

"Thank you for volunteering, good luck."

She moved around until she had spoken personally to every single runner, so they felt part of one big team.

It felt good being part of a common cause and working as a team. The siren to begin the race was coming soon, and Teddy looked around at Summer. She clapped her hands, and Teddy winked at her.

The siren blasted, and they were off. For the first ten minutes it was about getting into her rhythm.

"We are going to smash this, ma'am," Jack said.

She turned to him. "You feeling good?"

"Never better."

Teddy took a sip of water from the small water backpack she was carrying. It was thought too dangerous to take water from the water stations along the way. It would be easy to spike her drink.

Teddy laughed when one of the charity runners sprinted up level with them. He was dressed as a T. rex. "Hey, Mr. T. rex. How are you feeling?"

He gave a big roar and said, "It's hot in here, but fun."

"Keep going, Mr. T. We're counting on you to finish this."

"Yes, ma'am."

Teddy soon fell into a rhythm and could feel the adrenaline flowing through her body. It felt good to be using her energies to help others. She felt angry at herself for feeling so down about her life when she had so much.

"Ma'am? How are you feeling?" Robbie asked.

They were around halfway, and Teddy was just concentrating on putting one foot in front of another, looking forward to seeing Summer in the crowd very soon.

Before long she saw Annie and Summer waving furiously. Summer looked so proud of her. It was a long time since Teddy had seen that look from Summer. It gave her such a shot in the arm that she picked up the pace.

"Ma'am, be careful not to peak too soon. We have a long way to go."

"I know."

Teddy made sure to smile and wave to the crowd as she ran. Summer was right, Pandora's revelations didn't spoil the day, but how long would that last?

There was one thing for certain. She wanted Summer back, as a friend if that's all she could offer, but she prayed for more.

Summer had never left her heart, and never would.

❖

"They will just be another few minutes," Annie said.

Annie and Summer were both at the finish line waiting for Teddy. "I'm so proud of her," Summer said. "I never thought I'd see the real Teddy again, or if she still existed."

"I'm actually quite fond of her, as far as big sisters go, and I'm so happy she left Pandora and changed her life. It's having you back in her life, you know."

Summer turned her head to look at Annie. "No, this is all her doing."

"Yes, she's got to this point by training and eating well, but it's because of you that she's here, in this moment, about to finish her first marathon. You know that, right?"

Summer didn't want to answer that question, but just at the right time, cheers and applause rang out.

"They're coming," Summer said.

Teddy came into view, and Summer was so happy to see that Teddy didn't look near collapse. She looked strong and determined.

Annie moved right to the finish line, with Summer at her side.

"Come on, Teddy," they shouted.

Teddy crossed the line and picked up Annie and kissed her. "Put me down, you big, sweaty fool."

Teddy turned to Summer, ready to do the same, but Summer grasped her hand before she could hug her.

"Well done, Teddy. You were amazing. How do you feel?"

Teddy leaned over to catch her breath. "Surprisingly good. Although I'm sure I'll feel worse in the morning."

Teddy was given a sports drink and went around to congratulate the other runners.

It made all the awkwardness and arguments worthwhile to see Teddy look so happy. Summer hadn't seen that dazzling smile in years. It was making her heart thud with that love that had never truly left her.

CHAPTER EIGHTEEN

The Irish marathon was hot on the heels of the first one. The newspaper that paid for exclusive interviews from Pandora released one the day of Teddy's second marathon.

Summer seemed to be avoiding her since the new Pandora release, which surprised Teddy. After all, Summer was the one who'd told her to ignore the press and brazen it out.

Reading about her sensationalized sex exploits must have made her uncomfortable to say the least. But Teddy had to shut her mind to it, brazen it out, and get the second marathon in two days done if she could. It was a challenge that tested her body and mind to the extreme.

If it hadn't been for such a good cause, and the cheering crowds, then Teddy didn't think she could have made it, but she did, thanks to the energy from the crowds that had come down to see her.

The one thing that made her sad was that, unlike in Wales, Summer wasn't waiting at the finish line.

That night every part of her hurt, and she wanted to talk to Summer badly. They were staying at Hillsborough Castle, the Queen's royal residence in Northern Ireland.

Teddy hobbled along to Summer's rooms. She knocked on the door, and Summer soon opened up.

"Are you okay?" Summer asked.

"Sore. Can I come in?"

"Of course."

Teddy hobbled along to the couch.

"Are your feet all right?" Summer asked.

"They aren't in the best shape."

"Right, sit down. There is a first aid bag in one of the cupboards. Do you want tea? Or coffee?"

"Some juice would be good," Teddy said.

"Coming up."

Five minutes later, Summer came back with a glass of orange juice and a first aid bag.

"Put your feet up here." Summer patted her lap.

"I'll warn you, they aren't the nicest looking."

"Who cares, I've seen you in worse scrapes."

"When?" Teddy asked.

"When you climbed out of my window close to midnight. You were staying over, but we weren't meant to be alone and certainly not in bed together."

Teddy laughed. "Oh yes, I remember. I had gone out of the guest bedroom window and shimmied along to yours. It went perfectly—"

"Until we heard my dad shouting my name and walking upstairs."

Teddy laughed. "I was shitting myself. There I was in his daughter's bed, with very little on."

Summer covered her face and laughed hard. "We were in such a panic, you more than me. You jumped up like a frightened rabbit and pulled on your T-shirt and boxers."

"I know. I tripped trying to put them on and nearly fell on my face," Teddy said.

Summer giggled at the memory. "I know I shouldn't laugh at your plight, but it was funny."

Teddy raised her eyebrow. "Funny? I slipped on the roof outside your window and fell down onto the garden patio. That was so painful."

"Your arm was broken, and you had cuts and bruises all over your face. I wasn't laughing then. I thought I'd lost you. I was terrified."

"You were?" Teddy felt the atmosphere change.

"Yes, I was." Summer looked down. She didn't want to bring up these feelings. It was a reminder of how much they had lost. "Put your feet up."

Teddy slipped her sore feet out of her pool slides and onto Summer's lap. Summer checked them over thoroughly. They were in pretty bad shape.

"These look really sore, Ted. Thank goodness you've got some time before the marathon in Scotland."

"Yeah, it's going to be hard."

Summer took out some sanitizing wipes. "This will nip, okay?"

Teddy nodded. "Oh! It really does."

Summer remembered the paramedics coming to the scene in the back garden and started softly laughing.

"My pain makes you laugh?"

"No." Summer shook her head. "Remember the look on the paramedics' faces when they came into the garden and found Princess Edwina on the ground with just a T-shirt and your boxers on?"

Teddy shook her head. "I was in too much pain to be embarrassed. Our parents were furious. Mum gave me the whole talk about respecting your parents' rules and risking my safety."

"I know. I was grounded for a long time."

Summer finished cleaning the sores and started to bandage the blisters and cuts.

"You know, Summer…I would take the pain and everything that went with it if I had my time with you again."

There it was. The unspoken truth that lay between them. She was sure Teddy still had feelings of some sort for her.

"I thought we agreed not to talk about our past," Summer said.

"Our romantic past, maybe, but we were friends a lot longer," Teddy said.

"That's true."

"Sometimes when I'm feeling lost, I think that's what I miss most. You were my best friend since I was little. You took my hand when I was unsure of myself and made everything better."

Summer's heart ached when Teddy said that. "You remember us meeting at Queen Roza's play day?"

"I don't know if it's a true memory or if it's being told the story so often, and seeing the picture so often, that makes me see it in my mind. I remember the feeling, most definitely."

"What was the feeling?" Summer asked.

"You gave me confidence. You made me feel safe, just like you have since we've been working together."

This conversation was getting to some dangerous places, and Summer noticed she was no longer giving first aid, but she was caressing the top of Teddy's foot.

"Bring up your other foot."

Teddy put her other foot on Summer's lap. "Can we be friends again, Summer? I've missed you."

"I don't know if it's a good idea," Summer said.

"What Pandora said today—"

The thought of Teddy being with other women had hurt her for a long time. Summer's memories of their sexual relationship had hampered her from moving on to a new one.

Every touch from another felt wrong. Her body was too used to the woman she loved, and that love was all her body knew. Teddy clearly hadn't felt the same.

"You are a young woman. There is no need to hide an active sex life. You are single."

"But what she said—"

"And as for the selfishness—I know that's not you. You couldn't be selfish if you tried. I remember, I've been there with you. She's just trying to embarrass you and hurt you."

Summer remembered the quick fumbling touches when they were young, but after that they learned everything about each other's bodies, and Teddy always put Summer's pleasure first. She lived to make her happy.

Her skin felt hot at the memory, and when she looked down, Summer realized her hand had crept up to Teddy's knee.

"Shit, sorry. Let me finish taping up your feet."

"Summer—" Teddy tried to speak but Summer didn't let her.

"I think you should see a podiatrist when we get back to London."

"Why don't we try to be adults, Summer? Let's be friends again," Teddy said.

"Friends?"

"No one knows me better, and I know you."

"I thought you'd changed. I really did."

Teddy took her hand. "I'm Ted, Summer."

"Okay, friends. I better tidy up, and you need to get some sleep."

"Thanks for helping me," Teddy said as she hobbled to the door.

"Ted, you are doing a good thing. I'm proud of you."

Teddy nodded and opened the door to walk out. "Summer? All those relationships you read about…they weren't what you think."

What did that mean?

CHAPTER NINETEEN

Teddy and her mum were running together the next weekend. Just a slow gentle jog to keep Teddy ticking over. Robbie and Cammy were out front, and Boothby and Jones behind.

"How much money have you raised thus far?" her mum asked.

"I asked them not to tell me. I want it to be a surprise at the end."

"You're doing really well, Teddy. I'm proud of you."

"I could never have done this without Summer," Teddy said.

"I know she has been a huge help, but this is your achievement. Listen, your mama wanted me to have a word with you about—"

Teddy held her palm up. "Not about the Pandora sex thing. I already told Mama that if she mentions it to me I'll vomit and then run away to a far-off land."

George chuckled. "No, not the sex thing. She wants to have a special dinner when you complete your Race Across Britain and wanted to know if you would like to invite Summer's mum and dad."

Teddy slowed up her pace and said, "I'd like to, but I don't know if Summer would want it…Can we talk, Mum, in private?" Teddy indicated to their security people.

"Cammy," her mum said, "we're going to take a breather." She turned to Teddy. "Come and sit down over here." She pointed to a bench on the side of the trail.

They each took a big drink of water. Their guards fanned out, giving them some privacy.

"Tell me," her mum said.

Teddy scrubbed her face. "Spending all this time with Summer has made me realize—"

"That you still love her?"

"How did you know?"

"You look at Summer the way I still look at your mama."

"I've always loved her. No matter how hard I tried to bury it deep down."

"Then try and win her heart back."

Teddy looked down at her shoes on the forest floor. "She doesn't want this life."

"Show her that this life can be managed."

"She couldn't cope with this life. Summer has her health to consider," Teddy said sadly.

"I should have anticipated this before Summer was cornered that day. You were both just kids," her mum said.

"She came back, you know," Teddy said.

"What do you mean?"

"After she broke up with me, she came back weeks later, telling me she'd made a mistake. Me being a stubborn idiot told her I wasn't interested, and I lost her. I fucked up."

Her mum put her hand on her shoulder. "You were just kids. Your mum and I went through a similar thing, and we were adults."

"You did?" Teddy said.

"Your mum and I got outed, and the pressure on her was immense, but we couldn't live without each other in the end."

"That's the difference, Mum," Teddy said. "I don't know if Summer has feelings for me any more."

"Then work on being the best friend you can be. You care about her? Be the best friend you can be to her. Show her the love and care that she deserves."

Teddy nodded. "Thanks, Mum. I will. Oh, there was one more thing I wanted to ask you."

"Yes?"

"You know you always said I could have Hollow Lodge? Can I have it now? I'd like to work on it and make a home."

"Of course you can. I'll have the land agent get everything you need. Would you like him to engage a builder and get the place shipshape?"

"No, I'd like to work on it myself, slowly, at my own pace."

"Let's get going, then. Mama will be expecting you to peel those potatoes."

Teddy smiled. "You're right. Let's get going before I get a bollocking."

❖

"Andy? Can you imagine what we could do with this?"

Teddy, Andy, Summer, and one of the land agents who reported to the Duchy of Cornwall trust stood by a disused farmhouse in Cornwall. Annie had an engagement today and so couldn't join them.

Mr. Reagan had been showing them around buildings and land to give them an idea of what the new arm of Street Kitchen—Garden Kitchen—could achieve.

"There are many parcels of land underused and unused. Great scope for the type of program you were describing to me," Mr. Reagan said.

Mr. Reagan was nothing like the board trustees Teddy had spoken to before. He was very open to their ideas.

"This is amazing, isn't it, Andy?"

"It's perfect. There's farmland as far as the eye can see. We can teach our clients the skills of growing your own food, taking care of animals. The list is endless."

"With lots of accommodation," Summer said.

"Then there's the coast not far from here. Fishing, protecting fish stock, and life skills on the water," Teddy said. "Mr. Reagan, you said you had a converted farmhouse that could show us the potential."

"Yes, ma'am. It's currently hired out as a B&B. It's by the sea. I had it set up for you as if a new guest was coming, to give you an idea of what you'd be getting."

"Lead the way," Teddy said.

Mr. Reagan drove them to the coastal cottage, and everyone was overawed.

"It's so modern," Summer said as they walked through the rooms.

Andy walked to the front window with Teddy. "Look at the view of the sea," Andy said.

"This shouldn't be only for the wealthy few who can afford to rent it," Summer said.

"I'd love to go down to the beach," Teddy said.

"I have another appointment, ma'am, but you have the keycode to get in," Mr. Reagan said. "Could I leave this with you?"

Teddy shook his hand. "Of course. Thank you for today. It's been great."

They walked out front to where the cars were parked. "This is so exciting," Andy said. "Thanks for asking me along."

Summer smiled. "Teddy wants you to be a big part of this project."

"I can't do it without you, Andy."

"Thanks. I'll need to shoot off now, if you don't mind. My stag weekend starts tonight."

"Have you found out where you're going yet?" Summer asked.

Andy laughed. "No, and I'm nervous, to tell you the truth."

"Good luck then, Andy. See you soon and enjoy yourself," Teddy said.

Once he left, they walked down to the beach. The wind was blowing, but it was refreshing. Summer loved the sea air.

"It's so beautiful. Can you think of a better place for people to learn new skills and get away from the city?"

"No, I only wish we could bring people down now," Teddy said.

"We will in time, if it's a success. You have the means to financially back this scheme, and I've sounded out companies who would be interested in buying produce and sponsoring the scheme. I know you can make this work."

"Me?" Teddy put her hand to her chest. "You're the one who has gotten the big companies involved. You really are a genius at this kind of thing."

"I just knew there were lots of companies who would like your logo on their websites. Companies who would find a benefit in pitting themselves against the government."

Teddy picked up a pebble and threw it into the sea. "Is that how people see me? Pitted against the government?"

"Yes, I think so. The extreme reaction towards the unhoused is going very badly among the younger demographic."

"Good. That's what we want, isn't it?"

Summer saw how relaxed Teddy was here. She was really nothing like the ogre Summer had turned her into in her mind since they broke up.

"Teddy? I'm sorry that over the years I've not been the friendliest to you."

Teddy stopped and looked at her. "I haven't been the friendliest to you either."

"We both said some things we shouldn't," Summer said. "It's not easy being best friends with your ex-girlfriend's little sister."

"No, we maybe needed some more space after we broke up. Being angry—"

They both replied at the same time, "Was easier."

Teddy smiled at her. "We agree on something at least."

"I'm sorry, Teddy."

Teddy took a step closer. "Why on earth would you be sorry?"

"I've been inside the royal family. I know the gossip, the lies that are bought and sold. How many times have you read lies about your parents' marriage? I have, hundreds of times, and I should have known not to trust the stories about you in the press. That was what you meant in Northern Ireland, wasn't it? The stories about your...exploits not being what I think?"

"My exploits?" Teddy grinned and leaned in to Summer. "That's a delicate way of putting it, Ms. Fisher."

Summer pushed her back. "Shut up."

Teddy laughed, put her arms out, and spun around. "Isn't this so freeing?" The isolated beach had not a person on it as far as the eye could see. "I love this. I'd like a summer cottage near here, and a nice dog to take on walks and play with on the sands. It would be idyllic."

Summer watched as Teddy pulled off her shoes and socks. "What are you doing?"

"You remember we used to paddle at Loch Muick?"

Loch Muick, part of the Queen's Balmoral Estate in Scotland, evoked some wonderful memories.

She'd joined Teddy there in her summer holidays many times throughout the years. Summer usually stayed for a week, and they all had so much fun. The extended royal family would visit regularly, so there was a gaggle of kids everywhere. They would paddle, fish, go boating, and sunbathe, when there was any sun, but it was always freezing, even in the height of summer. The most she would do was paddle.

"You can't be serious. We've got to drive back in a few hours, we'll get wet."

"Oh, come on, live a little. It'll be good for my poor feet." Teddy put on a sad face.

"You go in, then."

"We can get dry up at the B&B." Teddy grasped her hands and pulled her to the shore.

"Teddy," Summer moaned.

"This is an order from your Princess of Wales."

Summer sighed but started to take off her shoes.

"That's it. Let's you and me have some fun like we used to."

Teddy waved up to Robbie and Jack, who were keeping watch up on the dunes. Jack gave her a thumbs-up back.

Teddy and Summer walked down to the shore. Teddy loved the sand between her toes, and she liked it even better when Summer jumped when her skin touched the cold, wet sand.

"Come on. We're not even in the water yet. You're such a soft city girl."

"Why did I even agree to this?"

Teddy took her first steps into the water. "*Woo.* It feels so refreshing."

"You mean bloody cold." Summer began to walk backward.

"No, no. You said you would." Teddy pulled her into the small waves lapping at her feet.

"Oh my God, oh God." Summer jumped up and down on her tiptoes.

Teddy laughed so hard. "God's not going to help you now, Cinders."

"This is not funny."

"Okay, okay." Teddy was loving this. It felt like no time had passed between them. She acted on impulse and scooped Summer up into her arms. "Do you remember what else happened on Loch Muick?"

Teddy wadded out into the water.

"Ted, put me down," Summer shouted.

"Ms. Fisher goes fishing."

Summer wriggled in her arms. "Don't you dare, Teddy."

Teddy felt so alive. This was the magic that was Teddy and Summer. It was a game they'd played as teenagers. Sometimes Summer got thrown in the water, sometimes the threat was fun enough.

"Don't worry. I wouldn't do—" Teddy's foot hit a rock on the seabed, and they both fell forward into the water with a big splash.

Summer screamed, and Teddy burst into laughter. She was lying over Summer, whose face was full of fury.

"Get off me, Teddy! Get off me now!"

"I tripped. I didn't mean it."

She got up and pulled Summer out of the water. They were both drenched.

"Ma'am? Are you all right?" Robbie asked as he and Jack ran down to them.

"It's okay, I'm okay. I just tripped."

"You did not trip," Summer said. "You were acting like a fool. You stay away from me."

Teddy wasn't laughing any more. Summer was shaking with the cold, and Teddy felt terrible.

"Robbie, can you help Ms. Fisher up to the B&B?"

"Yes, ma'am."

Robbie offered Summer his jacket and put it round her shoulders.

"Did you hurt yourself, ma'am?" Jack asked.

She had. Teddy felt two of her toes on her left foot radiating in pain, but she wasn't going to mention that now. It was just what she deserved.

CHAPTER TWENTY

Summer lay in bed and pulled the covers up to her chin. The shock of falling into the freezing water had only calmed when she took a long hot shower. Summer was so…angry? Was she? It wasn't only about Teddy. She was angry about putting herself in this situation.

Why was she here? Why was she having fun with Teddy, of all people? It had been a lovely day, as they planned for the future. They planned just like when they were young, and Summer was as excited by the future as Teddy was.

Deep down Summer knew why she was here. She'd painted it as obligation to Queen Georgina and Queen Bea, but the truth was it was for Teddy. It had always been for Teddy, from the first day she had taken her hand at the play day.

Ahead of her, all she saw was hurt.

There was a knock at the door.

"Come in."

The door opened slowly, and the first thing she saw was a large mug followed by Teddy appearing around the door.

"Please don't throw anything at me. I've got tea."

"I'm too cold to throw anything at you. Bring the tea."

Teddy came in and was wearing one of the matching dressing gowns provided by the B&B management company.

Teddy handed her the mug. "Here you go. Summer, I swear I didn't throw you—*us*—in, I was just joking that I would, but then I tripped on this rock and—"

"I know, I know. It's fine."

Teddy sat down on the edge of the bed. "I shouldn't have joked around about it. Something about this place, and just being here with you…It took me back to a happier, simpler time."

"I felt it. All those summer days spent at Balmoral. Just being kids and having fun. I think you were always the most relaxed there."

Teddy nodded. "I was. I could be myself, knowing there wasn't a camera around, and you'd let me hold your hand and show affection."

Now was not the time to talk about their past relationship, so Summer said nothing.

"I hope you don't mind—I sent Robbie to the town to get us some dinner, and I thought we could stay here tonight and head back in the morning."

"No, that's okay. By the time we get our clothes washed and dried, it'll be too late to go home. Did you put our clothes on to wash?"

Teddy drummed her fingers on her knee. "I put them in the machine, but I had no idea how to put it on. It has so many bells and whistles. It's like a robot washing machine."

Summer sighed. "What nonsense. Hold this."

Teddy took Summer's cup of tea and she got up from the bed. Her matching dressing gown rode up on her thigh, Teddy's eyes watching it all the way.

Just as Teddy was about to get up herself, she saw a black carry case with Summer's medications in it. She was used to Summer taking some meds throughout their time together, but there looked to be a whole lot more now.

Then she thought about all the times Summer had taken pain shots over this time they'd been back in each other's company.

And you dropped her in the freezing cold water. You idiot.

She hobbled out into the main living room, the pain in her ankle making her more angry at herself.

"Summer, I'm sorry. Please?" She hobbled into the kitchen and saw Summer on the porch, next to the washer and dryer. "Summer? I'm sorry. I would never have done it if I knew it would turn out like this."

"Look." Summer sighed. "It was an accident. I get it. A boisterous reliving of our youth."

"No, I mean, I saw all your medication. The shock of the cold water could have made you ill."

"I'm okay. I've just had my meds changed, so there's a new combination to take. I inject them each night into the pump in my forearm. I'm fine." Summer peered into the drum of the washer. "How much washing liquid did you put in?"

Teddy walked forward and lifted the bottle. "About half?"

Summer rolled her eyes. "It should be only a capful. Never mind." She selected the programme, and the machine whirled to life. "How do you survive without such basic skills?"

"My washing gets collected and washed at Kensington Palace."

"What about when you were in the army for a year?"

"There was a label put on the machine, so we knew what to do each time," Teddy admitted.

"You are so spoiled."

Thankfully Teddy was rescued by the front door opening and Jack escorting Robbie in.

"Sounds like the food's here."

"One pepperoni and one vegan veggie hot one," Jack said.

"Thanks."

"I'll be back later to have a final security check."

"Enjoy your dinner with Robbie. Good night."

Teddy brought the pizza boxes over to the couch.

"Vegan for you, Cinders, and pepperoni for me."

Summer laughed.

"What?" Teddy asked.

"Nothing." Summer tried to suppress her laughter.

Teddy sat down and opened her pizza box. "Well, it's clearly something, so just tell me."

"Okay, do you remember I used to make you wash your teeth or use mouthwash if you'd eaten pepperoni or any meat like that?"

Teddy laughed hard. "So you did. God, I forgot about that. You have to admit, Cinders, we had a lot of fun together."

Summer smiled. "We did. No one has ever made me laugh as much and cry as much."

Teddy pursed her lips and nodded. "Yeah, I think we both did."

There was silence, and now the electric and fun atmosphere had been deflated like a balloon. They both took the opportunity to eat some pizza.

❖

Later that evening, Jack came back for a security check. "Everything looks secure, ma'am."

Summer was curled up on the couch finishing her last piece of pizza, while Teddy was at the door talking to Jack.

"Thanks. I'll lock the door as soon as you're gone. I'll call you if there's any problems."

"Will Jack and Robbie be okay out there?" Summer asked.

"It's a two-bedroom, two-bathroom garden flat. I think they'll be okay. How was your vegan pizza?"

"Vegan cheese has improved so much since I was a young girl." It was then Summer noticed Teddy's limp. "Hey, you're hurt."

"No, no, it'll walk off."

"But you're coming to sit down now, please. It was the rock you tripped over, wasn't it?"

"Fine, yes, I twisted it," Teddy admitted.

"Come here."

"I'm beginning to think you have a foot fetish. First my blistered feet, now my ankle."

"Shut up, and feet up, Charming…" The nickname rolled off her tongue so easily. Just like it seemed to in the water with Teddy.

"I'm still Charming, eh?"

"You always were," Summer said, "but I have a vested interest in keeping you on your feet for the next marathon in a few weeks."

Teddy put her foot in Summer's lap.

Summer felt the ankle, and Teddy gave an intake of breath. "It's swollen. You're not going to be able to run on that."

"Don't be ridiculous. It'll be okay," Teddy said.

"The next run isn't a normal course, running around Loch Ness over really difficult terrain. It'll be impossible."

"Look, just don't," Teddy said firmly. "I made a commitment, and I'm sticking to it, even if I have to drag my way around the course."

Summer felt frustrated and angry at Teddy's inability to admit she was suffering and in pain. It was always the same, whether it was physical pain or emotional pain.

"Fine, I'll get the first aid pack and put a support on it."

Teddy got an ankle support and put it on. She was determined to show the pain wasn't bothering her as much as it really was.

"Summer, can you tell me about your condition? Don't just say you're fine or skirt around it, because the meds look a lot more complicated than I remember."

Summer put her napkins inside her pizza box and pushed it away.

"I'll tell you if you swear not to tell my mum and dad, or anyone for that matter, not even Annie, okay?"

"I promise. You might think a lot of things about me, but you know I'll keep my word."

"Right. My doctor says the device in my arm, and the meds in it, aren't controlling my condition as well as they used to any more. He wants to do a more invasive procedure, recoding the genes that cause my illness, but I'm scared of that to be honest."

"You mean gene editing? Why are you scared? Do you trust this doctor? He's looked after you a long time," Teddy said.

"I know, but there have been such a lot of horror stories about advanced gene therapy. Any time it's been mentioned in the past, Mum and Dad have wanted me to get it done. So I haven't told them the doctor's advice at my last appointment. The therapy scares me. Pathetic, eh?"

Teddy took Summer's hand without thinking about it. "Don't you ever say that about yourself. You are the bravest person I know. Remember I used to visit you in hospital? I was Roo's age. It was around that time that I realized children could actually die, and it was terrifying."

"Teddy—"

"No, let me finish. You were just that little bit older, you knew the truth, that you might have a life-limiting condition, but every time I came in to visit, you were smiling, joking, and I was so proud of you."

"Thank you. But you thought I was scared when I broke up with you."

"I'm sorry, it was anger and pain talking. You were thinking of your health and the effects of stress. Now you've explained the difficulties you've been having—well, maybe Cinders and Charming can't have a happy ending like you said. I wouldn't subject any partner I loved to my life. Excuse me, I'll go and get the dry clothes."

Teddy got up and walked away to the laundry area.

❖

Following the sound of music, Summer wandered out to the conservatory. Teddy only had on her boxers and vest top. Teddy always had a good physique, but she truly had grown into her adult body.

Summer gazed hungrily at her toned shoulders and arms and had to stop herself. In her mind she wandered over and wrapped her arms around Teddy's waist, as she had so many times.

What would Teddy think of her body? She had grown more curvy.

She wondered what Teddy's reaction would be. But she already knew. Teddy still had feelings for her, as she had for Teddy.

Without turning around Teddy said, "Why do we always end up feeling the hurt of the past?"

Summer walked up beside her and looked up at the clear, starry sky. "Because we haven't had an honest conversation about how we ended things."

Teddy said nothing.

Summer looked up at the stars. "It's beautiful out here."

"It is. Remember the way we used to watch the stars?"

"It'll be freezing."

"I'll put the outside air on. Computer, turn the outside air on hot."

Teddy took her hand, and they walked out onto the artificial grass. Teddy lay down on her back and patted the grass beside her.

Summer shrugged and said, "Why not." She lay down and looked up at the stars. "It's so clear out here."

"It is beautiful, and the sound of waves in the background too. We used to sneak up on the roof of Buckingham Palace or Windsor Castle, look at the stars, plan our future, and…connect."

Summer felt the touch of Teddy's hand as it clasped hers.

"I thought," Teddy said, "it might maybe be good to talk about how we ended and put the hurt and tears behind us."

Down here, and not looking at each other, it might be easier. "Okay, you start."

"I know what happened the day you were chased, but you closed down to me. What really happened? How did you feel?"

"Terrified, suffocated. I noticed the paps' cameras and tried to hurry down the road to the Tube station. When people on the street started to notice I was being followed, they all started taking pictures. I ran down an alley, and I was trapped. I was surrounded."

Teddy rolled on her side and looked down at Summer.

"I tried to call you, but it was hard when everyone was around me pawing me. Then eventually Quincy came and pulled me out."

"I'm so sorry you had to go through that, and all because of me, and who I am." Teddy stroked her hair. "I was a kid, Summer. I didn't handle it well. As soon as I got your call, I ran and tried to get a car and get out of the palace to help you, but Quin grabbed me and said she'd take care of it. I came to see you after at your mum's house, but you shut yourself away."

"I was scared, Teddy. My face was all over the media, and I just went into my shell. It took me a long time to come out. I missed the first six months of uni, and even then I was a figure of curiosity. People whispered behind my back, took pictures and video. It was hard."

Teddy stroked her cheek so tenderly. "I'm so sorry, and I'm sorry I was so stubborn when you came back to me. I was a stubborn, hurt kid."

Summer felt tingles all over her body, and her chest tightened. Just being close to Teddy like this brought back all those feelings of her youth. The very air between them crackled.

"We made such plans for the future," Summer said. "We were going to be the best Princess and Lady of Wales. But I never truly understood how much pressure and scrutiny there would be, and I couldn't cope."

Teddy continued to stroke her hair. "I understand. It is too much to ask anyone, especially someone with a health condition like you."

"My health was an excuse, Teddy. I was just frightened."

She leaned her forehead against Summer's and whispered, "I'm sorry you were frightened. I should have protected you. I've finally accepted my fate as heir to my mum, but I needed to understand what you went through. Just know…"

Summer reached up and rested her fingers on Teddy's face. Her lips were parted, and nothing seemed to matter except feeling Teddy's lips.

"Know what?" Summer breathed.

"That there will be no one else for me, and if I have to, I'll walk this path alone."

Teddy barely rubbed noses with Summer, then with lips parted they breathed each other in, before Summer felt the soft lips that she had been yearning for since she'd parted from Teddy.

The kiss was knowing, reconnecting, soft, and languid. Summer pressed her fingers into Teddy's hair and held on to the moment as long as she could. Their tongues touched softly, and then Teddy pulled away from the kiss. "Tonight we have this moment for those two kids who were so much in love."

"You'll meet someone eventually, and she'll be your Lady of Wales, then Queen."

Teddy smiled. "No, Cinders." Teddy grasped Summer's head lightly. "Now that I know exactly what you went through, there's no way. You need to concentrate on your health and look after yourself, but you know you are the only woman I've ever loved. I'm sorry, the kiss shouldn't have happened. I just needed to feel your lips one last time. Goodnight, Cinders."

"Teddy, wait."

"No, I said what I wanted to say. I know this life isn't what you wanted."

Teddy walked out, leaving Summer confused and aching for her.

❖

Kurt showed Pandora the image on-screen. It showed Teddy and Summer frolicking on the beach in Cornwall.

"I fucking knew it. Summer Fisher, I knew that it was her game. Get me out of the way and jump into my place."

Kurt poured them each a gin and tonic. "When my photographer followed them to Cornwall, she wasn't expecting anything like this. We can make a lot of money from this picture."

Pandora, who was sitting with her legs up on her coffee table, grasped the glass from him.

"This isn't about money," Pandora said. "This is about principle. Teddy and I were getting on perfectly well until Summer came to work for her. Summer is a manipulative bitch, and Teddy's gullible."

Kurt flopped down on the couch beside her. "So, what do you want to do with it?"

"Get me more pictures like this, and then it'll all come down to timing. Cheers!"

❖

Summer was dreading coming through to get breakfast and running into Teddy. Last night had blown her mind and brought back every feeling and hurt from their break-up. This was exactly what she feared would happen if they worked closely together.

But the fierceness of Teddy's feelings had surprised her. All those other women that Teddy'd been with didn't alter Teddy's feelings towards her. And if she was honest, didn't alter her feelings for Teddy.

Why couldn't she move on? The way Teddy kissed her showed her exactly why.

"Fucking bastards." Teddy's voice was loud and clear.

She hurried into the living room. "What's wrong?"

Teddy pointed to the TV screen. "Crawford fucking Blackmore. Look what he's done."

Summer watched the police report:

"Housing charities were incensed this morning to find out the government had asked the police and local council workers to take part in an effort to remove the unhoused from the streets of London. Tents were slashed to make them unusable, and then the bedding of the individuals sleeping in the tents was thrown into a bin lorry to be destroyed. The leader of the opposition has said the actions were cruel and unfeeling."

"I can't believe the prime minister could sink so low," Summer said.

"He is not going to get away with this. I'll call Annie and see if she can meet us at Street Kitchen as soon as possible, and you call your contacts in the news media. I *want* them watching and filming us for the first time in my life. Let's go."

Arrangements made, Jack and Robbie got them on the road to London as soon as possible.

Teddy was not going to take this lying down.

CHAPTER TWENTY-ONE

A ndy, Jack, Robbie, and Teddy finished packing up the van. The TV journalists and cameras were across the street, waiting to film what came next, after the tip-off from Summer.

Three days had passed since the prime minister's cruel actions. They had pooled resources to come up with everything they needed.

Volunteers from other London charities had come together with Street Kitchen staff to distribute all the equipment they had gathered. Businesses had donated food, camping gear, and warm clothes in large quantities to replace the items the government had destroyed.

Teddy worked closely with Summer to make sure they had everything they needed. Azi had also joined them on the streets that evening, filming everything that happened.

Summer had advised the police of what they would be doing, just so there were no complications and the Princess of Wales wouldn't be arrested. That wouldn't be a good look.

They headed out about seven at night with their army of volunteers. All of them had the Race Across Britain donation number on the back of their shirts and on the sides of the vans that followed.

Summer had organized doctors and other healthcare workers to go with them, so they could give medical assistance. As word spread that the princess was doing this, crowds started to appear, much to the chagrin of Teddy's protection officers, but the crowds would ensure these pictures would go around the world.

Teddy talked to a young man while one of the doctors gave him some meds for a chest infection. Teddy handed him a pack with toiletries, new winter outerwear, and food ration packs.

"Thanks, Princess."

"No problem, Joel. You go in to Street Kitchen tomorrow. I'll tell my friend Andy to watch out for you. He can help with everything you need. I hope you feel better."

The cameras flashed as she gave him a hug and shook his hand.

Teddy stood and walked back to the van, waving to bystanders as she went. There were people waving from windows in the buildings above. The pavements were packed, and the road was virtually brought to a standstill. Teddy and Annie waved to everyone as they met up with Summer at the van door.

Summer was beaming. "You see? There are some very good aspects to media attention. Every one of these pictures is going around the world, showing Crawford Blackmore for what he is."

Annie laughed. "That warms the cockles of my heart."

"I think we better get you and Annie off the street now before the police get any more worried," Summer said.

Teddy hugged them both at once. "We did it."

Lali was trying to get Bea back to the waiting car quickly. But, as ever, Bea was generous with her time. Bea had spent the afternoon at a new school for young adults with special needs.

Bea always gave everything during her visits, but then Lali started getting messages from Bastian and other colleagues, and requests for statements. When she read the headlines, she tried to expedite Bea's walk to the waiting car.

"Ma'am? I need to show you something in the car."

Bea waved goodbye to the staff and patients and got into the car.

"Okay, what's happened?" Bea said with worry.

"No one is unhealthy or injured, so just relax. Teddy, Annie, and Summer have been out with some of the staff at Street Kitchen, helping…eh, just watch."

Lali called up the news channel on the phone.

"The Princess of Wales and the Duchess of Edinburgh, and their friend and PR agent, gave out sleeping bags, tents, food parcels, and bags of hygiene products after the outrage at the government's actions a few nights ago. The centre of London was nearly brought to a standstill."

"Well done, Teddy," Bea said. "I'm so proud of them."

"Number 10 has been kicking off. They want a statement," Lali said. "They say the Queen needs to coordinate with Bastian and ourselves and either say nothing or praise the government's actions."

"What's the old adage?" Bea said. "Never complain, never explain. I'm not going to condemn my daughters for doing exactly what I would do, but I'll speak to George about it."

Chapter Twenty-two

A few days later Teddy, Summer, and Annie were having coffee at Teddy's to go over the great publicity they got from their impromptu event and to think about next steps. "I'm going to talk to Robbie for a few minutes, okay?" Teddy said.

Once Teddy left the room, Annie said, "What's going on? There's a weird tension going on between you two. I'm used to the outright hostility, but this is different."

Summer leaned onto the table in front of her. "We had a moment in Cornwall."

"Really?" Annie moved her chair up closer to her, with the biggest smile on her face.

"We ended up staying over because Teddy was being a fool and got us wet in the sea and twisted her ankle. We decided to wash our clothes and stay in the B&B overnight. Then we talked about how we broke up and—"

They were interrupted by Teddy rushing in. "Annie, Mum's had an accident."

Annie jumped up. "What? What kind of accident?"

"Not life-threatening. She took Roo skiing at the ski centre. I don't know what's wrong, but I think her leg is bad. Come on."

"You two go. I'll finish up here."

"Thanks," Teddy said.

"Let me know how the Queen is," Summer said.

"We will," Annie said.

Her mum loved alpine sports, and so did Teddy and her sister and brother, and they were all going on an alpine holiday together in a few months' time. Her mum had promised to give Roo skiing lessons ahead of the holiday and to spend one-on-one time with him. Her mum booked the ski centre for a few hours so they could have some privacy.

Teddy and Annie headed out to the car and got in the back.

"What could have possibly happened?" Annie asked. "Mum is an exceptional skier."

"I know."

When they arrived at the palace, they ran up the stairs and down the corridor to their mums' private rooms.

Cammy was at the door and opened it for them. "Your mothers are in the bedroom."

"Thanks, Cammy." Teddy burst into the bedroom and saw her mum lying on top of the bedclothes in shorts, with her leg encased in an exoskeleton cast. Rupert was standing beside their mama, looking worried.

"What happened?" Teddy said.

"Everything is fine." George winked at Teddy.

"Yes," their mama added, "your mum was a little careless when she was skiing."

Now Teddy looked at Annie. That was not true. It couldn't be true.

"Mum has a bad break, and she's going to have surgery to repair it," their mama said.

"Absolutely. Can I talk to Teddy in private?" their mum said.

Mama nodded and said, "Come on, Roo and Annie. Why don't we ask the kitchen for ice cream?"

"Sounds perfect," Annie said. "Come on, Roo Roo."

Once they were gone, her mum patted the bed. "Sit down."

"What happened?"

"Roo lost control and was heading at speed for a metal pole and fence. I got there in time, and instead of your brother breaking his legs or arms, I got it. My leg got wrapped around a part of the fence, and two bad breaks."

"Are you in pain?" Teddy asked.

"Not too awful, with the help of the painkillers. The hospital put this exoskeletal cast on it till I have surgery. It was thought less disruptive if I waited at home, rather than causing mayhem at the hospital because the Queen is there. My doctor and nurse are coming in every hour. Now I need a couple of things from you. The first is easy."

"Name it," Teddy said.

"Support Roo. He's blaming himself and feeling bad about this whole accident."

"Of course I will, Mum."

"He's a sensitive boy. The other thing you're not going to like. I'm having surgery on Wednesday, and I'm going to need rehab."

Teddy had no idea what was coming.

❖

Summer was watching TV at her parents' house when she heard her phone ring. After hearing about the accident, she didn't feel like being alone.

"Hello, Teddy? How's your mum?"

"She's okay. Her leg was badly broken...I wondered if I could come and talk to you?"

"Yes, I'm at my mum and dad's."

"I'll be ten minutes, then."

Summer told her parents, "Teddy's coming over."

Her mum shot up. "She is? I need to tidy up."

"No you don't, Mum. You know Teddy doesn't have airs and graces."

"How is the Queen?" her dad asked.

"She's broken her leg badly, I think."

"We'll just say hello and let you two talk," her mum said.

The doorbell rang, and Summer let Teddy in. When Summer led her into the living room, her parents bowed and curtsied.

"Mr. and Mrs. Fisher, it's so good to see you again."

"Diana and Ryan, you know that, Teddy. Come here."

Her mum pulled Teddy into a hug that looked to Summer as if it was gratefully received.

"Is the Queen doing okay, Teddy?" her dad asked.

"She took a bad fall trying to get in between Roo and a steel barrier, but she will heal with treatment."

"Glad to hear it," her mum said. "We'll let you two talk, then."

As Summer's mum and dad were leaving the room, Teddy said, "I've missed both of you, Diana and Ryan."

Summer's heart melted as she watched her parents smile with happiness.

Once the door was shut, Summer said, "Thanks for saying that. You made their day."

They walked over to the couch and sat down. "It's true. I lost a second set of parents when we broke up."

"How's your mum, really?"

"Really? She has a bad double break in her leg. Roo was going to hit if she didn't come between him and a metal pillar. Poor kid is feeling so guilty. Like it's his fault."

"Poor Roo. It could never be his fault."

"I know. I'll make sure he knows it. Mum is having surgery on Wednesday, and then there will need to be a lot of rehab. Which is what I wanted to talk to you about."

"You need to cancel your charity races?"

"No, I can do that. I'm now a senior Counsellor of State, along with my mama. We can step in when Mum is ill, incapacitated, or just can't perform a function because of another reason."

"What do you need to do?" Summer asked.

"A few investitures. Knighthoods and the like. They'll be shared out within the family, but that's not why I'm upset."

"You're upset?"

"Angry and frustrated, more like," Teddy said. "I have to do the State Opening of Parliament."

"Wow. That is a big event," Summer said.

"There's no way Mum could do it. The heavy robes and gown would be impossible, and then there's the stairs. Impossible. But you realize what doing this entails? Sitting there in front of all the MPs, the House of Lords, reading out the government's new policy to cut benefit payments and get the unhoused off the streets, just like we were fighting against last night."

Teddy stood up and started to pace angrily. "Doing it with people claiming it is being done in the Queen's name, all the while Crawford Blackmore is laughing at me."

"You won't be condoning what you're reading. You will be there representing the Crown. A neutral position. Think how many your mum has given. Do you think she believed in them all? Do you not think she would have been horrified at some, and want to cheer at some others? But you wouldn't be able to tell from her expression. You know as well as I do, that's what a constitutional monarch has to do."

Teddy flopped down on the couch. "I'm not very good at being neutral."

"I doubt many people are. But in a way the better you do at representing the Crown like this, the more it will hurt Crawford Blackmore. It's well known there's no love lost between his party and this system of government. He'd be much happier with the title of President Blackmore."

Teddy had the tiniest conspiratorial smile. "You know, you might be right."

"You should know that I'm always right, after all the time you dated me."

Teddy chuckled. "Very true. I suppose I'd better let you get back to your family."

Summer didn't want the night to end just yet. "Can you give me a lift home?"

"Yes, sure. As long as you're ready to leave."

"I'll just let Mum and Dad know."

CHAPTER TWENTY-THREE

Teddy was surprised that Summer wanted a lift home but was happy to oblige. Jack and Robbie were off shift after their unexpected stay in Cornwall, and she had DS Taylor and DC Bell with her this evening.

As they drove to Summer's flat, Summer said, "Do you want to come in for a drink? I'd like to talk to you about something."

"Yes, that would be great."

When they arrived, Teddy leaned over and said to Taylor, "I don't know how long I'll be. I'll let you know."

"Yes, ma'am."

Summer brought Teddy a glass of wine. Teddy wasn't expecting to be asked in, especially after Cornwall. She was kind of nervous and wasn't sure what to say, so she took a large gulp of wine.

"How's your ankle?"

"Not bad. Robbie thinks I could do some light training in a couple of days."

"Do you feel better about the State Opening of Parliament?"

Teddy turned in her seat on the couch so she was closer to Summer. "After talking it through with you, yeah, as much as I can be. I don't have to like it, but I'll get through because it's my job now."

"I'm glad. It's a horrible situation," Summer said.

"You always make things seem better. It feels like you have been showing me the right way since I was little. Talking me through things, encouraging me. I've missed that since we've been apart."

Summer brought her knees up on the couch and faced side-on to Teddy. "I care about you. Not many people looking in would know what an emotional person you are, but I know. You hurt easily and need encouragement from time to time."

"Well, I needed it today. Mum says her actual crown will sit on the dais in front of me. I don't need to wear robes or vestments, just formal dress uniform. The uniform that I felt a fraud in."

"That's something I've been thinking about. You feel that you could have achieved more in your military service."

"Yes."

"Why don't you go and achieve your dream? Go to Royal Marine officer training."

Teddy wasn't expecting her to say that. "But…"

"No buts. I mentioned it to you before. Learn to live with not going, or do something about it. You're young, fit, and getting fitter every day. It would change your life, I think, give you such a shot of confidence, to achieve something that you have wanted since you were a child."

"And what if I fail?"

Summer reached her hand across the back of the couch to where Teddy's hand was set and held it. "Then you can look at yourself in the mirror and know you tried. Think about it?"

Teddy felt tingles of excitement. Excitement at being so close to Summer, excitement at the possibility of attempting to meet a dream she had wanted for so long.

"I'll think about it, maybe talk to Quincy and Mum."

Summer smiled and held up her wine glass. "Good."

Teddy entangled her fingers in Summer's. "You have a beautiful smile."

"I do?"

Teddy laughed. "You know you do. I've missed it."

"I know. Who would have thought, just a month ago, we wouldn't be arguing and in fact getting on well," Summer said.

"It's been fun, hasn't it? You, me, and Annie helping people in a practical way, and pissing off Crawford and his cronies. My mama was really proud of us."

"Can you imagine—your mama used to demonstrate against the government, the monarchy, and now she's part of it all."

Teddy laughed softly. "She jokingly says that she wanted to take down the system from the inside."

"Quite right. I love your mama, and your mum."

"They love you, believe me. No other girl could measure up to you."

"No one could measure up to you, with my mum and dad too.

No matter what the press said about you, they would say *That's not the Teddy we know*." Summer paused, then added, "Can I tell you something?"

Teddy rubbed her thumb on the back of Summer's hand. "What?"

Summer hesitated and looked down. "It doesn't matter."

Teddy didn't believe that, but she didn't want to force her. Summer looked up at her with a fire behind her eyes. A want that surprised her. She had seen that fire in Summer's eyes before.

It had been the night Teddy finally expressed her love for Summer. It was Teddy's eighteenth birthday. Her parents had thrown a big party for Teddy on the Windsor Castle grounds, for all her friends and family.

There were fairground rides, street food venders, an outdoor dance floor and band, and a fireworks display for later in the evening. The noise of music and laughter, and flashing lights filled the grounds of the thousand-year-old castle. It was everything that Teddy wanted to share with Summer.

Teddy didn't know when she first started to fall in love with Summer. She thought it must have been the moment Summer took her hand for the first time when they were children. Since then her feelings developed as she grew older and knew what love and attraction were.

She was sure that Summer felt something for her. They were always doing things together, but with Summer being that little bit older, Teddy didn't know if it was just close friendship or more.

Teddy watched Summer across at the shooting gallery with some friends, trying to win a prize with no success.

She had promised herself that she would tell Summer how much she loved her tonight. She was turning eighteen, and Teddy hoped that Summer would now take her seriously. Teddy took a drink of the lager she was having at the bar with some friends.

"First legal drink, big sis? How does it feel to be eighteen?"

Teddy smiled at her little sister. "It's not exactly my first."

"Can I have one, then? Go on, they won't serve me."

Teddy turned to the barman and said, "Can I have a non-alcoholic lager, please?"

"Thanks a lot." Annie scowled at her.

"Mum would kill me," Teddy said and handed her the bottle.

"So? Are you going to gaze longingly at Summer all night or tell her how you feel?" Annie said.

Her little sister couldn't help but know Teddy's feelings for Summer. They were written all over her face every time they were together.

"I'm waiting for the right time."

"There's no right time. The fireworks are in half an hour. You're going to miss your opportunity," Annie said.

"You think?"

Teddy had set up the most romantic moment she could. Earlier in the evening, she took a bottle chiller, holding champagne and two glasses, up onto the Round Tower. It was a romantic gesture to show Summer how deeply she felt, but Teddy was going to lose her opportunity, just like Annie said.

"I should go?" Teddy asked.

"Yes."

Annie took Teddy's lager and shoved her on her way. "Go, good luck."

Teddy's heart was pounding as she walked over to the shooting gallery. Summer saw her and smiled. There was no turning back now.

"Teddy, you need to help me. I'm hopeless."

Teddy's stomach was doing flips inside, but she was trying to show off uber confidence. She took the air gun from Summer. "No problem." If there was one thing she could do, it was shoot. Military cadets had prepared her for a military life.

At first her hands were shaking. Summer watching with her friends only added to the expectation.

Teddy took a few deep breaths, lined up the target, and she made her shot.

"Bullseye!" the man running the stall said. "Pick your prize from the top row."

Summer and everyone around them were clapping.

"Which stuffed animal do you want, Summer?" Teddy asked proudly.

"The dog holding a heart."

Teddy asked for it, and she handed it over. Summer was jumping on the spot and hugging the bear tightly.

This was her chance. "Summer, do you want to come and watch the fireworks with me? I've got a special place in mind."

"I'd love to."

Teddy let out a breath. She'd done it. She'd asked, but now came the hard part.

It had taken them fifteen minutes to get up onto the roof. Teddy knew there wasn't much time left.

Teddy led Summer by the hand over to the edge of the turret where she had left the bottle chiller.

"What's in there?" Summer asked.

Teddy took out the bottle and handed Summer the glasses. Summer put down her plush stuffed dog and took them.

"Some champagne to make the moment more special," Teddy said.

"You are sweet."

Once the glasses were poured, Teddy said, "To the future."

"To the future."

Summer took a drink and looked out over the fairground. "It looks beautiful from up here. Your mums gave you a great party."

"They did. It's been great. Even better is spending time with you."

Summer looked at her with some sort of recognition in her eyes. Did Summer feel the same as she did?

There was a bit of an awkward silence then. Summer cleared her throat and said, "How long till the fireworks?"

"Any minute now."

Summer shivered.

"Are you cold?"

"A little," Summer said.

Teddy was brave. She put her glass down, spooned Summer from the back, and put her arm around Summer's middle.

"I'll keep you warm."

To Teddy's surprise, Summer pulled her in tighter. Teddy had to say the words that she had been rehearsing for years.

"Oh, look—it's starting, Teddy." Summer put her glass down on the turret wall and pulled Teddy's other arm around her waist. "I'm so glad you brought us up here. It's special. A special memory," Summer said.

The fireworks were going off like beautiful bombs in the air. Summer was right—this was special. Now was the time to tell Summer.

Teddy was so nervous that her arms were tremoring.

"Are you okay, Ted?" Summer asked.

"Yes—um…"

This was so much easier in her head. She placed her lips to Summer's ear and whispered, "I love you, Summer, I'm in love with you."

Summer turned around in her arms. "Teddy—"

But Teddy was determined to finish what she said. "It's always been you for me, ever since you took my hand as a little child."

Summer gazed into her eyes while bangs and explosions were going off above them.

"I can't love you, Ted."

Teddy's stomach tightened. She didn't say she *didn't* but *couldn't*. Teddy was certain that she did feel something.

"Why can't you?"

"The age gap. Your parents—"

"It's only three years. I'm eighteen now, Summer, and my parents love you. You know that. I've been waiting my whole life to share my feelings with you. Tell me you feel nothing."

Summer looked down. "I can't tell you that."

Teddy put her fingers under Summer's chin and raised her head to meet her gaze. "Tell me the truth."

"I've always been your friend, like Annie, but this last year my feelings have been changing. We've always had this deep connection, Teddy. I…"

Teddy rested her forehead against Summer's. "Please tell me."

Summer's hands caressed Teddy's cheeks, and then she ran her fingers into Teddy's hair.

"I love you too. I've tried to hide it, but being here with you now, I can't."

Teddy's heart pounded like a drum. She wasn't going to waste a second more. She pressed her lips against Summer's, and Teddy felt the last piece of love in her heart fall into place.

The kiss was soft, tender, and everything that Teddy had dreamed. Summer then deepened the kiss and moaned. Teddy placed her hands on Summer's backside and squeezed.

The kiss became more demanding, and suddenly Summer broke away from her and with eyes full of passion said, "I love you, Ted."

Teddy saw that same passion in Summer's eyes here. But she couldn't make this more complicated again. It wasn't fair to Summer.

It took everything in her, but Teddy stood up. "I better go."

Summer stood and grasped at her hand. "Don't go."

Teddy's heart started thudding. "Why?"

Summer took both her hands and pulled her closer. "You know why."

Teddy cradled Summer's head in her hands. "You know you don't want this."

"Then you shouldn't have kissed me under the stars in Cornwall." Summer's lips drew her closer, but inside she was saying *Get out. Only heartbreak will come of this.*

But when Summer said, "I want you, Teddy," she was powerless to resist.

"Tomorrow you—"

"I don't care about tomorrow. I care about you."

"Are you sure you want me to stay?"

"Yes, call Taylor and tell her you're staying."

After she made the call, Teddy kissed her. Not soft and tenderly. Their kiss was breathless, needy, and hungry. Hungry was exactly how Teddy felt.

As they kissed, Summer led Teddy to her bedroom, and as soon as the door was closed, Summer started to undress Teddy.

She was sick of keeping her feelings deep inside, her logical brain holding her back, taking Teddy away from her. She didn't want to be frightened any more. She wanted Teddy.

In a frenzy they pulled off their clothes down to their underwear. Teddy lifted Summer back onto the bed and then lay on top of her. Every nerve ending in Summer's body was on fire. She never thought she'd ever feel that again.

She grasped Teddy's hair while Teddy kicked off her boxer shorts. Summer immediately felt a wet heat on her thigh.

With new confidence Summer rolled on top of Teddy and watched Teddy's hungry reaction as she took off her bra and her breasts were freed. Teddy's hands cupped them, and her eyes closed briefly before Summer leaned forward and allowed Teddy to place her hot, wet mouth on them.

Teddy sucked Summer's nipple in her mouth and rolled her tongue around it. With every suck, an electric jolt went to her sex and set off a white-hot burning fire.

Her hips started to rock on Teddy's stomach, and Teddy clearly had enough waiting. She rolled Summer under her again and sat up to pull Summer's underwear off. Then Teddy groaned as she put her thigh between Summer's legs and felt the wetness there.

"Teddy. Touch me."

Teddy leaned over and kissed her while her hand grazed her breast, then squeezed. Every touch felt right, felt natural, the thing that had been missing, that her heart had been yearning for since they split up.

Teddy lightly held Summer's two hands above her head in one of her own, while her other softly caressed its way to her sex.

Summer pulled away from the kiss. "Teddy, please."

"I'll take care of you. This time I will."

She slipped her fingers into Summer's wet, hot sex. Summer flexed her hips, hungrily trying to make Teddy's fingers stroke exactly where they needed to be.

Summer didn't wait long before Teddy's two fingers found their way to her core. Summer gasped. It had been so long since she'd felt that sensation, that completeness of being closer to your love than anyone else.

"I've got you, baby," Teddy said.

Summer broke free from Teddy's hold above her head and held on to Teddy's strong shoulders, and her hips quite naturally moved in time with Teddy's thrusts.

Teddy's body was both familiar and new. Teddy's body had changed in the intervening years. It was more solid, stronger, but it was utterly familiar, as if they had never been apart.

Summer pulled Teddy as close as she could as her orgasm started to build. "Yes, yes, Ted." Her arms and her thighs started to shake. This intensity had been long gone from her life, and Summer had thought forever gone, but no. It was simply the case that her body had been aching for the right touch.

Summer's breathing became shorter and raspy.

"Come for me, baby," Teddy said.

She held on tightly around Teddy's neck, and as the white heat from her sex erupted all over her body, she grasped Teddy's hair.

"Oh God, oh God," Summer gasped as the orgasm lost its intensity and waved warmth to all her extremities.

"I missed you so much, baby," Teddy said.

Summer tried to get her breath back quickly so that she could explore Teddy's body, but Teddy, as giving as she ever was, kissed her way down Summer's body, licking and sucking as she went.

"It's too soon…Ted…"

But she didn't listen, and Summer jumped when she felt Teddy's tongue hardly touching her clit, but enough so that her second and then third orgasms rocked her body.

"Enough, Teddy. Come here."

That was Teddy. Giving to a fault, and always putting herself last. She kissed Teddy's lips, feeling as close as they ever had been.

Teddy stroked her hair, gazed lovingly into her eyes, and said, "Hello again, Cinders."

"Hello again, Charming."

She knew how Teddy liked to come, as close to her as possible. So she wrapped her legs around Teddy's hips and pulled her as close as she could.

Summer whispered in her ear. "I wish we had your strap-on, so you could be inside me. Remember how you loved your Intelliflesh cock?"

"Jesus Christ, yes." Teddy's hips thrust faster and her breathing became shorter.

But as her orgasm hurtled towards her, Teddy forced herself to slow down. She rolled her hips, feeling and appreciating every sensation she could. Because Summer might think this was wrong tomorrow, and it might be the last time Teddy was this close to her true love.

Her body gave her no choice but to thrust faster again as the rage of passion propelled her towards the precipice.

"Summer...fuck."

Teddy kissed Summer as her orgasm set her body on fire. The passion was rocking her to her core.

I love you.

❖

Teddy sat at the window in Summer's bedroom, dressed only in her T-shirt and boxers. She'd woken early with Summer cuddled into her chest. She'd lain there awhile, but the longer she lay, the more worries and fears crept into her head.

Last night had been finding that missing puzzle piece, but how long would she have it? Until Summer woke up? This was her greatest wish and her greatest fear. She'd been young when she'd had her heart broken before.

Teddy turned her head and gazed at a beautifully serene looking Summer Fisher. She almost wished that Summer wouldn't waken, because that would mean her heart would remain intact. But that couldn't be.

Summer moved and stretched out her arms before her eyes fluttered open. When Teddy caught her gaze, Summer smiled.

That was a good start.

"Hi," Summer said.

"Hi."

"What are you doing over there?"

"I couldn't sleep," Teddy said.

"You look worried. Come over here."

Teddy slipped back into bed.

"Should I be worried that you look worried?" Summer said.

"I kept thinking that you would say you'd made a mistake, that last night was a mistake."

Summer caressed her face. "No way. I knew what I was doing. I simply couldn't find the words. Do you remember me trying to say something but I said it didn't matter?"

"Yes." Teddy put her hand on Summer's hip.

"That night in Cornwall. You asked me to tell you how I felt when I was harassed and chased?"

Teddy nodded.

"You told me that you handled it badly. That you were just a hurt and angry kid."

"Yes, I was. I didn't feel like I could protect you and take care of you. Then when you came back to me that day, do you remember?"

Teddy wouldn't answer her calls, her texts. She asked Annie to give her sister messages but got nothing in return. Summer was distraught, and Annie could see that, so she set up a false meeting down at the stables, to talk about their mama's birthday gift.

When Teddy arrived, she went to the stables in search of Annie, who would probably be grooming her horse. Next to Annie's horse was not her little sister. It was Summer. The girl who had trampled on her heart.

"What are you doing here?"

"You wouldn't reply to calls or texts," Summer said.

"This was a trick." Teddy turned to leave.

"Please, Teddy, I want to talk to you."

Teddy took a step towards her. "Do you know how long I've been trying to get you to answer my calls? I was ignored. You broke up with me by a text. I'm not interested in anything you have to say."

And she walked away.

"I'd internalized all that anger towards the press, the people that chased you, and I took it out on you. I was too stubborn. I wanted to lash out and hurt you too."

Summer put her hand on Teddy's neck. "I understand that now, but have you considered that I was a young, scared kid too? I'd been fighting my illness all my life. You might've thought I was brave, but I was scared of my illness. Every time I thought I was better and beginning a normal life, my body would say *No, you're not.*"

Teddy nodded. She remembered cradling Summer as she cried from the pain in her body. It wasn't really until she was thirteen that the doctor got her condition under control.

"You know I had anxiety about confined spaces, and people not giving me room. I was poked and prodded all my life, and I was cornered. I still have issues with that. Then the stress—I knew that it made me ill, and I was scared."

"I'm really sorry I reacted the way I did."

"That's the point I'm trying to make. We were kids, but I'm not a kid now. That's what I realized when we talked in Cornwall. You are an adult and have a different perspective on it now, and so do I. It was easy for me."

Teddy couldn't help but feel a build-up of excitement. "What are you trying to say about us?"

"In Cornwall you said that kiss was for the two young people who were so much in love. But this"—Summer pulled her close so their lips were almost touching—"this kiss is for the two adults who have loved each other our whole lives."

Teddy lost all the air from her lungs. Was this real? Just as she was losing herself to Summer's kiss, she pulled back.

"Wait, you know what my life means. I can't change what or who I am."

"I know that."

"I promise you that you'll be protected," Teddy said.

"I understand now, and I just can't live without you, Charming." Summer smiled.

That name melted her heart, and she let go.

CHAPTER TWENTY-FOUR

So, you have the State Opening of Parliament in three weeks," Summer said, "and then an investiture?"

Teddy and Summer were walking hand in hand to their special tree at Windsor.

"Yes, but that's all business. I want it just to be us this lunchtime. Then we can visit with my mums after."

Summer stopped and looked back at the castle. "Maybe we should have visited your mums first."

"Just come with me. I've got something special planned," Teddy said.

"Okay, you win."

When they arrived under their special tree, Teddy put her arms around her. "I've dreamed about being here with you."

"Me too," Summer said.

Teddy sighed happily. "You know I love you, right?"

"You know I love *you*, right?" Summer said.

They both laughed and then Teddy leaned in for a kiss. As their kiss became more passionate, Summer felt something.

She grinned at Teddy. "You didn't."

Summer remembered the sensation of an Intelliflesh strap-on growing with excitement. Intelliflesh, a material designed for the movie industry, could be made to any shape, and like real skin attached to your nerves to give you full sensation.

It had made the sex toy industry boom with happy customers.

"Come with me." Teddy took Summer's hand and led her over to Hollow Lodge.

"What are you up to?"

Teddy unlocked the door and walked into the empty house. "Remember we used to dream about living in this house? Next to our dreaming tree?"

"Yes."

"It's ours now." Teddy smiled.

"Ours?" Summer looked around the big entrance hallway.

"The Queen gave it to me, to us, if you'll live with me. Come."

Teddy guided her into the front drawing room. There was no furniture in it, nothing but a picnic blanket, cushions, a picnic basket, and champagne.

"You did all this for me?"

Teddy nodded. Summer pulled Teddy into a kiss and let her hand wander down to Teddy's crotch.

She moaned when Summer touched her ever-growing strap-on through her jeans. Summer's kiss became more passionate, and she frantically unbuckled Teddy's belt. She undid it and pulled Teddy's strap-on out of her tight jockey shorts.

"Baby," Teddy moaned.

Summer pumped it in her hand. "You know how many times I've fantasized about you and me like this? I need you, Teddy."

Teddy looked around for a surface. Any surface. There was an old sideboard by the wall. She guided Summer over to it and began to pull at Summer's jeans. Summer helped by pulling her T-shirt and bra off.

Teddy pushed down her jeans and underwear and allowed Summer to palm her strap-on as it got ever harder.

"I missed your cock, Teddy."

Teddy pushed her face into Summer's breasts, while Summer stroked her. It felt so good, everything was so much more intense.

"Inside, Teddy."

Teddy pulled Summer forward and placed the head of her cock at Summer's entrance. She was so turned on that she was shaking inside. Teddy moaned as she eased her way inside Summer, and Summer gasped.

"It's bigger than I remember. I feel so full."

Teddy thrust her hips while holding on to Summer's hips. They moaned into each other's kiss as the thrusts became faster.

"Yes, baby. You feel so good." Teddy moaned.

"Closer and deeper." Summer linked her legs high on Teddy's waist, and Teddy leaned over so they were almost lying down.

It was as close and as deep as they could get. Summer held Teddy's hair and whispered into her ear, "Fuck me, Ted. Come inside me."

"Oh yeah." Teddy held the back of Summer's head protectively as she thrust faster.

"I'm coming, Ted. Now."

Teddy felt Summer stiffen and pulse inside against her strap-on. Then Summer cried out and hung on to Teddy's neck tightly.

Teddy said, "It's coming, baby, it's coming." Her breathing became erratic, and then she cried out almost in pain.

"Fuck, I'm shaking," Teddy said as her breathing calmed down.

"That was so good, Ted." Summer started laughing.

"What?"

"I think we're going to need a shower before we visit your family."

Teddy laughed and stroked the damp hair from Summer's brow. "I love you, Cinders."

Summer kissed her nose. "I love you, Charming."

CHAPTER TWENTY-FIVE

Teddy showered and got dressed quickly, allowing Summer to take her time. She whistled as she walked down the corridor towards her mums' drawing room. She was energized and saw nothing but rainbows ahead. She couldn't remember the last time she felt this high and optimistic.

She made a conscious choice not to let those little worries creep into her head. The ones that niggled in the back of her brain. Things were rosy now, but what about when they came out? Would Summer truly be able to cope with the intensity that was her life, and her future life?

Summer was worth it. Teddy wasn't going to mess this up.

She knocked on the door to the drawing room and walked in to find her mum looking severely pissed off, her leg with the brace up on a footstool. Quincy, who was there too, stood up and bowed her head.

"Mum?" Teddy bowed her head.

"Thank goodness you're here," Quincy said. "Your mum is a little frustrated."

"Frustrated? I can't exercise, my diary is cancelled for two months, and my son is blaming himself for me being hurt."

Teddy sat down on an armchair. "I'm going to see Roo after we've talked. He'll be okay."

"I'm used to *doing*. I've never had an idle day in my life," her mum grumbled.

That was very true. Whereas her mama could lounge by the pool or on the beach, her mum always liked activity, swimming in the pool or in the sea, while on holiday. Even on days when she had precious little time to herself, she would help chop wood at Windsor, walk the dogs, run, or build her model ships.

"Where are the dogs?"

"Tommy took them out," her mum said.

Tommy was one of the footmen who took care of the dogs if her mum was busy or away.

"Tomorrow's the big day, then? When will you get home?" Teddy asked.

"The next morning. It won't come quickly enough, believe me. I'll be doing all my rehab at Windsor. We're most comfortable here."

"Where's Mama today?"

"The children's service dog training centre. She loves her days with the children and the dogs. She'll be home soon enough for us to enjoy the weekend together."

Her mum pushed herself up and yelped in pain. "Argh. What time is it?"

"Five o'clock, ma'am," Quincy said.

"Teddy, can you hand me my pain shot?"

"No problem." Teddy went over to the side table and took the pain shot syringe and one of the vials that went into it.

"Here you go, Mum."

"I hate taking these things," her mum said.

"It's not for long," Teddy said.

"So, what did you want to talk about?"

"First of all, thank you, Quincy, for being part of this meeting. I know you don't like to miss an event with Mama."

"I'm happy to. I have a well-trained staff to step into my shoes," Quincy said.

"It's two things really. The first is that I've been thinking about my future and how I can be useful to the country as well as doing something I'm passionate about."

"You are being useful, Teddy. The work you are doing for charities for the unhoused is excellent, and you've only just started. I read the plans for Cornwall. Offering people training in agriculture, practical skills that can help in them getting a job."

"Yes, the Duchy of Cornwall trust aren't too pleased at using perfectly sellable parcels of land and buildings to our cause. It makes enough money as it is to fund my Princess of Wales office," Teddy said.

"The trust were fairly resistant to my attempts to modernize when I was Princess of Wales, and then because I became Queen unexpectedly early, they have had the run of the trust themselves for a long time. Now here you are with some radical new ways you want to use the land and holdings. It may be time to move some trust members on, and get some younger faces in."

"I'd have your support to do that?" Teddy asked.

"Of course. You are Princess of Wales now. You do what you need to do, to make the Duchy more modern," her mum said.

"Thanks. I will—with your guidance—make some changes. Summer has given me great ideas. One of them was what I wanted to talk to you both about."

Teddy was nervous as to how they would react to her wanting to try for Royal Marine officer selection. Would they think it was pointless, since she wouldn't be able to fight on the front line, given the security risk, and would they think she was capable?

The parachute regiment and the Royal Marines slugged it out over which service had the toughest training and was the most elite regiment. Very few could survive the gruelling training.

"I need your honest opinion. You too, Quin."

Teddy's stomach twisted, and her heart beat a little faster. *Just get on with it and say it.*

"I would like to try for Royal Marine officer selection. It's always been my dream, but until recently I didn't believe that I could do it."

Her mum and Quincy exchanged a look. Uh-oh. But soon, smiles appeared on their faces.

"Teddy," her mum said, "if this stupid thing wasn't on my leg, I'd jump up on my feet and hug you so tightly."

Quincy stood and shook her hand. "That is the best news, ma'am."

"You think it's a good idea? I know I can't fight on the front line," Teddy said.

"It's the best idea. I'm so proud of you. It's the perfect training for a future Queen. I enjoyed my time in the army and navy. I couldn't fight either, but I was able to do jobs that allowed others to fight."

Quincy said, "Yes, there's lots of jobs that will be suitable. I'm proud of you too, Teddy."

"Where did this sudden inspiration come from?" her mum asked.

"That was the other thing I wanted to talk to you about." Teddy cleared her throat. "Well, it was Summer who encouraged me to follow my dream, and we are back together."

Quincy immediately said, "I'm so happy for you both. Summer is such a great girl."

But she was surprised that her mother was quiet.

"Mum?"

"I need to be serious for a moment. Does she realize what that will mean for her? Summer struggled to cope with it before. Can she now?"

"We are both adults now, Mum. I didn't protect her before."

"You mean *I* didn't protect her. I should have realized your relationship would come out soon, and she would need protection, especially with her illness," her mum said.

"She does understand, and I'm determined that she is protected this time. I know that the public purse won't pay for a guard until Summer is at least engaged to me, but I'm willing to pay out of my pocket, if Quincy would recommend someone."

"No, I will pay, Teddy. It's my mistake from the last time around, and I owe it to her and her parents to take care of her."

"I will be happy to recommend someone who will be perfect for the job," Quincy said.

"So how do you feel about it, Mum?"

Her mother's face broke into a smile. "I couldn't be more happy. Your mama and I always thought Summer was the best thing to happen to you. Just take care of her. Your mama is going to go crazy. Summer is her dream girlfriend for you."

Teddy laughed softly. "Oh, I know."

"With Your Majesty's permission"—Quincy looked to the Queen—"I'll start sounding out some people and give you a list."

"Thank you, Quincy."

Just then Annie burst into the room and threw her arms around Teddy's neck. "You did it. I'm so happy."

They all laughed.

"You heard, then?"

Annie kissed her cheek and moved over to her mum for a kiss. She hung her arms around her mum's neck and said, "Although what she sees in you I'll never know."

❖

The morning of the race in Scotland, around Loch Ness, the media was flooded with pictures of Teddy and Summer, outing them for the first time. Teddy was awake well before Summer and was terrified of what she would say when she woke up.

The pictures were mostly of them in their private space, taken by paparazzi. One was especially troubling. It was taken when they kissed under their dreaming tree. That tree and Hollow Lodge were in a very private and guarded area of the estate.

Teddy held her hand to her mouth. She felt Summer move behind her. "Teddy?"

"Morning, baby."

"What's wrong?"

Teddy handed her the computer pad and said, "We've been outed. The paps have some private photos. I suspect Pandora is behind it. She did say I would regret breaking up with her."

"I see."

Teddy's eyes closed in resignation. *It's going to be over.* "I'm sorry my life exposes you to this. If you want out—"

Summer sat up on the edge of the bed. "Teddy, look at me."

When Teddy turned to Summer, she saw annoyance on her face.

"I thought you wanted to marry me. *Want out?* Do you have no faith in me?"

Summer took Teddy's hand. Was Teddy sitting here, worrying that she was going to run?

"No, but—"

Summer kissed her hand. "I told you, I'm a grown-up now. I'm not leaving you for anything, far less stupid pictures."

"How do we handle this, then?"

"We give the press what they want. We'll go to the start line, hand in hand, looking relaxed and open. You get a kiss at the start and at the end. It makes Pandora's pictures less sellable. We give them better pictures for nothing, and we can be ourselves."

Tears welled up in Teddy's eyes. "I thought I'd lost you again. Thank you for being brave and facing this life with me."

"I'm going to be even braver now I have your support. I'll have the gene therapy as long as you are at my side. Then we can hopefully have a happy, safe life."

Teddy kissed her softly. "I'll be with you every step of the way."

Later that morning, Teddy and Summer walked hand in hand down to the start line at Loch Ness. The crowds had swelled with this morning's revelations. Summer thought the publicity would swell the donations. Not quite what Pandora had in mind.

At the start line the crowds whooped and screamed as Teddy kissed her childhood sweetheart. Her destiny.

Next to her a woman in a Nessie costume jumped up and down with joy.

"Go and run, Charming."

EPILOGUE

"Come on, Wales, fucking faster, faster!"

Teddy's combats were soaking wet and weighed down with mud, and her gun was slung over her shoulder.

The sergeant major was screaming in her ear as she neared the ending of the final marine test—a ten miler across country and through obstacles, like the sheep dip where you were submerged through a tunnel.

She felt like she would drown, but Teddy got through it and over the various jumps.

Her legs had nothing left in them, but still she ran. She shivered with the cold, but still she ran. If she thought a marathon was bad, this was a million times worse. She pictured Summer in front of her at the finish as she had been at the Scottish marathon.

That's who she wanted to finish for, to make her proud, to make her family proud. The opening of parliament ran through her mind. Teddy hadn't put a foot wrong that day, and the Queen was so proud of her performance.

Then she thought of the conclusion of the Race Across Britain, which brought in fifty million pounds. It was a huge success.

She'd found pride in her life at last, and she wasn't going to let up making her country, family, and the woman she loved, Summer Fisher, proud of her.

Teddy crossed the finish line first and was given applause by the commanding officers, then had a hot drink pushed into her hands. She took her gun off and drank from the warm mug.

I did it. I made all my dreams come true.

No, that wasn't right. Summer had made her dreams come true.

❖

Teddy stood in dress uniform in front of the rest of her class of recruits, and now officers.

The commanding officer came to the lectern. "Families and friends, there was one recruit who displayed every ethos of the Royal Marines. I will allow Her Majesty the Queen to make the presentation of the silver sword to the officer who finished top of their class."

Teddy marched forward and met her mother below the platform. She was wearing her Royal Navy uniform.

"I couldn't be more proud than to present my daughter, the Princess of Wales, with the silver sword. Congratulations."

Teddy shook her mum's hand and saw her wink before handing her the sword. Teddy put the sword into her scabbard and allowed herself a look up to her family in the viewing gallery.

She searched out Summer's face and saw she had been crying and dabbing away tears.

There was a lot of expectation on her shoulders, but now that she had Summer, the girl who had taken her hand all those years ago at a children's play day, she could face anything.

Teddy saluted her mother and said, "Thank you, Your Majesty."

About the Author

Jenny Frame is from the small town of Motherwell in Scotland, where she lives with her partner, Lou, and their well-loved and very spoiled dog.

She has a diverse range of qualifications, including a BA in public management and a diploma in acting and performance. Nowadays, she likes to put her creative energies into writing rather than treading the boards.

When not writing or reading, Jenny loves cheering on her local football team, cooking, and spending time with her family.

Jenny can be contacted at www.jennyframe.com.

Books Available From Bold Strokes Books

Back to Belfast by Emma L. McGeown. Two colleagues are asked to trade jobs. Claire moves to Vancouver and Stacie moves to Belfast, and though they've never met in person, they can't seem to escape a growing attraction from afar. (978-1-63679-731-1)

The Breakdown by Ronica Black. Vaughn and Natalie have chemistry, but the outside world keeps knocking at the door, threatening more trouble, making the love and the life they want together impossible. (978-1-63679-675-8)

The Curse by Alexandra Riley. Can Diana Dillon and her daughter, Ryder, survive the cursed farm with the help of Deputy Mel Defoe? Or will the land choose them to be the next victims? (978-1-63679-611-6)

Exposure by Nicole Disney & Kimberly Cooper Griffin. For photographer Jax Bailey and delivery driver Trace Logan, keeping it casual is a matter of perspective. (978-1-63679-697-0)

Hunt of Her Own by Elena Abbott. Finding forever won't be easy, but together Danaan's and Ashly's paths lead back to the supernatural sanctuary of Terabend. (978-1-63679-685-7)

Perfect by Kris Bryant. They say opposites attract, but Alix and Marianna have totally different dreams. No Hollywood love story is perfect, right? (978-1-63679-601-7)

Royal Expectations by Jenny Frame. When childhood sweethearts Princess Teddy Buckingham and Summer Fisher reunite, their feelings resurface and so does the public scrutiny that tore them apart. (978-1-63679-591-1)

Shadow Rider by Gina L. Dartt. In the Shadows, one can easily find death, but can Shay and Keagan find love as they fight to save the Five Nations? (978-1-63679-691-8)

Tribute by L.M. Rose. To save her people, Fiona will be the tribute in a treaty marriage to the Tipruii princess, Simaala, and spend the rest of her days on the other side of the wall between their races. (978-1-63679-693-2)

Wild Wales by Patricia Evans. When Finn and Aisling fall in love, they must decide whether to return to the safety of the lives they had, or take a chance on wild love in windswept Wales. (978-1-63679-771-7)

Can't Buy Me Love by Georgia Beers. London and Kayla are perfect for one another, but if London reveals she's in a fake relationship with Kayla's ex, she risks not only the opportunity of her career, but Kayla's trust as well. (978-1-63679-665-9)

Chance Encounter by Renee Roman. Little did Sky Roberts know when she bought the raffle ticket for charity that she would also be taking a chance on love with the egotistical Drew Mitchell. (978-1-63679-619-2)

Comes in Waves by Ana Hartnett. For Tanya Brees, love in small-town Coral Bay comes in waves, but can she make it stay for good this time? (978-1-63679-597-3)

Dancing With Dahlia by Julia Underwood. How is Piper Fernley supposed to survive six weeks with the most controlling, uptight boss on earth? Because sometimes when you stop looking, your heart finds exactly what it needs. (978-1-63679-663-5)

The Heart Wants by Krystina Rivers. Fifteen years after they first meet, Army Major Reagan Jennings realizes she has one last chance to win the heart of the woman she's always loved. If only she can make Sydney see she's worth risking everything for. (978-1-63679-595-9)

Skyscraper by Gun Brooke. Attempting to save the life of an injured boy brings Rayne and Kaelyn together. As they strive for justice against corrupt Celestial authorities, they're unable to foresee how intertwined their fates will become. (978-1-63679-657-4)

Untethered by Shelley Thrasher. Helen Rogers, in her eighties, meets much younger Grace on a lengthy cruise to Bali, and their intense relationship yields surprising insights and unexpected growth. (978-1-63679-636-9)

You Can't Go Home Again by Jeanette Bears. After their military career ends abruptly, Raegan Holcolm is forced back to their hometown to confront their past and discover where the road to recovery will lead them, or if it already led them home. (978-1-636790644-4)